"Gaby . . ." he said, and it was an invitation to which she utterly consented. His hands reached out and deftly, lovingly grasped her bare shoulders, drawing her to him.

The kiss was long and passionate and so easy, so graceful, she was astonished. Their tongues fit, their mouths fit, their bodies fit, as if they had always been here doing what they were doing.

Somehow they walked to the bed, somehow her towel dropped to the floor, and he sat on the bed as she stood before him, inviting his touch. As he studied her with his hands, she was flooded with a kind of desire she hadn't felt since she was very young, an ardor that impelled her down beside him and against him, having to hold him, having to touch him.

"I've never seen you undressed before," she murmured in wonderment as he moved against her, and the feel of his skin against hers, the weight of his body, made her gasp . . .

CAROLYN FIRESIDE

BERKLEY BOOKS, NEW YORK

AUTHOR'S NOTE

I have taken the liberty of rearranging social history to suit my private purposes, but always lovingly. The observant reader may note, for example, that Dean & DeLuca opened in East Hampton a year or two later than here described.

ANYTHING BUT LOVE

A Berkley Book / published by arrangement with
the author

PRINTING HISTORY
Berkley edition / October 1982

For information address: Berkley Publishing Corporation,
200 Madison Avenue, New York, N.Y. 10016

A condensation of this novel was published in *Cosmopolitan*.

ISBN: 0-425-05710-0

Berkley Books are published by Berkley Publishing Corporation,
200 Madison Avenue, New York, N.Y. 10016.
The name "BERKLEY" and the stylized "B" with design are
trademarks belonging to Berkley Publishing Corporation.

A BERKLEY BOOK ® TM 757,375
PRINTED IN THE UNITED STATES OF AMERICA

For Judith Weber,
who made me do it,
and with special thanks
to Ned Stewart.

Thus began the dualism of love—two souls rolling through space and never at rest until they join together to complete the universe.

—Okakura Kakuzo,
The Book of Tea

Anything But Love

Prologue

CANNES,
May 1982

"CANNES is a paradise of excess. Too many flowers. Too many yachts. Too many bronze-on-blond nymphettes. Too many palm trees fronting too much perfectly aquamarine sea, sheltered by profusions of perfectly formed clouds, too white not to have been painted on the azure sky. . . .

"Cannes is the archetypal movie set," warbled the lead-in to the *Esquire* piece I was mentally composing *in medias res*. Stuffed, I was, like the proverbial pimiento in the olive, into an elegant corner of the extravaganza of bullshit, hustle, and relentless glamor that was the Carlton Terrace in mid-May.

I'd never been to the film festival before, but the regulars claimed they could detect subtle nuances in each year's hysteria and, from them, could predict the future of the international movie business—at least, until the next festival.

To me, the perennial boy reporter hunting for a

scoop, it was astonishing that anybody could even find anybody else in this melee. But the movie sharks can spot power in total darkness; the din and the overflow stopped no self-respecting *handler* in his illusive pursuit of the big deal. Still, the stars always ended up with the moguls: power gravitated to power. And it was this process of natural selection that drew the great director Federico Fellini across the terrace to the table of my famous companion. After the requisite kisses and quips, Denise loftily introduced me as "the journalist, Terry Barron."

Fellini, luckily, had been pleased by an interview I'd done with him a few years ago in *The Times* and seemed genuinely glad to see me again.

The presence of fame reduces us all to adolescence: To me, the offer of Fellini's hand was as thrilling as copping Frank Sinatra's autograph must have been to the bobby-soxers back in the forties. Bathing in the afterglow of the grasp, I didn't care when, almost immediately, Fellini and my legendary Denise began a barrage of industry intimacies that left me out.

Taking advantage of the free minute before they'd wrap their tête-à-tête, I allowed my imagination to track the scene around me. With a hint of a lead for my piece already concocted, I rewarded myself with yet another surreptitious glance at my watch—the gold Rolex that Denise had given me for my twenty-fifth birthday. It was the first expensive gift I'd ever gotten from a woman, and I wore it as a sort of *memento mori*, reminding me that the American gigolo evenings at Elaine's had passed with my twenties.

"Terry Barron! Checking the time behind my back?" Although she waved gaily at the disappearing Fellini, Denise Sullivan's celebrated smoky delivery let me know that she was pissed. "Even at my age," the three-time Oscar winner continued, "even at my age, I'm not about to play second lead to anybody's next appointment!"

"Denise, my dear," I coochie-cooed, with that custom blend of tough Irish street kid and cool Oxford don that never failed to enchant her, "you know you're always the headline in my newspaper!"

"Right," she retorted skeptically. "And I'm Gloria Swanson, and you're Bill Holden, and this here's Sunset Boulevard." And with that, she flashed that famous lost-little-girl grin that only her public took at face value. Denise Sullivan might have been a vulnerable gamine to the millions, but to me she was a real scrapper. Right now, she was looking for a fight.

Something was bugging her, but what? Had Fellini approached her about playing somebody's mother? Did a town lousy with starlets make her feel her age? And what did she care, since she looked a good ten years younger than her organic forty-eight? And since she had only recently snared the world's greatest catch, a dashing Italian tycoon who was a count to boot. Guido had immediately taken to buying her houses the way ordinary moguls present their ladies with Bulgari necklaces, and her most recent bauble was an unpretentious little thirty-five-room cottage on Cap-d'Antibes.

My trip to Cannes had been a last-minute affair, which had created an immediate problem. It was clearly useless to try to get a hotel room in a town that was booked a solid year in advance, but a cable to Denise took care of all that. My longtime friend and lover didn't wait to telex back. She called. Denise, a truly generous and complaisant girl, didn't even ask why I needed to crash in Guido's villa. She just ordered me to come as soon as possible and get a tan. Guido was in Italy consummating a gigantic deal, and the hot tub at the villa, she suggested spicily, promised delights never even dreamed of in the U.S. of A.

The hot tub delivered. As did Denise. For two full days we played. Good, dirty fun between chums. Never serious enough to break up a marriage. That, Denise constantly reminded me, was the secret of my success with women. Fun in the sack, and no strings.

Partially as a thank-you for our couple of days of pretending that she wasn't famous, Denise had responded royally to my request for wheels. At my disposal, she placed a gorgeous little number that De Lorean had customed for the count. It was as black and sleek as a Nubian princess, and it hugged the road like it was making love to it. I'd driven into Cannes for the first time only that morning, and the hour-long ride from the *cap* was as flawlessly intoxicating as a TV commercial for the Riviera. Anyone who took the wheel of the Princess felt instantly famous, and I was exploiting that euphoria to bolster my courage for the trip I'd soon be making to Mougins, thirty minutes down the coast.

What waited at the end of that road was my real reason for rushing to Cannes. The *Esquire* article I'd dreamed up with my editor was an afterthought. The thought of what waited at the end of the road had my stomach in knots and my pulse pounding in my temples.

For Denise was right. I was preoccupied. And a little melancholy. And scared. Over the years, Denise had learned to read me better than I could read myself. Even when I deceived myself, she always caught me at it, and now was no exception. I had, in fact, shifted my attention far away from her. But for more than a story. For a quest. And for a girl.

A girl who had captured my heart, then fled with it into a dark place where I could not follow. A dream girl whose glowing image would live again for me in forty-five minutes in a tiny medieval town on the Côte-d'Azur. A girl named Gaby.

BOOK I

chapter one

NEW YORK,
April 1977

"*Merde!*" The blare of the downstairs buzzer had come from nowhere, disturbing Gaby's equilibrium almost enough to jog the perfect kohl line she was drawing along the bottom rim of her right eye. Luckily, the shock made her drop the pencil before the line ran amok.

The digital clock-radio by her bed announced eight thirty in no uncertain terms, and although her date wasn't due until nine, the last thing she needed now was a charity-soliciting neighbor or a kid playing tricks with the bell.

Deciding to ignore the nuisance, she made a moue at herself in the mirror and picked up the pencil just as the buzzer rang again, this time with hurricane force. "Not a chance," she murmured, "not without an invitation," and was proceeding to finish the eye when whoever was downstairs switched to a new tactic—one nerve-fraying, unbroken ring.

Steeling herself against the infernal screech, Gaby persevered with stubborn concentration, completing the line, then reaching for the mascara. Suddenly, the buzzer stopped. For a moment, Gaby could still hear the memory of the noise echoing over Stevie Wonder's "Songs in the Key of Life," then, as the uninterrupted strains of "Isn't She Lovely?" glided from the sound system, she began applying the mascara.

Even without the near-disruption, she was definitely running behind schedule. The remainder of her makeup would take about another ten minutes. She'd already bathed, powdered, and perfumed, and the gown had arrived from the cleaners the day before, pressed before it was ever worn, having received the royal treatment that, given the price tag, it was born to. Her hair always took the longest, so she saved it for last, although she'd started it early that mroning. The two tiny beaded braids on either side of her face had been inspired by a girl at work who'd come back from Jamaica wearing them; she'd begun at 9:00 A.M. After she'd negotiated the braids, she'd set the baby-fine, chestnut mane in huge rollers, which still waited to be taken out.

All this had to be done in—let's see—fifteen minutes, and that didn't allow for getting dressed. If the guy was prompt, she'd still be in jeans and sweat shirt, uncoiffed and possibly lashless. Served him right, she grumbled, for being a blind date.

Even now, she couldn't understand how she had let Laura Pendleton talk her into it. She'd gone to plenty of MOMA openings alone; after all, she worked there, and it was often officially part of the job. She was past the point of needing an escort, especially a man she'd never met, especially a journalist! Yet another hot young reporter who thought he was this year's answer to Carl Bernstein *and* Bob Woodward. And this one had sounded on the phone like a real ladies' man, so he probably walked around dreaming he was a better-looking version of Robert Redford. She wondered if he'd wait till after Jackson's opening to pounce on her; maybe he'd just jump her when she opened the door. Five years in the publicity department of the Museum of Modern Art had taught her more about young journalists than she ever wanted to know; their horniness was matched only by their arrogance. They practically plagiarized her press releases, then didn't even bother to give her the time of day.

The finest trembling of the hand holding the mascara wand made her realize she was nervous. A year from now, when Jackson Pendleton had made her face famous everywhere *Vogue* was sold, she'd probably take dates for granted, wouldn't even accept the calls of a man who made less than a million a year, but right now, after so long—over a year since Mark had left and her seclusion began—she was scared. And the bout with the bell hadn't done anything to steady her nerves.

Abruptly, her own doorbell chimed, completely blowing her cool. The distractor downstairs had obviously pushed all the buttons until he found a turkey who would buzz him in blind, then dashed upstairs to her door. She rose from her dressing table, furiously determined, marched through the bedroom, down the steps, across the living room, and to the door.

"Yes?" she demanded tersely.

"You in there?" a male voice thundered back.

"Go away, I don't want any," she snapped.

"You did last Wednesday."

"Hey, just what in hell do you want?" she barked, using the time to start removing the rollers, which she let drop to the floor at her feet.

"I want to go out with you!"

"Go out with me? What is this?" she paused, roller in hand.

"This, Ms. Blake, is what they call in New York a date. Have you had a change of heart?" He didn't sound pleased.

"What?" She felt herself freeze.

"I'm Terry Barron," growled the voice on the other side of the door. "I'm here to take you to Jackson Pendleton's opening. Remember? Or were you hit on the head with a heavy object after you accepted my invitation?"

"Listen, Mr. Barron"—Gaby's ire returned—"Is it considered good form in New York to show up half an hour early?"

"Half an hour early? Ms. Blake, if you'd answered the buzzer like a sport, I was prepared to apologize for being half an hour late."

"Before you go accusing me of eccentric behavior, Mr. Barron," she continued haughtily, escalating the removal of the rollers, "let me point out to you that you are almost half an hour early."

"And may I point out to you, Ms. Blake, that it is almost ten o'clock?"

"Check your watch, Mr. Barron. Mine says eight forty-five. What does yours say?"

"Mine, like everybody else's who's on Eastern Daylight Time, says *nine* forty-five. Didn't you remember to set your clock ahead last night?"

His words stopped her mid-roller.

"The time changed last night, Ms. Blake"—she could hear the smirk in his voice—"and some scuzzy cad leaked it to the press. Don't you read the papers, Ms. Blake?"

Oh, Lord! She'd set her hair so early in the morning, she hadn't run to the corner for a paper! She hadn't even turned on the radio all day. She felt like a total fool, and, as always when she felt like a fool, she was reduced to monosyllables. "Oh," was the most she could manage.

"Would you still like to go to the party?"

"Yes."

"Are you ready?"

"No."

"Will it take you longer than five minutes?"

"Yes."

"Then can you pass a magazine under the door so I can amuse myself while I wait?"

"Ummm." Penetrating her humiliation was the blossoming suspicion that this guy was rude and snide and sullen, possibly even drunk. Sure. A mean drunk. Probably balding. Beer-bellied. Oh, what a night this was going to be!

"Or would it be easier," He persisted, "if you just let me in? I promise I won't attack you." He damned sure wouldn't, promises aside.

"Sure, come in," she submitted with palpable resentment. Kicking the curlers out of the way, she unlocked the three locks, grudgingly turned the knob, and pulled open the door to reveal her nemesis—who was not balding, not beer-bellied, not falling-down drunk; who was, in fact, a taller, blonder, bluer-eyed version of Robert Redford, but better looking.

It took Gaby twenty minutes to get dressed, during which it occurred to her that she hadn't so much as offered to take his Burberry or serve him a drink. Actually, she hadn't even managed to say anything charming, just silently, swiftly indicated the couch in her flight toward the bedroom stairs.

As she blitzkrieged the rest of her makeup, she tried

to psych herself out of the new surge of nerves his dazzling presence had induced in her. Even if she'd been a girl who dated a lot, he was just too handsome to be alone with easily. And not only was she out of practice, but she was shy to begin with. Well, be that as it may, it was too late to turn back. Her only recourse was to convince herself that, when her soon-to-be-famous face was made up, when she was properly dressed, she would feel up for the game. If Jackson Pendleton, the grand master of fashion photographers, pronounced her a beauty, then she was a beauty, by God, but . . .

Since it was her *drôle de fameuse*—her ''funny face,'' as Jackson had pronounced it—that had attracted the photographer to her, she knew her looks, whatever they were, weren't conventional. Not everyone, Jackson had lectured her, would find her beautiful. She was a specialty item, and why should she assume that she was Terry Barron's kind of dish?

And even if he did like her looks, chances were he was the kind of guy who would treat her like a real bimbo. And even if he didn't assume she was dumb, he would, with justification, find her weird at best, graceless, more likely. Poise! Poise! she repeated with conviction, as she slipped the long, two-tiered burnished peach satin Halston over her head, fastened it, then reached for the brown satin sandals. And then it hit her.

The reason why she hadn't taken his Burberry was because he didn't have one. Because he wasn't in black tie. Because he was a journalist, and for the investigative reporter, there is no black tie. How dare he! Jeans, cowboy boots, work shirt, tweedy jacket, aviator shades. For a Sunday night opening at MOMA!

The turkey! There was no way she could wear the Halston!

"Ms. Blake," his voice floated up from downstairs, disturbing her hostile reverie, "it's after ten!"

"I'll be right down," she caroled as pleasantly as she could.

"Is this an ashtray?" he called again.

"Is *what* an ashtray?"

"The . . . the onyx round thing on the coffee table. Is it an ashtray?"

"Yes," she replied, staring at herself in the mirror, rigid with fury. She had so much wanted to wear the Halston.

"Hey." His voice was softening, as if he had serious doubts that she would ever reappear, as if she had to be coaxed gently, like a cat from a tree, or talked down, like an airplane pilot in a storm. "We really have to get a move on. Jackson and Laura'll be gone before we get there!"

"Five minutes!" she yelled with a semblance of conviction.

But what the hell *was* she going to wear? What *should* she wear? Just how do you dress to your escort? Maybe, it struck her, you dress *like* him. But, instead of cowboy boots, you pull on your high, high burnished gold boots from Charles Jourdan over your jeans. To which you add a perfect little brown belt with a small but exquisite gold clasp. You turn in the sweat shirt for a flawless, jade green silk men's shirt, custom ordered from Turnbull & Asser, over which you throw the silky tweed Ralph Lauren hacking jacket that keeps improving with age. And, finally, you comb out your hair into a mane so that, when the beaded braids show, it's a knockout contrast. Rapidly, she collected the evening's necessities—invitation, makeup, money, credit cards—and dumped them into the tiny version of a camera case, zipped it, slung the long strap over her head and across her torso so the bag rested on one hip, checked herself rapidly in the mirror, and breathing deeply, headed for the stairs.

It was the third week in April, but the evening was as warm as Memorial Day weekend. As they descended the steps of the brownstone, the East River breeze wafted their way, salty, sultry, and innocent as a Truman Capote heroine.

"Nice place you got here." Terry waved his hand as if to indicate all of Beekman Place.

"Thanks." She smiled a very small smile.

"How much of it is yours?" he persisted.

Aware that she was being set up, she decided to meet the challenge. "Not much. Just the building."

"Your own building?" She thought she could see the wicked gleam spring to his eyes as she nodded modestly. "I'm shocked, Ms. Blake." She had been right; even in the misty glow of the sulfurous lights, the sweet blue eyes were icy. "How does a humble career gi—*person* . . . acquire a brownstone on Beekman Place?"

Under the urging of his resentment, Gaby found her nervousness transforming itself into anger. "How, Mr. Barron? Simple. By being born rich."

"So you're not a poor little proletarian, after all?" he persisted as they walked toward First Avenue.

"No more than you're a member of the PLO, Mr. Barron," she snapped back.

"*Touché.*" He acknowledged her rejoinder with a mirthless grin. "Are you an heiress?"

"Is this *What's My Line,* Mr. Barron?"

"Just trying to get to know you." But the hostility was unmistakable. "Come on, clue me in. Where's the money from?"

"Shipping. Boston."

"What a coincidence, Ms. Blake." He commenced what was obviously going to be a major attack. "I'm from Boston, too. Bet we didn't go to the same high school. . . . Hey! You're not from the Blakes of R.H. Blake & Co.?"

"As a matter of fact, I am." They had made the corner of First and Fifty-second, to find the avenue's wide vista almost deserted in the Sunday evening dark.

"New York is a wonderful place!" he remarked nastily, as he scoured the thoroughfare for a cab. "Never in our mutual home town would Mr. Terry Barron of the bogs of South Boston be escorting Ms. Gaby Blake of Louisburg Square *anywhere*. . . ."

Over the rise of the hill that First Avenue takes above UN Plaza to make Beekman Place, four empty cabs appeared in squadron formation. "Sure you wouldn't rather walk?" She couldn't resist saying it. "Aren't taxis a little decadent for a man of your principles?"

He ignored the comment and deftly commandeered a Checker, then proceeded to hand Gaby into the vehicle with a politeness so arch that it infuriated her.

"Museum of Modern Art, driver," Terry shouted through the five small holes in the plastic partition.

"Whatyasaybuddy?" called the cab driver without turning his head.

"Museum . . . of . . . Modern . . . Art," Terry shouted each word separately, as if he were singing them. "Fifty . . . third . . . between . . . Fifth . . . and . . . Sixth!"

"Gotcha," yelled the driver, then proceeded north, making a stylish left onto Fifty-third and heading west.

"An heiress. What do you know?" Since Barron was not prepared to drop the subject, Gaby simply retreated into a corner and refused to be provoked any further.

"Do you work?"

''Yes.''

''Where?''

''MOMA.''

''Gives you something to do when you're not shopping, right?''

Silence.

''Ever married?''

The question startled her into a spontaneous, ''No.''

''No Boston fiancé?''

''No.''

''Well. Enjoying New York?''

She refrained from responding.

''This thing tonight must be a real drag for you,'' he pressed her. ''I bet you go to these museum things all the time.''

No comment.

''Ms. Blake, gimme a chance!'' he said with profoundly bogus bonhomie. ''If I were interviewing you, I'd be on the verge of suicide. Come on. Say something!''

And, as the cab eased across Fifth and began to pull up toward the museum entrance, Gaby obliged him.

''Mr. Barron, here we are. Now that we've arrived, you needn't feel obliged to so much as acknowledge my existence. It is not my fault that I was born rich, and I refuse to be made to feel guilty because of it. And, after meeting you, I'm actually grateful for my background since it instilled in me some manners, which you seem to be entirely lacking. But there are moments, such as now, when I do envy someone from your . . . *class*''—he was paying the driver, so she proceeded to open the door nearest her as she continued—''because if I were less well-bred, what I would do right now, Mr. Barron, is to suggest in no uncertain terms that you *fuck off*.'' And with that, she descended to the sidewalk and strode proudly through the revolving doors, not once looking back.

Having divested herself of the creep, Gaby made it solo through the revolving doors, past the barrage of *paparazzi*, and into the thick of the crowd—all gorgeous, mostly distinguished—either leaving or arriving. The MOMA lobby was stocked with Manhattan's most fabulous flora and fauna, a living advertisement for the strictly A-list guests waiting within. Thank God, Mark was in California, so at least she didn't have to worry about running into him.

Invitation in hand, she was successfully making her escape into the center of the throng when someone gripped her shoulder. As she whirled around, she saw the invitation being snatched from her and looked up to find the creep grinning down at her.

"Found ya!" Terry Barron was all smiles as his hand moved from her shoulder to her back to steer her toward the ticket-taker.

"I'm a big girl. I can find my way in by myself," she protested icily.

"I don't doubt it, but why should you have to bother? See, we're here!" He had already handed in both their invitations and was leading her across the main lobby, where more famous and fabulous faces were arrayed like glittering art treasures against the shadows of the Sculpture Garden beyond the far windows. "Listen"—he urged her to face him—"I'm sorry I was such a jerk, really. Let's call the mix-up a victimless crime, let bygones be bygones, and start over, okay?"

The worm turns, thought Gaby, deciding against total capitulation in favor of a meager smile. That seemed to be all Barron needed, for he, quite astonishingly, grasped her hand and led her across the floor as though they were teen-aged sweethearts at the senior prom.

"Hey," he beamed down at her, "isn't this better than sparring?" She couldn't resist a small, bitter shrug of the shoulders, but allowed him to hold onto her hand just as an exquisitely beautiful woman drifted toward them.

To Gaby's great surprise, the lady spotted Barron, shouted, "Terry, *caro,*" hurried to his side, and embraced him.

As he stepped back to take both her hands and hold her at arm's length, he replied merrily, "Marina, *cara,* lovelier than ever!"

And it wasn't merely empty flattery, for the woman before them, of a Proustian uncertain age, was truly a great beauty. The honey-colored hair, worn short and brushed back from the aristocratic features, fit like a frame around a classical portrait. The sea green silk gown—Givenchy, for sure—was perfectly elegant and draped itself with flawless understatement around the lean, toned body. The unforgettable face was one Gaby had admired only recently on a *W* cover, but the photo hadn't done her justice.

"And who is your charming friend, Terry?" the lady inquired.

"Oh, gosh, excuse my rudeness," he apologized, like a young boy at dancing school. "Marina Raffaelli, Gaby Blake."

"A pleasure, my dear," Signora Raffaelli told Gaby warmly, then turned back to Terry. "Have you seen Jackson and Laura?"

"No, not yet, just this minute got here," Terry said. "Where is the guest of honor?"

"Right through there." She indicated the gallery from which she had come.

"Guess we'd better make an appearance," Terry mused.

"And I must find my party. Again, a pleasure, Gaby." Signora Raffaelli bestowed a final radiant smile. "You'll have a wonderful evening with this one, I assure you." Then she was off, waving to a group of friends awaiting her nearby.

To Gaby's surprise, Terry had retained her hand for the entire interview without even being aware of it.

"Marina's quite a woman," he murmured noncommittally as they resumed their course toward the gallery.

"Yes, she seems like quite a woman," Gaby acknowledged as she wondered how a lady of Signora Raffaelli's breeding could know, much less publicly embrace, a boor like Barron. And how dare he, the foe of the affluent, be such a hypocrite as to hold one building against her when the woman he had just embraced held an empire at her fingertips? Who *was* Terry Barron, anyway?

They caught Jackson between conversations, suave and charming as always. "Gaby! Terrific, kid!" He pulled her to him for a warm, brief hug, "And Terry." He released Gaby and shook Terry's hand. "Hey, you guys don't have a drink. Bar's over to the right, if you're up for the hard stuff. Circulating champagne, if you're not."

"Think we'll hit the bar." Terry lightly took Gaby's elbow without consulting her. "That bubbly's too delicate for my brutish Irish soul."

"Catch you two later," Jackson called as they departed. "And if you run into Laura, tell her Shirley MacLaine's looking for her!"

"Sure thing," Terry agreed, as Gaby felt herself being steered toward the bar.

The press around the bar was fearsome. The bartenders were totally indifferent to the relative celebrity of the drinkers, and Bob Fosse and Henry Kissinger were having equally hard times getting served.

"This is going to take a while," Terry decided. "Why don't you wait here where there's air?"

To her surprise, she submitted without a word, seating herself on a wooden *moderne* bench in the center of the tall, narrow gallery. The show had been hung with partitions dividing one or two larger galleries into a maze of smaller, more intimate spaces, leaving a couple of good-sized white, windowless rooms to accommodate bars and food tables. Against the walls, Jackson's smart and very important photographs seduced the eyes of even the idlest viewer, and although Gaby had been involved in hanging the show, the impact of the work still stunned her. Even before she had met him, Gaby had enormously admired Jackson Pendleton's genius, not only for fashion photography, in which he was the acknowledged master, but in the more daring painterly areas that now comprised this show. She had always admired him, but then she had met him, and that memory led her eyes back across the gallery to his actual form, as vivid as the most striking of his photographs.

Jackson Pendleton was at that point in his late forties when a successful, good-looking man blooms with the assurance of his place in the great world. Six foot and trim, with a tennis player's grace and a gentleman's generosity, he managed, in a town that didn't make it easy, to be both envied and admired. He had the straightest nose, the squarest jaw ("Common as dirt in East Texas," he was fond of saying with that slight, disarming drawl), the most deceptively soft hazel eyes behind tortoise-shell aviators. His chestnut-colored hair, graying at the temples, was brushed slightly back in a style as sinuous and sexy as his Meledandri dinner jacket.

Gaby had met him over six months ago during the

planning meeting for the show. She had tried to talk in a businesslike way about the press release she was putting together, but he had instead cupped her chin in one hand while, with the other, he removed her big, tinted glasses.

"You have beautiful eyes. How dare you hide them?" He had folded the glasses and, handing them to her, continued, "If you can't see, get contacts." He had paused a moment to study her face. "You really *do* have beautiful eyes. Wanna have lunch?"

Over some kind of exquisitely prepared fish, at one of the wonderfully secluded little tables at the Box Tree, he'd quizzed her graciously about herself, so graciously that her natural shyness receded in the face of his sincere and flattering interest in her education (New York University's Art Institute, where her specialty had been photography until she switched to the film school, where she'd made enough contacts to land the MOMA job right out of school), her private life (she'd only alluded to the old, dead relationship, then decided she was his to command when he immediately, gently steered the conversation into more pleasant waters), her age (she'd said twenty-three, but she realized that he'd caught her half second's hesitation before she'd answered and probably knew she was shaving off a couple of years) and, finally, her ambitions.

"Ummm," she'd smiled, relaxed by his flattering interest and the excellent Meursault '71, "I'm doing pretty well at MOMA. I've been there long enough to get a couple of promotions, and in time, I guess I could become a department head. But, you know, those PR jobs are for women like me who don't have to live off their salaries, who don't absolutely *have* to work, and I'm not ambitious, really, because I don't have to be. I guess I believe I'm destined for something greater, but I haven't got much of a bead on what it is. I guess I'm like a lot of other girls my age. We're all waiting to be discovered—as something or other."

"Well, then," he said as he motioned the waiter over to refill their wine glasses, "I'm your man. I'm here to discover you."

"What do you mean?" She thought, for a moment, that he was coming on to her, and found she didn't mind at all.

"Frankly, dear, I'm propositioning you," he stated flatly, looking her directly in the eye.

Before she could respond, he went on. "And this is my proposition: If you decide to work with me, if you do exactly what I tell you to do, you'll be on the cover of *Vogue* in less than a year."

Her heart had leapt in secret joy and overwhelming disbelief as he continued, "I've got the best eye for beautiful women in the business, and I see you as *the* top model. It won't be easy. Or fun. For starters, you'll be going against girls who are still in their teens or who are peaking in their early twenties, so you're going to have to compensate by sacrificing a lot and sweating like hell. You, Gaby darlin' "—he patted her hand—"will be starting at a disadvantage, except for one thing: I think you've got it. If you want it. Do you?"

She nodded demurely but determinedly, desperately wanting to believe him.

"All right, my girl"—he'd shot it at her like a challenge—"then we're about to get to know each other very well. And just to prove how honorable my intentions are, why don't you come over to dinner on Thursday night? I'd like you to meet my wife." And her fleeting disappointment over his honorable intentions at lunch on Tuesday was swept away by the real delight of that dinner on Thursday.

To Gaby's surprise, it was a treat seeing Jackson and Laura Pendleton together. Somehow, acknowledging that a man as devastatingly attractive as Jackson Pendleton could still be in love with his wife was a comfort, as was the fact that his wife was not young, not gorgeous, but was as elegant, as warm, and as generous as her husband. It had been Laura who, over the months, had shown Gaby how to dress, how to exercise, how to walk and pose and smile. Gaby quickly became a regular at the Pendletons', and she loved it, for Laura and Jackson's affection for each other was reflected in the sunniness of their home life, which encompassed two teen-aged boys, a dog, two cats, a couple of birds, a cook, a maid, and a constantly rotating collection of fascinating people.

To Gaby, an only child raised in the frigid and repressive confines of blue-chip Boston, and ultimately rejected by it, being welcomed into the bosom of this loving and talented bunch was a dream. Here were people she wanted to please because they were so pleasing. Both Laura and Jackson were tough taskmasters, but their demands were so obviously based on her own well-being that, for perhaps the first time, she felt all her innate rebelliousness dissipate in favor of hard and willing work. And now, all that work was going to pay off.

Jackson had done a fabulous series of contacts of her, and when he had flashed them at *Vogue's* Grace Mirabella, she had flipped. So *Vogue* had given them the go-ahead for a new, ground-breaking layout starring Gaby, and the shooting was to begin next week. Now, gazing at Jackson across the gallery, Gaby knew she would do anything for the Pendletons, but that, unlike her own estranged mother and stepfather, they would never ask, much less demand, too much of her.

"One Perrier, coming up!" She was rapidly brought back to the present by Terry Barron, who was towering over her, offering her a drink. Compared to Jackson's absolute elegance, he looked as callow and disheveled as a character from *Animal House*.

"Let's drift over this way," Terry urged her, "toward the bag lady series, okay?" As they walked, Gaby waved politely to the museum officials and to the artists and filmmakers she'd come to know through the museum, while Terry called out familiar hellos to an astonishing number of famous people. She realized she wasn't doing much talking, and she sensed it was intimidation as much as her lingering anger that kept her quiet. She suspected that she was acting like a total bitch, but none of his attempts to warm her up seemed to be working. As he paused to kiss Lauren Bacall, Gaby, standing back, confronted her confusion about his position in this luminous crowd. Granted, he was a great-looking guy, but he was still green and awfully rude.

My God, it suddenly struck her, what if he's a gigolo? What if he's been to bed with every rich and beautiful woman at this party? Maybe he lived off these women, whose connections brought him assignments for articles that rarely got written. A year lived largely in solitude was definitely putting her at a disadvantage.

Laura Pendleton hadn't told Gaby much about Terry when she'd arranged the date, just presented the proposal as based on mutual convenience, since she and Terry were both invited, and as a chance for a nice, casual evening. That it certainly wasn't, but Gaby made a mental note to get the dirt on this guy from Laura as soon as possible. Until then, she'd just smile and be silent and feel herself turn invisible as her escort continued to glow.

* * *

An hour later, surfeited on famous names and faces, Gaby helped herself to a glass of champagne and wandered out into the Sculpture Garden. From within the museum, the hubbub floated like the ghost of a vanished fête; above the garden's far wall, windows glowed, neon with luxury, in the towering buildings across the street and to the north. Through the grating in the wall, a single cab appeared and disappeared like a black-lit disco dancer boogeying toward Fifth Avenue. In the museum's dim light, the garden revealed its stark, almost Japanese dimensions. Against it, like mythic monsters idling in the cement desert, rested the great Rodin, the Henry Moore, the Noguchi, and Gaby's special favorite, Hector Guimard's wrought-iron Art Nouveau *folie*, the Paris Metro entrance.

The few guests who had retired to the Sculpture Garden with their supper plates were beginning to wander back inside, and Gaby was left with the blossoming depression that always signified she was missing Mark. For the first time in months, she felt acutely alone.

A budding star she might be, but tonight, none of Terry's famous friends granted her more than a word in passing. To give Barron his due, he was paying attention to her, but not the kind she needed to quell the panic. Maybe she just wasn't ready to be social again.

She'd felt more comfortable, she realized, in the empty days right after Mark's exit, when misery was a natural state. She'd felt awful for that year and a half, so vulnerable that she seldom went out and took pains to avoid meeting men, substituting the make-believe romance of the books she was reading at the rate of one a day.

Expecting to die of love, she'd almost disappointed herself by surviving. Hoping to starve to death, she found, to her dismay, that her passion for chocolate doughnuts and pizza with everything on it was undiminished by grief.

She read, she ate, she started smoking because she hated herself. She stopped running, dancing, exercising, and skiing. She worked as hard as ever at MOMA, but now maintained a distance from the rest of the world, which alienated everyone, women confidantes as well as suitors. She didn't bother to call back the friends who left messages on the answering machine, and, eventually, they stopped calling. But she kept the machine long after she needed it, wanting more than anything not to miss Mark's call when it finally came.

He had left just after New Year's. Then came Easter without a word. Then a silent July Fourth, Halloween, and Thanksgiving. By Christmas, she felt she had bottomed out, but on New Year's, realizing it had been a year since he'd left, she consumed an entire *gâteau St.-Honoré* from Dumas and put the machine away.

Then, in March, at the opening of one of the Museum's film series, she'd overheard someone say, "Mark Groseman." She'd almost fainted, then, discreetly, over the drone of the filmmaker who'd cornered her, she'd begun to eavesdrop. Pauline Kael and a reviewer from *Newsweek* were discussing *Torture Garden,* a horror movie Mark had shot on a shoestring in New York while they were still together. After he'd hit Los Angeles, he'd hustled it to an old college chum who was now a production executive at Epic Pictures. The studio had opened it wide in the middle of the country, and to everyone's shock—the executive's most of all—it had begun to do big business, so much so that it was now being released in the major markets. To coincide with the Memorial Day super release, the reviewer had persuaded his editor to fly him to LA to interview Mark. Pauline Kael and the *Newsweek* guy couldn't praise

Mark's potential highly enough, suggesting, among other things, that at Mark's age, Hitchcock hadn't had his virtuosity.

Although Gaby continued to smile and acknowledge whatever it was her companion was pontificating about, she felt every pulse point in her body start to throb. It was extraordinary that the man next to her seemed not to hear her thundering heartbeat, not to display alarm at the way she must have paled. But he merely droned on as her thoughts raced as fast as her heart.

She had cut herself off from most of her friends because they were actually *their* friends, because the very mention of Mark's name made her flinch. She had pretty nearly stopped going to movies, since they reminded her of Mark and, consequently, hurt her. She rarely risked reading the entertainment section of the *Times* for fear of seeing him praised for something he'd achieved without her support.

She had spent a year and a half in solitary, sheltering herself from any news of him, cursing him, and now that time proved to have been a total waste. Mark Groseman was alive and well and living on the brink of the Big Time. She, on the other hand, had gained fifteen pounds, gotten totally out of shape, and become a relative recluse.

He had already outgrown her in New York. By now, in LA, he must have totally forgotten her. He was gone, and he was never coming back. She would never be part of his success, and, at twenty-six, she had too many years left to waste them grieving in her apartment. So she made herself lose the weight, get back in shape, stop smoking, do all the work on her post-Mark version of herself. And, just when she was ready to venture forth into the world, Jackson Pendleton had entered her life, bathing her in priceless promises and a dazzling future, but leaving untouched the same old set of insecurities.

"Hey! Why'd you run off?" She looked up to find Terry standing beside her, a glass of champagne in each hand. "Hamill, who pronounced you quite a dish—and he should know—took it personally, your splitting like that."

"Sorry," she replied, setting down her own empty glass and accepting one of his. "You seemed sort of . . . involved."

He sat down beside her with just enough deliberation to make her aware he was feeling the booze. "And you seemed sort of upset."

"About as upset as you are high. Just a little."

"Yeah, but I switched from bourbon to the kids' stuff. What are we going to do for you?" He swayed almost imperceptibly as he waited for her answer. "You're lonely for someone, aren't you?"

She didn't raise her head, just shrugged.

"Don't worry." He draped his arm lightly around her, as if they were teammates walking off a softball field. "We'll cheer you up!"

"We will?" She managed a faint grin.

"You bet." He patted her back reassuringly. "Let's split from here. At this point, we're both o.d.ing on wit and glamor. Let's move down in the world." And, for some reason, she trusted him enough to allow him to take her hand and lead her away.

"We didn't say good-night to Jackson and Laura." Gaby remembered after they had made it to the sidewalk.

"Don't fret. Tell them I dragged you out against your will." Terry pulled out a pack of Camels, extracted a cigarette, lit it and dispensed with the match in one fluid gesture, like Sinatra. "Blame it on my boorish, working-class upbringing."

"Oh, pul-eez, don't start that again!" She was surprised to find, now that she was mobile, that the champagne had made straight for her head. "Please!"

He grinned and made a mock bow. "Okay. Agreed. The only Marx I quote tonight is Groucho."

Gaby responded with a little curtsey. When Terry suggested they go uptown to that boîte of the literati, Elaine's, Gaby emphatically shook her head no. "You promised we could get away from wit and glamor. I don't want to spend hours watching you talk to the same people you were talking to inside. Elaine'll forgive you if you don't show up just this once, won't she?"

"Costello's?" It was the longtime newspaperman's hangout in the east forties, a shirt-sleeved version of Elaine's, but to Gaby it was, for tonight, off limits. She said no. Then she said no to Studio 54. No to Regine's. No to Bobby Short.

Suddenly, her face seemed visibly to brighten. "I know where I want to go! Trader Vic's!"

His pure shock was unmistakable. "Trader Vic's?"

"Yeah," she beamed, "Trader Vic's. I want whatever they have that's closest to a piña colada."

"Oh, well then." His ruggedly handsome features began to relax until they were almost cherubic with relief. "You should've said that to begin with! I just happen to know that the bartender at David Kay's makes a legendary piña colada——"

"Trader Vic's." She was *telling* him. "Don't worry. Nobody you know would dream of being seen there, so you're safe. Liz Smith will never be any the wiser!" And she patted his cheek gently, like a nanny calming her charge.

Terry was determined to behave like a good sport, but as he took her arm and steered her toward Fifth Avenue, he mock-muttered, "Whatever happened to the women's movement? I remember the good old days of 1971 when you could fight it out with a dame. Whatever happened to sexual equality? Next, you'll be expecting me to light your cigarettes!"

"I don't smoke," she told him loftily, as they turned uptown toward the Plaza and Trader Vic's.

As they strolled along a Fifth Avenue deserted except for occasional bands of Japanese businessmen, across Fifty-eighth and up the Plaza steps, she described to him her childhood memories of the Plaza, a monumental fairy-tale palace to a small girl from Boston. How she and her New York cousins had played tag in the bowels of the hotel while the adults enjoyed tea at the Palm Court. And that the crowning reward for keeping out of the grown-ups' way was a trip to the amazing Deco jungle that was Trader Vic's, where the Shirley Temples arrived in coconut shells, each shaded by a tiny paper umbrella, which Gaby had always carried back to Boston as a treasured souvenir.

Tonight, the coconut shell contained a thick, sweet delectable potion that she knocked back as fast as Terry downed his Wild Turkey. After her third round, she completely lost her way back to the table from the ladies' room and realized simultaneously that she was drunk and that she might never find Terry again. She did, though, and they both laughed at the fact that her skill as a Plaza explorer had faded with the years.

She was too high to be sure how high either of them was, but as long as she was seated, she felt sober enough to keep up her end of a steady stream of giddy, funny, wisecracking conversation, which flowed so easily she forgot they had just met.

Later, standing at the base of the Plaza Fountain, Gaby, unable to stop giggling, admitted, "I'm drunk, I think, and embarrassed," to which Terry replied, "No reason to be embarrassed about having a good time, but you should be embarrassed about forgetting these, after you made such a fuss," and he withdrew from his pocket three tiny pink paper umbrellas, which she accepted with a slightly shaky curtsey.

He refused to tell her where they were going next, just hailed a cab and gave the driver an obscure address somewhere downtown. The cab whisked them through the empty post-midnight streets like a magic stallion, making every light once they'd hit Park, then turned east in the forties, plunging toward the East River Drive. The luminous skyline panorama from the drive thrilled her as much as the river breeze languidly whipping her hair. "God, this really is a trip!" she exclaimed and received a warm squeeze of the hand in return. Now they were turning off the drive and heading for a destination deep in the Wall Street Area.

"I'm not going to give you the satisfaction of asking where we're going. I'll just sit still and take my medicine."

"It won't hurt for long," he assured her, "and after the pain comes the most exquisite pleasure. You'll see."

The cab was stopping in what looked like the middle of nowhere. The only recognizable architectural feature was the bridge far above them. As they climbed out, Gaby murmured, "I hope you're trustworthy, because if you leave me here, I'll never get back uptown."

"Sure you will. By day, this area is really busy." They were standing still as she waited for him to spring the surprise. Finally, the strangeness of the place and a sneaking suspicion that it would all turn out all right made her say, ''All right, I give up. Where could we be going this close to the Brooklyn Bridge?''

''The Brooklyn Bridge!'' he announced merrily.

''What do you mean, the Brooklyn Bridge?''

''The Brooklyn Bridge. You've been living in New York . . . how long?—three years . . . five years? —and I bet you've never even been to Brooklyn. Have you?''

She had to admit she hadn't.

''So I'm taking you on the grand luxe tour, starting with the bridge. You lucky girl . . . woman . . . person!''

She responded with the obligatory ''hrrmph,'' then asked him just how they were going to get across the huge expanse.

''Simple.'' He took her hand and led her toward a steep flight of steps leading up to the bridge. ''We're going to walk.''

''Walk . . . across the Brooklyn Bridge?'' She stopped dead in her tracks. ''You must be crazy. You *are* crazy! Even if I was foolish enough to risk my life walking across a totally deserted bridge at two o'clock in the morning, I would certainly not risk my feet. Look at these heels! If I don't get the heel caught and plunge to my death, I'll be crippled for life. Terry, really, I'm just not a free agent in these boots.''

''Baby''—he retained her hand but with his free one, lifted her chin—''with the amount of alcohol you've got in you, you'll think you're wearing your Adidas. Believe me, you're in absolutely no danger of maiming or death.''

''So you'll protect me, huh?'' She cocked her head at what she hoped was a jaunty angle.

''You bet,'' he proclaimed, his grape-jelly eyes staring deep into her suddenly misty ones. But the expected kiss never came; he merely dropped his fingers from her chin, patted her cheek, and began to lead her up the steps to Brooklyn.

"Your kingdom, madamoiselle." He indicated the glittering city for her approval.

"Thanks. Since you were so kind as to offer, I'll take it." She turned from the skyline to face him. They were just staring at each other, two tall, slightly drunk people, suddenly silent in the middle of the Brooklyn Bridge.

"Did anyone ever tell you," she asked him abruptly "that you look like a taller, funkier Robert Redford?"

"Actually yes," he responded. "But did anyone ever tell you you look like a younger, hipper, sexier Audrey Hepburn?"

"No," she answered, refusing to drop her eyes, "but they will," and on they continued across the bridge.

On the first third, Gaby screamed that she would be swept off the open expanse by a strong wind, while Terry assured her it would never happen, had never happened. To get off midbridge, he noted, you had to jump. She considered that reasoning and solemnly accepted it. The boots, given his careful shepherding, were less of a problem than the sliver of traffic roaring by in the cracks between the wooden slats that formed the pedestrian walk.

"Suppose one of the boards goes? Right now? We'll be plummeted into traffic?"

"Never happen. Not while I'm around. You know, luck of the Irish!" And, with that, he irrationally dismissed her fears.

She was forced to ooh and aah at the monumental spider's webs extending from the double pinnacle miles above her, the twin towers of the bridge becoming a single *trompe l'oeil* turret with a divine mirror reflection. Terry had been right; from fear she had progressed to ecstasy, and reveled in the warmth of the night, the benevolence of the breeze, the imperial openness.

"Now, turn around," he urged her, and she wheeled carefully about to confront the skyline waiting at the end of the filigree road on which she stood. "God!" she gasped, "the Emerald City!"

"Worth the trip?" he asked, lighting a cigarette on the first try, despite the river breezes.

At the River Café, a chic converted barge on the Brooklyn docks with an astonishing eye-level view of the Manhattan skyline, the bartender introduced Gaby to a mysterious concoction far surpassing a piña colada. It was called a Golden Cadillac. When she wolfed it down, demanding another, Terry warned her, "Go a little slower. They're dynamite."

With an atypical insouciance, Gaby insisted, "At this point, I doubt that I'd even feel it," to which he replied with an irresistibly crinkly smile, "That's what they all say, and it's the last thing they remember until the next morning!"

"What time is it, anyway?" Gaby asked later as they stumbled across the pebbly yard of the restaurant.

"Do you really want to know?" he laughed, checking his watch as if to be prepared for her decision.

"Ummm. Yes . . . no, *no*! No, I don't," she decided. "Anything else on the agenda?"

"Well . . ."—he contemplated the possibilities as they reached the sidewalk. "As long as we're here . . . come on, this way," and he led her into a stark, deserted street of warehouses fronting on the docks.

There was no traffic on the river, not so much as a sign of anyone in the alley, and she could hear her boot heels beating a tattoo on the pavement. Craning her neck to look up, she was surprised to see, like a village built into a mountainside, great, glowing buildings towering above her.

"What's that up there?" she asked him.

"Brooklyn Heights." He steered her toward some steep steps. "Our next destination. Truly, the best view in New York."

"Gee, I didn't even know this was here!" she exclaimed as they mounted the stairs to confront a broad promenade running parallel to the river, backed by elegant townhouses whose rear river views had been enhanced by the addition of balconies or huge picture windows.

"This is my equivalent of your neighborhood. All you get to see from Beekman Place is the other side of the river. What I get to see is Manhattan."

"It's fabulous." She was struck by the glorious skyline, as well as by the calm and the sense of the past around her. "Could I just sit down for a minute and stare, like the out-of-towner that I am?"

So they sat, not needing to speak, satisfied with the progress of their trek. Then he lit a cigarette and gently urged her to talk about herself.

She told him about her dreams, about a lot of her past, omitting, for some unfathomable reason, Mark's existence in her memories. Omitting, too, the terrible break with her family, she tried to explain to him that she was an *ordinary* rich girl, from old Wasp money with little glamor. The Blakes were a Boston patriarchy in which the jet set was considered to have been spawned in the vile behavior of the Duke and Duchess of Windsor some forty years earlier. "You know, being a rich provincial in New York doesn't really give you any social advantage whatsoever. It's still the way it was in the days of Edith Wharton. In fact, it's worse. You can't buy your way in, not when you're me. A redneck rock star has a better chance of breaking into the great world than someone with my background.''

''Or a bog-bitten Irish reporter . . .'' he growled.

''No . . . well, yes, I guess you're right. Anyway, the Great World—I want it as much as you seem to. It's just that at this moment you're the prince and I'm the serving maid—'' Suddenly a thought struck her. ''Hey, don't get me wrong. I *know* I'm lucky. It's great not having to struggle for a living. I appreciate that. But, you know, even people with charmed lives have problems and hang-ups and disappointments.'' She turned toward him. ''You haven't talked about yourself at all. Your story's a lot more interesting than mine.''

Unexpectedly, he gently put his hand on her shoulder. ''It's too late, and the story's too long—and too rambling. Later . . . You know, you really are a beautiful woman.'' She felt he was about to draw her to him, and she realized how much she wanted him to. ''I think Jackson's taste is once again right on the dollar.'' To her dismay, he released his hold and sat back, examining her as if she were a contact sheet. ''You'll be a famous face. Very soon.''

''Thanks,'' she replied, more puzzled by his reticence than pleased by his confidence in Jackson's taste. ''That's good to hear,'' and she proceeded to catch herself in a yawn.

''Tired?'' he asked.

''Yes.'' She felt, for the first time, her exhaustion. ''But I hate to give up while it's still dark.''

''Next time we'll see the sun come up,'' he assured her. ''When I tell you the story of my life.''

''Promise?'' she glanced at him, waiting for his word.

''Cross my heart,'' and he did. ''But listen, I live only a couple of blocks from here. Why don't you stay at my place and then get a cab back to New York at a civilized hour tomorrow?''

Unexpectedly, her heart leapt. ''Well, actually . . . maybe I'll take you up on that.''

Gaby knew she would never forget the walk to the apartment, through the lush and dreaming streets of Brooklyn Heights. You just never know how things are going to turn out, she told herself. You just never know at the beginning of an evening where you're going to end up. Terry had his arm loosely around her, and finally admitting they were both far too tired to be witty, they strolled in silence, but serenely, as if they were used to being together. With a start, Gaby realized that, for the first time in a year and a half, Mark had slipped from her thoughts for as long as an hour at a time. This Terry Barron, this blondish, incredibly blue-eyed brute, was really some guy. And he thought she was beautiful, and he wanted her to spend the night.

''Okay, home,'' he proclaimed as they paused before a regal grey stone Victorian apartment building.

''Good evening, Mr. Barron,'' the ancient doorman greeted him, without any indication that a lady's presence at this time of the night was at all scandalous.

''Good evening, Sean,'' Terry responded amiably, then allowed the doorman to lead them to an elevator and to drop them on the fourth floor.

They emerged into a small square anteroom that contained two doors. ''Big apartment,'' she surmised.

''Yeah, two on a floor. Brooklyn Heights was very grand when Beekman Place was a cow pasture.''

''Let's hear it for Brooklyn.''

''Why not?'' he agreed, turning the key in the lock. The apartment was huge; she couldn't tell how huge, but the central hall was as big as a disco. Before he disappeared into the cavernous depths beyond, Terry escorted her into the living room and urged her to make herself comfortable. She was glad for the momentary chance to examine his domain without being observed, but the more she looked, the stranger things became.

The living room ceilings were high, the windows plentiful. But what puzzled Gaby was the decor. It was "early Boston Irish parlor" style, replete with lace curtains and doilies on the arms of bloated, upholstered furniture. The walls were decorated with unspeakably awful prints of Paris scenes, painted by artists who'd never been there, and paint-by-number woodland brooks. The only feature that made her realize she was not in Curley's Boston was the huge color TV proudly placed before the windows with the river view.

When Terry returned, he found her sitting on a couch, inwardly mortified by the fact that she was posing among pillows with embroidered inscriptions. She knew it would be tough to get romantic on top of "My Country 'Tis of Thee," but she aimed to try.

"Would you like something to drink?" he asked her.

"No, I've had more than enough, but why don't you sit down for a second?"

"I will as soon as I close the doors. I don't want to wake up anybody."

"Who is there to wake up?" Gaby asked, hoping for a dog.

"Well, my mother."

"Your mother?"

"Yeah, after my dad died, Mom decided to move down here. This is a co-op. We own it."

"You live with your mother."

"Yep, with my mother, my two sisters, and my grandmother."

"And they're all here."

"All but my sister Sarah. She's in Montauk with her

boyfriend.'' Through her shock, Gaby guessed Sarah had to go that far away to get laid.

''So, listen, you sleep in my room, and I'll sleep out here.''

As her world collapsed, her manners improved. ''Oh, I couldn't do that.''

''Of course you can.'' He took her hand and raised her to her feet. ''Mom would never forgive me if I let a beautiful girl sleep on the couch. I've put out one of my sister's nightgowns, some towels and a toothbrush, and made up the bed. Right through there. Bathroom's attached.''

She nodded mutely.

''All set?'' he inquired. And New York's number one stud took her hands in his, lightly pecked her on the forehead, and whispered, ''Sleep tight.''

''Come on, baby! You're making love, not playing statues!''

The room was as steamy as a tropical rain forest, and Gaby was starting to sweat. The exquisite manly form of Tom Matthews grabbed her, whirling her toward the thick carpet beneath them as the sexy, insistent beat of the Rolling Stones enveloped them. Now she was on her back, her chestnut hair fanned out around her, the thick white satin of the Lagerfeld shirt opened to her waist. Tom's lean, perfect body insinuated itself next to hers, and his hand moved rhythmically along the satin, toward her breast, with passionate concentration. She smiled, she moaned, she moulded her torso to his. She laughed, she murmured, she examined his model-perfect features at close range as she wondered why Terry Barron hadn't called. He already had her number; Laura Pendleton had given it to him so that he could make the MOMA date, but he hadn't used it since. Conventional women's wisdom always said that if you'd had a great time, the guy had too; according to that, he should have been calling her constantly, but no. The night they'd met, she'd decided to check him out with Laura, but afterwards, bathed in the remembered glow of the evening, sure that she would hear from him, she'd decided it was bad luck to bring him up. Instead, she spent some time at the library, reading back articles he'd done for *Esquire* and *New York*. She even bought *Sports Illustrated* for the piece he'd done on Bjorn Borg, and was thrilled to discover the extent of his talent.

When he called, she'd be prepared. She'd done her homework, could even quote him. When he called. But he hadn't.

Now Tom had maneuvered himself across her, and she raised one Calvin Klein tuxedo-clad leg, wrapping it around the matching gabardine of her partner's back, the black satin pump dangling from her toes. The music grew more frenzied as her temperature continued to soar. She could feel the sweat binding the hair at the base of her neck to her skin, the heat of Tom's body reaching hers even through the layers of clothing.

Instinctively, she and Tom moved together so that she was astride him, her head thrown back in rapturous abandon. And just as she decided to call Laura after all, Tom raised himself and buried his face in her chest, the music climaxed, and someone above Jackson shouted, "All right, guys, we got it!"

Immediately, she rolled away from Tom, who rose and helped her to her feet. "Terrific, Gaby! It really felt great," and he kissed her politely. "Thanks. Thanks, Jackson." He grabbed a towel from a nearby table and began to dry himself off.

Gaby was staggering toward the miragelike magnificence of a can of Tab beckoning seductively in the distance, but before she got to it, she was swept up in the fatherly embrace of Jackson Pendleton.

"Jackson, was it good?" She looked pensively up at him.

"Good? My love, it was revolutionary! It was hot! It'll be a classic! Once *Vogue* hits the stands, you'd better have an unlisted phone!" They walked languidly, arm in arm, toward the table with the Tab. As she was gulping gratefully, he said, "Ran into a friend of yours in East Hampton."

"Yes?" she paused. "Who?"

"Terry Barron," he continued casually, turning off the bright shooting lights.

"Oh?" she asked with apparent indifference. "I don't know if I'd exactly call him a friend. I only saw him that once, the night of your opening."

"Well, *he* thinks he's your friend. Went on and on about what a great time you both had. Said he's going to call you as soon as he and Denise get back to town."

"Denise?" she shot back before she could stop herself.

"Yeah. She flew in from the Coast for a couple of weeks. They're coming to New York next week, then she's off to Paris."

"Funny," she mused. "He didn't mention . . . Denise."

"Honey, he must've assumed you knew about Denise. *I* thought you did."

"Well, I don't," Her thirst had vanished with Denise's introduction. "Denise who?"

"Baby," he told her, "Denise is Denise Sullivan."

"Oh, my God." Her hand, propelled by shock, flew without bidding to her mouth. "*The* Denise Sullivan?"

"The one and only," he replied, then patted her affectionately on the rear. "Come on, get dressed, and we'll grab some lunch!"

And as she changed back into real life, it all became perfectly clear. Denise. Denise was *the* Denise Sullivan, of Southampton, New York, Los Angeles, Palm Springs, Antibes, Acapulco, Venice, etc. *The* Denise Sullivan, winner of three Academy Awards and several opulent alimonies. She was one of the most glamorous women in the world. And Terry Barron was her lover.

chapter two

CANNES,
May 1982

THE assemblage of meeting-takers on the Carlton Terrace continued to build, but the sun, apparently having been sufficiently entertained, was withdrawing gracefully behind the waterline. My appointment was a half hour out of Cannes, and I had forty-five minutes to get there. Luckily, Denise was meeting François Truffaut at seven, so we plowed our way off the terrace and through the chaos of the lobby to the elevators. Denise was to see Truffaut upstairs in somebody's suite, so she paused, traded a kiss for the car keys, and disappeared into the first available elevator. Only someone who'd known her as long as I had would have guessed she was pissed at me for my inattention; Denise is some actress.

Despite the press, the doorman got the De Lorean to me in record time, and as I spoke sexy love words to my beautiful creature, she responded by purring, then springing into life with the grace of Makarova, around the driveway and onto the Croisette. The crowds on the boulevard were unbelievable; people were making deals while crossing the street, cornering producers, seducing distributors, chasing stars, ogling starlets against the lavish background of palms and blue sky and flowers and gigantic garish billboards pimping for movies I'd never heard of. As the black cat and I slinked together out of town, I breathed a sigh of relief and took the coast road. It was just what I needed in this car—challenging enough to engage my attention yet allow my thoughts to wander to the man I'd soon be meeting.

Monsieur Corday. I was curious to know what his game was, curious to know the nature of his involvement with the object of my grand passion. No, I was more than curious. I was nervous, nervous and afraid. Almost as afraid to meet the man as I was to view the treasure that I had craved and he had captured. What had Gaby meant to him that he would plunk down a fortune simply for the privilege of bathing in the reflected glory of her image? I wondered if he was equally uneasy about meeting me, for after all, he had intimated that he was contacting me because Gaby had wanted it. Maybe in that last year, she had missed our friendship, strange as it was. And it was strange. Right from the beginning.

The evening we first met had lasted almost twenty-four hours and taken us from the vaunted halls of MOMA to my mother's living room in Brooklyn, from bedrock antagonism to an affinity that karma had fashioned out of what should have been romance.

I remember when she first opened the door after a bizarre delay; she was half-madeup, hair not done, clad in jeans that were going at the knees and a Rolling Stones t-shirt so faded the logo looked like palimpsest. She was, even then, the most striking woman I'd ever seen—a sort of wild combination of Audrey Hepburn and one of Gaugin's Polynesian nymphets, ethnically untraceable, incredibly alluring. She was tall, probably five-ten or so, and her body still possessed a long-legged coltishness that only narrowly skirted awkwardness in favor of infinite charm. The shape of the face revived in me the sensual thrill of Modigliani's sweet temptresses, the oval motif repeated in the eyes, huge half-spheres of Coke-bottle green with flecks of amber; the nose was perfectly suitable in almost any culture, the cheekbones high and gentle as an Olympic downhill slope, the mouth, a perfect, irresistible Lolita rosebud. And the mahogany-auburn mane made her look like a lioness-in-training. She was adorable—and snobbish, frigid, unsociable, a real rich bitch of a brat.

Which only proves you can never tell endings from beginnings. We endured a cab ride of such genuine bad feeling that I was prepared to volunteer for the Foreign Legion, if it still existed, rather than spend another minute in her narcissistic company. But that all changed, and only a few hours later I was leading this ice princess, all giddy and laughing, across the Brooklyn Bridge and realizing for the first time in my life that the root word of *enjoyment* is *joy*.

That first night, she talked about her plans, her dreams, her life, even a little about the family from which she was estranged. But there was something she didn't tell me, some enormous disappointment that had produced that terrified shyness I'd taken for arrogance. She was quite a lovable sort of girl, in more ways than one, and there was a moment on the Esplanade when I was determined that we would plunge into an affair. What halted me was my awareness of her vulnerability.

This was a girl who'd been hurt; I'd have staked my reputation, both as a perceptive journalist and as a man who knows and likes women, on it. She'd been hurt, and she was very, very sensitive, and given my present relationship with Denise, what I had to offer as a lover wasn't substantial enough to risk hurting her again. So I changed my course, but I just couldn't sail away. It's unusual, even in this enlightened age, for a man and a woman to ease into the same groove so effortlessly. We liked each other too much to call it quits, so I decided to play it the hard way. Since we couldn't become lovers without losing each other, we'd have to do the impossible; we'd have to become friends.

chapter three

EAST HAMPTON, NEW YORK, *August 1977*

GABY was reaching up for a tin of biscuits when she heard a woman's voice behind her whisper to a companion, "That girl! She's on the cover of the new *Vogue*! Isn't she fabulous!"

Restraining herself from freezing midreach, Gaby turned in toward the shelf. Pulling the red tin down from the top shelf, she let her back disguise the grin that sprang unbidden to her face. When she had slowly, casually turned around and strolled toward the register, the ladies were already outside on the sidewalk, casting one last, confirming glance in her direction.

It was Wednesday, midweek, but it was a week that culminated in Labor Day, and Dean & DeLuca was almost as crowded as it normally was on a rainy Saturday afternoon. Jackson, still waiting to be served at the cheese counter, was mildly agitated by the fact that the two tennis-clothed ladies in front of him had been sampling every cheese they decided not to buy. As

Gaby approached him, he muttered, "They have now sampled twelve triple crèmes. Just can't make up their minds. Sometimes I wish this wasn't the greatest delicatessen since Fauchon. If it wasn't so good, we wouldn't have to put up with this."

"More like Cartier than a deli, I'd say," she quipped, indicating a cheese that was a steep eleven dollars a pound. The two matrons had finally decided on half a pound of "the closest thing you have to Jarlsberg," after which Jackson took a pound and a half of *mascarpone* while Gaby grabbed a couple of *marron* sorbets from the freezer case, and they both charged to the register.

Along the ironically skinny length of the store was displayed the best of every kind of luxury food, from fresh produce and probably fifty kinds of mustard to an endless variety of crackers, biscuits, and pickles, and, as Jackson had just bemoaned, more triple crèmes than can be found anywhere outside the Food Halls of Harrods in London. Great bowls of homemade salads of every kind, platters of smoked meats and fish, caviar and barbecued ducks competed with lavish displays of fresh herbs, fresh pasta, breads, cakes, dozens of kinds of imported candies, and elegant cooking supplies.

To spend more than five minutes in Dean & DeLuca and not grow ravenously hungry was impossible, even, Gaby imagined, for a Zen monk. But if a monk could be pardoned for a momentary deviation from cold noodles, not so Jackson Pendleton's pet model. She was not permitted so much as one icing-covered apricot, not a single fresh lychee. Fame. Grr. It just had to be worth the hunger.

They were back in Jackson's silver blue 1967 Cadillac convertible, cruising along Main Street, a verdant, Georgian thoroughfare lined with sparkling white renovated houses and twenties Tudor cottages, a vista broken in its broad center by a pond lush with water lilies. Turning left toward the ocean, they passed lanes bordered with increasingly large, increasingly manicured cottages, extending, as the road began to widen, into baronial mansions hidden behind hedges at the end of long drives, their gatehouses fronted by fences luxuriant with climbing roses.

When the road opened up, it did so to disclose, on the right, an eighteenth-century vista of extraordinary serenity: a still and elegant pond on which floated several swans with ugly ducklings in tow; on the left, a bend in the road became a lane running parallel to the beach, and lying straight ahead was a great dune, which sported, atop its gentle height, the Maidstone Club, the apotheosis of the Deco Tudor manor house indigenous to the South Shore of Long Island. The sun was high, and everything gleamed with the insouciance with which only great financial security can endow a scene.

"Well, Gaby, do you?" The irritation in Jackson's voice shifted her wandering attention rapidly back to him.

"Jackson, I'm sorry. My mind was wandering . . ."

"So I noticed. What could it be, a thought so important it outweighs my always pithy conversation?" He smiled, patting her white-muslin-clad thigh without taking his eyes off the road.

"Well, actually," she turned toward him, "I'm just blissing out because . . . because two ladies in Dean & DeLuca recognized me—*me*!—from the *Vogue* cover! Me! Jackson, I've been recognized, for heaven's sake!"

"Baby," he shot her a brief, bittersweet smile, "in another six months, you'll have those same ladies stopping you in the street. The price of fame is loss of privacy, so enjoy what's left of your anonymity while you can."

"Oh, Jackson, don't act like Scrooge. I'll be able to handle it!" She noticed, suddenly, that Jackson had turned on the radio on which Carly Simon was singing, "You're so Vain."

"So, anyway," Jackson continued, "you want to drive back into town with me to pick up Laura and Philippe?"

"Which train?" she asked idly.

"The four fourteen."

"And it's now . . . what? Two thirty?"

"Just about," he answered, not bothering to check his watch. "We'll have lunch when we get back to the house. Something light."

"I don't want something light. I want a pizza!" she protested.

"You can't have it," he replied tersely.

"Then I wish I could at least go out in the sun!"

"Not a chance," he lectured her, "not if you want *Vogue*. Grace has this crazy bias against tans with evening gowns." He smiled compassionately. "Sacrifice Number Three. No privacy. No food. And no beach."

On the radio, Carly had given way to Billy Joel, who was crooning to some lucky girl that he loved her just the way she was. Hmmmm. Some girls sure had all the luck.

"You know, Jackson, I'll stay around the house when you go back to town, and finish *The Thorn Birds*." She would be sorry to see it end; for the few days during which she had been caught up in the novel, all the passion and sensuality that her new, glamorous life entirely lacked had flowed back into her thoughts.

"Yep. I think I'll lie around and read. Unless reading dulls the eyes the way pasta rounds the corners."

"No, you can continue to read—for a couple more weeks, at least," he joked as he turned off Georgica Lane onto a narrow road leading across a gently inclined field to the dazzlingly white *moderne* factory of a beach house that had appeared in *The New York Times*, *Vogue*, *Architectural Digest*, *Town and Country*, and almost every other notable publication with the exception, as Laura pointed out, of *National Geographic*.

Staggered on three levels, the house featured external industrial stairways sinuously clinging to two silo-shaped turrets. A swimming pool, built into the lowest level, still considerably above ground, opened off the studio-sized wall of glass forming the living room window and overlooked the ocean beyond. The house, certainly the most avant-garde in this nest of beachy mansions, had garnered substantial critical comment from the more traditional neighborhood, until the chic crowd that Jackson and Laura drew there had made it a must subject for conversation. Since then, the praise excited on the house's behalf in *The New York Times* had made it a stop on everybody's tour of East Hampton, and in the five years since it had gone up, it was coming to be widely imitated—in one case, right down the road from the original.

Jackson pulled up the stark driveway and then they both began hauling the next few days' supplies around to the back deck, which led to the magnificent restaurant-sized kitchen, which Jackson alone ruled. As he unpacked the provisions, Gaby perched atop a rattan-seated stool, leaning against the huge slab of waist-high chopping block that extended the thirty-foot length of the room. The circular pan racks above her head displayed their gleaming copper pendants like chandeliers in a ballroom.

When he'd finished the groceries, Jackson poured them each a chilled glass of Pouilly-Fumé, then prepared the lunch of cold lobster, his with *mayonnaise verte,* Gaby's with lemon. When the plates were arranged as beautifully as a still life, Gaby and her host carried them out to the canopied kitchen deck, which looked out onto a small, wooded area containing the herb garden and some riotous wild flowers. Although the canopy sheltered Gaby from the sun, Jackson insisted she take the added precaution of a wide-brimmed Ecuadoran farmer's hat. Although her body was covered from head to foot, the baggy, Indian muslin pants and loose shirts were sheer and loose enough to allow her to feel cool.

"Can I have one more glass of wine, Jackson, pretty please?" She moved her chair closer to his in play-intimacy.

"Well, just this once!" he laughed. He rose, grabbed both the empty glasses, and disappeared into the kitchen to refill them.

By the end of the second glass, Gaby was feeling the wine. "I can't believe it," she giggled, stretching seductively as the languor overcame her. "Two glasses of white wine, and I'm high! The clean life! Wow! I bet two puffs of a joint would have me hallucinating!"

"No," he patted her hand, "it would do worse. It would make you eat everything in the refrigerator, which is why you can't do it. Okay," he told her, "it's about three thirty. I hate to make you feel bad, but I'm going for a swim before I meet the train. Why don't you have a nap before your run?"

"Okay, I'm off," she sighed, as she rose and walked through the Bauhaus cathedral that was the living room, up the curved white metal staircase, and down the hall to the east tower room.

The room was at the top of one of the silo turrets, a small, round chamber like the princess's in a fairy tale, three quarters glass, including the roof, with a view made up entirely of ocean and sky. At night, you could choose to sleep under the stars. For the faint of heart, afraid of being wakened by the sun, white drapes could be drawn. Gaby had immediately decided to forego the drapes, for waking up in that light helped her pretend that she was at sea, on her way to any number of exotic places, with a handsome and courtly lover sleeping beside her.

The wine had already lulled her half to sleep, and as soon as she had stripped off her clothes and insinuated herself under the cool, white sheets, she drifted into a light and lovely doze in which, from a distance, she heard the car drive away. When, suddenly, the phone rang down the hall, she bolted from bed, wide awake, and ran into the master bedroom.

Jackson and Laura's bedroom was perhaps the most famous room in the entire house, and it was all Laura. The color of the walls was eloquently sandy, and the seemingly thousands of floral patterns were rescued from any hint of garishness by their neutral shades: sands and greiges and peches and ochres, nothing so strong even as pink; there were beige roses against off-white meadows sheltered by mother-of-pearl orchards. The bed, love seat, and chairs were comfortably upholstered in various neutral florals, and the tables and occasional furniture were glass, blond wood, and wicker. In almost colorless, exquisite Chinese bowls, off-white roses emitted a fabulous bouquet.

The phone rested on a glass Parson's table at the side of the bed, and Gaby had to hurl herself across the king-sized expanse to grab the instrument before it stopped ringing. As she reached for the receiver, she knocked the fragile little touch tone off the table, from which it clattered dully onto the silvery boards of the gleaming wood floor. "Oh, shit!" she cried, stretching to retrieve the casualty and rapidly calling hellos into the receiver.

"My God, girl," came the hearty voice of Terry Barron. "What's wrong? Intruder interrupt you when trying to call the cops?"

"Smart ass," she retorted, settling back onto the cushions, phone crooked in her neck. "Are you calling from out here?"

"Yep. Drove out last night. Real late. What're you doing?"

"Right this minute? Nothing. Jackson's gone into town to pick up Philippe de Valmont and Laura and the maid. I'm all alone. In the master bedroom. And I'm not wearing a stitch. Wanna join me?"

"Be over in a flash," and he pretended to be hanging up.

"Can't wait that long," she joked. "I'll just have to get dressed. Hey, what're you really doing?"

"Nothing," he told her. "Denise is in Southampton for the day, visiting some rich European ex-relatives who are too rich and too European for me. Thought maybe I'd take the car and drive to Montauk. Wanna come?"

Gaby mulled over the offer, then decided, "I don't really think I can . . . I mean, I don't think I should, not until they're all back at least. Why don't you come by here? If you leave now, you'll have a few minutes of my fabulous company before the arrival of the great Valmont. Did you ever meet him?"

"No, but the word is he's the greatest soccer player since Pelé."

"Oh, puleez. Philippe de Valmont is only the greatest design talent since Balenciaga. That's what Jackson says. I resent the guy already,'' Gaby admitted.

''And you need help making that clear, eh? You can count on me, nefarious creature. Gimme half an hour.''

''Okay. If I'm in the shower, just come in.''

''Best offer I've had all day. See you in thirty,'' and he hung up. Gaby replaced the phone on the table, straightened the bedclothes, reluctantly left behind the sensual fantasies that the beautiful room instantly conjured up, and settled instead for the nonfattening, nontanning luxury of a long, hot shower.

Gaby stuffed her hair under a cap and stepped into the shower stall. As the hot water first pelted her body, then gently caressed it, she thought of Jackson running backwards in front of her, camera in hand, and she running toward him barefoot down the beach, against the setting sun, in black Valentino chiffon, in absolutely magnificent red satin Lagerfeld, in green Valmont velvet; at one point, he tossed a beach ball as she ran and as she leapt to catch it, he took the picture. The whole sequence was going to be great. Jackson was not only terrific, he was fast. They had hauled the dresses along in the car for a practice run. If it worked, they'd bring out the crew and an editor and shoot for real, and from what Jackson said, the prints he'd developed that morning, but which she wasn't to see until this evening, were really promising.

Thinking about the Valmont gown made her realize she'd better get a move on. Regretfully, she turned off the water, stepped onto the carpet, dried herself with a towel the size, texture, and color of a cloud, then slathered herself with Floris body lotion.

Most of her makeup was still intact, and as soon as the mirror unfogged, she patched up the highlighter, the eyeliner, and applied one more coat of mascara to her lashes, as her fantasies took her forward to the impending dinner confrontation with Denise.

The dinner at which she was finally going to experience the phenomenon that was Denise Sullivan. Denise Sullivan, the woman who had everything—including Terry Barron.

Since that weird night in Brooklyn, Gaby and Terry had become something like buddies. He'd delivered on the promise he'd made through Jackson and called her as soon as he had gotten back to the city at the beginning of June. Denise had left for Europe the day before, and Gaby was convinced that, out of loneliness, he'd called everybody else looking for something to do before he phoned her. But he'd sounded, at least, genuinely glad to be in touch with her and, picking up on the easiness they'd achieved in the course of their one evening together, had insisted she go with him to a Yankees game. Astonishing herself, she said yes, although she was bored by baseball and not altogether thrilled about acquiring the company of an artful dodger like Barron. If he wasn't a playboy, he was a gigolo; either way, he was probably after her money. And even if he wasn't after her money, he didn't strike her as the dependable type—if only because of his mysterious commitment to Denise Sullivan. She'd intended to play it cool at the game, but found, to her dismay and delight, that she was having fun. Terry knew his baseball and was able to make it interesting to her. They laughed and joked and cheered and took comfort in each other's company, just like the first time. They ended up having pizza afterwards and then, surfeited on junk food, had wandered the lanes of Greenwich Village until the small hours. When they parted, they parted friends. He'd put her in a cab, kissed her chastely on the cheek, and told her he would call her.

But as the cab snaked upward through a deserted Sixth Avenue, her elation turned to depression. She knew, she just knew, that he'd never call again, and if he did, it would probably be seven months from now, the next time he was stuck with nothing to do. Anticipating her disappointment, applying it against the scenario of the disaster with Mark, she'd tried to unpuzzle in advance why someone who obviously enjoyed her company, who laughed at her jokes and traded innocent insults and furtive giggles on instinct, would keep his distance. When he hadn't called in two days, she'd patted herself on the back for her paranoid perspicacity. So secure was she in her safe sadness that, when he called on Sunday afternoon, she was almost disappointed, but only for a second, and when he insisted she join him for Chinese food that night, she totally overlooked the fact that he was calling at the last minute. From then on, they'd developed a pattern of talking to each other every couple of days, spending a week night or two and at least one weekend day together. He never came on to her, and she never knew why; then she stopped wondering and realized that, for the first time in her life, she had a real friend who was a man—a friend who admired her, who appreciated her, who shared his humor and his contacts and his trust with her. They were totally equal, the kind of relationship Gloria Steinem and the crew at *Ms.* would applaud, and on those rare occasions when the core inequity—the fact that he had someone in his life and she didn't—raised its ugly head, she told herself her burgeoning career would make a romantic commitment impossible, in any case. And if Mark *had* been around, they'd never even have had the time to become chums. Still, she had dreaded Denise's return.

She liked walking into P. J. Clarke's and having

people check out her and Terry because they were such a striking couple. She liked going to a tennis match and being greeted casually by his cronies. She even liked staying over at his house, where, in the morning, she always found her clothes freshly pressed by his warm and loving mother, who would also have prepared a breakfast so huge that Gaby was relegated to yogurt for the rest of the day. And best of all, she liked knowing that, without the eventual complications that sex brings to affinity, there was no reason for her ever to lose him. You lose lovers, not friends, she assured herself, and forced herself to quell her curiosity about the nature of his relationship with Denise. If he didn't offer to explain, she wasn't going to ask. That seemed to be one of the unarticulated rules of the relationship, and she obeyed it.

Finally, though, he'd opened up to her, just as he'd promised he would that morning as the sun came up on the Brooklyn Heights Promenade. He was Boston Irish, all right. His father had worked in the post office all his life, a deeply passionate Democrat who loved the Kennedys and prided himself that among his nephews were a psychiatrist and a Jesuit. Terry had, early on, developed a sense of rebellion and adventure and, a straight-A student in high school, had managed to maintain a record as both a model scholar and a brawler. Too attracted to the action outside the cloistered walls of Catholic school, he had joined the Marines after graduation then was promptly sent to Vietnam in the tough days around Tet.

He never talked about his experiences in Nam, but did mention he'd come back radicalized as well as redirected. Reapplying to the colleges he had not bothered to decline before the service, he rejected Harvard for Boston College and was as surprised as anyone when Harvard came back with a full scholarship. If he was surprised by Harvard, he was shocked when, several years later, he found himself the recipient of a Rhodes Scholarship. It was in England, at Oxford, that he'd mingled with the sons of the very rich and powerful, even been invited to their houses, had charmed their sisters, impressed their parents, and made enough journalistic contacts to come back to New York with an excess of self-confidence and an entree to top magazine and newspaper editors through the tycoons who employed them. Sure, he was cocky, but with reason. He had started noodling with writing in Nam, found, on his return, that he liked it, and by the time he came to New York, at home both in Society and the locker room, he was well on his way to being accomplished. Journalism offered him the same blend of action and solitude that he'd always craved, and his obsessive interest in sports and the street found an outlet in his writing. He was a young man with the ability to live comfortably in conflicting worlds, and he wrote of them both perceptively.

He'd met Denise early on in his New York debut, at a dinner party given by the parents of a friend. They'd ended up lovers that night and, four years later, they were still "together." In 1973, he was a brash kid in his twenties and she was a star in her forties, and her accepting him into her bed outstripped even his most glorious fantasies. He had been dazzled then; to his possible discredit, he was dazzled now, and even though Denise was incapable of traditional fidelity, she still exacted from him the obedience that a glamorous older goddess can always demand of a younger, lesser male mortal. They fought constantly—bitter battles; the clash of Irish temperaments clearly meant they were not intended to live together, and besides, the disparity in their ages and professional levels prohibited a conventional marriage with children and a vine-covered cottage. Denise veered between predicting he would grow up and leave her and excoriating him for being such a baby. He had actually tried to break it off, had experimented with pseudo-serious relationships with more suitable women, but the inexplicable lure of their love battles always drew him back when she wanted him. Surprisingly, she hadn't objected to his friendship with Gaby and was said to be looking forward to meeting her. Gaby, of course, resented Denise's patronizing hold over Terry and, as she applied her lip gloss, was rehearsing the ladylike put-downs with which she would vanquish the golden gorgon, when she heard cars pulling up outside the house and voices laughing down below.

chapter four

CANNES,
May 1982

EVERY ocean departs the day in its own style, like a guest leaving a party. Cruising along the Gold Coast, I marveled as the navy of night began to stain the technicolor aquamarine of the Mediterranean. The can-can flourish of this Riviera sunset seemed so extravagant compared to my recollection of dusk on the Atlantic coast. There the ocean greets night as if its arrival were a state visit; the water darkens gradually, like a carpet being rolled out for a potentate, moving gracefully, elegantly inward from the horizon toward the shore.

And as I thought of Long Island and the close of those long, languid days, and, of course, of Gaby, an image shot into my mind with such vividness that I could almost see it projected like a movie on the road before my eyes. It was a scene I'd completely forgotten because I'd underestimated its importance in all our lives. Looking at it now, from the vantage point of five years down the road, I wondered what would have happened if what I'd seen then had prompted me to make some comment, some gesture, to alter the pattern of what lay ahead. But maybe by then it was already too late, maybe it wouldn't have mattered. Nevertheless, having recalled it and recognized it as the turning point, I knew I would always be haunted by the lurking suspicion that, if I'd done something then, Gaby would now be sitting beside me, laughing and joking and being.

That late East Hampton afternoon, I had driven over to Jackson Pendleton's glamor factory of a beach house. Denise was doing something or other and wouldn't be back for a couple of hours. Since we were due to dine with the Pendletons, I'd left a note for her saying I'd gone on ahead and suggesting she meet me there. As it turned out, I arrived at Jackson's at the same time that he was pulling into the driveway with Laura, their maid Olga, and their weekend guest, the brilliant young couturier, Philippe de Valmont. Valmont must have been a couple of years younger than I was, around thirty, a tall, incredibly lean man of a physical type only possible in countries that have once had royal families. No American could fail to recognize him as an aristocrat; it was almost intimidating, especially in a country that measures worth in productivity of goods, not in ancestors. The very presence of Philippe de Valmont suggested that our puritan system of values was not only misconceived, but vulgar and, finally, callow. Centuries of careful breeding had gone into developing that incredibly narrow face; it occurred to me then that aristocrats and race horses, being equally the products of breeding, do actually resemble each other, especially in the stark simplicity of the lean, sculptured faces. Valmont's coloring suggested universal royalty; only men with a "de" before their names have that neutral-colored hair, which the alchemy of any particular scene turns to gold or bronze or, eventually, to the purest, most priceless pewter. The greyish-bluish eyes gazed at you with the self-possession of centuries of being obeyed, and his nose was fine as a stallion's, as perfectly in proportion to the high cheekbones and sliver of a mouth as in any portrait Valasquez ever painted. I'd met a lot of fancy and powerful dudes in my travels, but this guy was the genuinest article I'd come across. With the manners of a fifteenth-century Venetian diplomat, he gracefully requested to be shown immediately to his room to change from the probably thousand-dollar white linen suit that, disgracefully enough, was displaying the wrinkles sustained on the Long Island Railroad. Jackson grabbed Valmont's Vuitton weekender and escorted him to his quarters in one of the tower rooms. Laura and I, wineglasses already in hand, wandered outside, toward the ocean. As we passed by the east tower, Gaby, who was staying in the identical room to Philippe's in the north silo, called to us out the window. "Hi," she shouted, over the sound of the waves. "I'll be down in a second. Where's Jackson?"

"Showing Valmont to his quarters, mademoiselle. Come on down!" I shouted back.

"Okay, be right there!" She waved one final time and disappeared from the window.

Since "right there" to Gaby meant a good ten minutes, I was still waiting for her when Jackson returned with a vodka-tonic for himself and one for Valmont. Moving to the deck by the swimming pool, with the waves washing in the distance and the late afternoon sun sparkling on the water with a glorious, final brightness, I sipped my wine and slipped into a kind of romantic lethargy.

I was lured out of my reverie by Jackson's exclaiming, "Philippe! Your drink's waiting for you." Out of instinct, I turned to greet him as he stepped through the door, unprepared for the wave of outraged jealousy that swept over me. Having been accustomed to being a good-looking guy, my physical self-esteem is rarely shaken, but Valmont made me feel like the hunchback of Notre Dame. The bastard just glowed. His hair was bronzing out to match the sunlight, slicked back, which on American men looks greasy but on him looked elegant. For a second, I nastily suspected that the perfect tan had been helped along by artificial means, then realized that this guy was so rich he could afford to have a legitimate tan all the time. He was dressed in gracefully pleated pants of what must have been the lightest-weight flannel ever woven, and a plain white shirt with the collar open and the sleeves rolled up. Tennis shoes were the only thing we had in common, but his were worn yet clean, funky yet elegant.

"Jackson, Laura," he enthused elegantly as he walked around the pool to gaze at the ocean, "this is a paradise!" His English was disgustingly good; in fact, the French inflection made my native language sound better coming from him than it did from me. Jackson, Laura, and I just sat there, sipping our drinks, staring at his statuesque presence against the ocean, and I silently struggled with myself to overcome the jealousy.

"Hi, guys." Gaby, also dressed in white, her hair restrained into one great braid like an Indian maiden's, had stepped onto the deck. "The sun's going in, so I guess I can come out," she continued, as Valmont turned slowly back toward the house to greet her. And as he turned, she stopped—stopped dead in her tracks, as if she had been physically struck with something. She paused only for a second, then walked to my side without taking her eyes off him as Valmont made his way back around the pool.

"Hello, I'm Gaby," she said to him as he took her hand.

"Yes," was all he said, but for the moment that he held her hand, the frame froze, as they say in the movie business; everything stopped in that second as Gaby Blake lost her heart to Philippe de Valmont.

chapter five

EAST HAMPTON, NEW YORK, *August 1977*

"DENISE! Certainly not. You must never touch that hair!"

They sat over the remains of a Chinese banquet, concocted by Jackson with a speed and style equaling his prowess with a camera. Philippe was assuring Denise Sullivan that the hairstyle she had worn continuously for the last fifteen years was a trademark that should not be altered.

"But, Philippe, my darling," persisted the great lady herself, "don't you think I'm getting a little long in the tooth for a Buster Brown?"

"Denise!" Jackson broke in, backing up Philippe, "Denise Sullivan without bangs is like a day without sunshine!"

"Jackson, my precious," she lightly took him to task, "don't be cute about my future."

"Never." Rising from the table, he bent over her and bussed the bangs-covered forehead. "Don't you agree, Terry?" He turned toward his other guest.

"We have this discussion five times a day." Terry pretended scorn. "I refuse to talk about Denise's hair after seven at night. It's a house rule."

"Look at how cruel he is to me!" Denise presented a Bernhardt-like gesture of tortured woman, then blew Terry a kiss. "Tell me, Laura," the star persisted, turning a perky shoulder toward her hostess, "is Jackson so hard on you?"

"Certainly not." Laura smiled gracefully. "I don't allow it!"

Laura, with her two teen-aged children safely stowed with friends in Europe for the summer, was free to pursue the interior design enterprise that had begun as a lark and surprisingly blossomed into a real business. Gaby had to admire her; she was accomplished and enviable, but so easy with her good fortune that her generosity canceled out the jealousy that such a woman would normally inspire in another. Laura was, in fact, the only person at the dinner table who had even bothered to speak to her during the meal.

From the moment Denise Sullivan had breezed into the mellow evening, the show had begun, and the show was all hers. No great beauty, Denise presented an initial impression, at least to Gaby, of extraordinary ordinariness. She *was,* in fact, a little long in the tooth for the caramel-colored pageboy she'd been sporting. But the freckles were as vivid as they must have been when she was a girl, the nose as pert, the mouth as generous, the scrapper's blue eyes just as challenging. She was a little woman, no more than five-two or three, and she dressed in a tomboyish, tailored style reminiscent of Katherine Hepburn but with the little-girlishness of Margaret Sullavan. Her baby aqua slacks and camp shirt picked up the blue in the eyes Gaby had instantly wanted to scratch out.

As soon as Denise had catapulted herself into the group, the conversation had turned to the star herself, where it remained, almost without moving, for the rest of the dinner. Soliciting the men's advice on everything from her investments to her coiffure, she occasionally managed to hurl an idle comment at her hostess, and even at the maid, but Gaby, of course, had become immediately invisible. She wondered now if it was deliberate, if Denise was somehow punishing her because of her friendship with Terry. Which, after this evening, was on very rocky ground. Not remark one from him either. Well, he was Denise's plaything, and that was that. Not that he hadn't warned her, but it still hurt.

Jackson had been so preoccupied with preparing the meal that his initial lack of attention had been excusable; even now, in his role as host, he was simply being polite to his most luminous guest.

But the worst of all had been Valmont. In the moment when they'd met outside, she'd felt some kind of energy flowing between them, some kind of attraction, which she was sure was mutual. And yet, since that moment, he had paid her absolutely no attention. He, the perfect gentleman, had managed to keep up a pretty steady flow of witty conversation, directed mostly toward Denise, since that was unavoidable, but occasionally including every other diner except herself. As Denise rattled on, Gaby was left to toy with her food or sip her Perrier as she brooded. Her relief was enormous when the company finally moved toward the living room. To her surprise, Terry caught up with her outside the living room door, explaining under his breath, "I'm sorry. Sometimes she's a bitch."

"Thanks," she muttered coldly and made a beeline for the living room, leaving him behind. He was sorry! Big deal!

Over brandy and coffee, Denise continued to regale the company with the radiance of her presence, then drew Jackson aside to discuss the possibility of his doing the publicity shots on her new film.

"I'm going outside," Gaby mumbled to no one in particular, then got up and walked out to the swimming pool. Of one thing she could be sure; she might be beautiful, she might be hot, but in this A-list group, she was sure as hell dispensable. She felt the way she had after Mark had left—like the worst, the least valuable person in the world. She wanted to cry at the realization that the depression she'd considered totally past had returned, worse than ever. "Oh, shit!" she murmured.

"Such language. From a lady." the soft, seductive voice caused her to whip around.

"Oooops," she laughed at Philippe de Valmont. "You weren't supposed to hear that."

He took her hand and led her around the pool until the view of the black ocean was unobstructed. "I think you are having a very bad evening, yes?"

"Yes." She smiled almost sheepisly.

"But it is only because you do not understand."

"Understand what?" she asked him sharply.

"Stardom," he replied, his eyes still fixed on the water. "You do not yet understand stardom. When you do, tonight will look very different."

"I'm not sure I understand you," she said, as much to keep him near as to figure out what he meant.

"You will, my dear Gaby." His accent caressed her name. "You will. In the meantime, I would like to see more of you. Halston is giving a little party for me next Thursday at Studio 54. So silly, but one must do what one must. Would you do me the honor of allowing me to escort you?"

She wanted to shake her head to make herself wake

up, but she decided against it; if this was a dream, why end it by waking? If not, well. . . .

"I'd love it, Monsieur——"

"Philippe, yes? Now, I have been traveling for what seems to be days. All the jet lag I was spared on the Concorde was more than compensated for by the hideous Long Island Railroad, so I am going to retire. For you, I would suggest you go back inside and behave like a—how do you say?—a good sport. Agreed?"

"Of course." She grinned.

"Until tomorrow then." He took her hand, brought it to his lips, and kissed it gently. "Until tomorrow." Then he left her to stand alone by the sea, pondering the recent past—and the wonders that came out of nowhere.

The huge box had been delivered by an actual liveried chauffeur that afternoon. It was huge and shiny white, with no logo, no ribbons. She had accepted it with her most gracious smile, then turned, kicked the front door shut with her foot, and run to the couch, setting down the box with a delicacy that suggested there were explosives within.

Resting elegantly on the layers of snowy tissue paper had been a small, fine envelope, from which she had breathlessly extracted a card, over which an elegant European hand had briefly paused:

Because the rose did not do you justice. Philippe.

The roses—six perfect white blossoms—had arrived moments after her return from the Island, so rapidly that Gaby had had to assume Philippe had ordered them by phone from East Hampton. She had retained the card for more than a moment, enchanted by it, then carefully placed it on the coffee table.

She'd been thrilled with the roses, but when she parted the layers of the tissue paper, Gaby had gasped. Cradled within had lain a dress of heart-stopping exquisiteness, a costume recalled from every little girl's fondest fairy tale, a fantasy, a tribute, a masterpiece. Now, strolling with Philippe beside her down the long lobby entrance to Studio 54, she caught her reflection in the mirrors lining the corridor and knew, with fabulous pleasure, that she did justice to the costume.

A gown fashioned for a gypsy empress, it combined black satin, black velvet, and gold crimson braid, in a confection that was dazzling. The ebony satin camisole, its tiny black straps lightly caressing her shoulders, plunged to a deep décolletage bordered in gold and red, then laced tightly to a fantastically tiny waistline, from which billowed a full skirt, a multitude of black chiffon layers shot with gold. She had chosen dark stockings and black satin pumps with the high red heels of a flamenco dancer, a narrow band of black velvet encircling her neck, and had piled her hair high with an ingenious blend of art and artlessness that Philippe had praised as perfect dishabille. Rich ruby lipstick and nail polish picked up the red in the dress, and the huge but almost invisibly fine hoops of her gold earings completed the picture of perfectly naughty elegance. Entering the dark and cavernous pulsating barn of a disco, she acknowledged the frank stares of admiration with ease, and allowed Philippe to steer her in the direction of the dance floor.

"Gaby, my dear," Philippe said, "there are Jackson and Laura," and, once her eyes accustomed themselves to the black light, she saw the couple walking toward them through the press of famous gyrating bodies.

"Hello," Philippe called as they approached. "How do you like our Gaby tonight?"

"Better than my wildest fantasy," Jackson exclaimed, pressing her hand, then turning to Philippe. "What say we get a couple of shots of you two on the dance floor?"

Gaby was surprised to hear Jackson talking business. "You mean I'm working? I thought this was supposed to be fun!"

"My idea," Jackson explained. "When I heard from Laura that you'd be wearing a brand-new model Valmont, I thought it would be worth at least a couple of rolls of film. So I brought the camera."

Philippe turned solicitously to Gaby. "It is up to you, my dear. Whatever you prefer."

Contemplating the possibility of real live glamor on the pages of *Vogue*, Gaby decided. "I have to admit, Jackson, it's a great idea for at least part of a spread, even if it is entrapment."

"Come on, doll." He hugged her affectionately. "In a few months, you'll thank me."

"Jackson, that's what you always say!"

"And I'm usually right."

And he was going to be right. Gaby had been modeling just long enough to be able to develop a feel for a good shooting, and this was a great one.

As it turned out, Jackson followed Philippe and Gaby all over Studio 54, onto the dance floor—where she knew in an instant Valmont was the best, yet most subtle attention-drawing dancer on the floor—then along the bar packed solid with the very glamorous, to the huge couches that lined one corner of the main floor, up the steps to the smoking lounges upstairs, high into the balcony of what had once been a TV studio, where couples made out or observed the phantasmagoria of the dance floor, laughing and joking, the noise of their conversation drowned out to silence by the pounding music surging up from the floor.

Despite the fact that she was working, Gaby was having the best time of her life. Philippe was an enchantment—polite, interested, graceful, attentive. His manners were so elegant they at first surprised her, then delighted her, then relaxed her. He seemed simply to know when she wanted to dance, when she wanted a drink, when she felt like taking a breather, and most wonderfully of all, how to introduce her to Halston, Liza Minnelli, Jacqueline Onassis, to any number of famous celebrants at the party given for him, and to make her feel part of the dazzling company. He was so at ease with his own glamor that she caught it, sparked to a new self-confidence bred of being exquisitely accompanied.

Toward the end of the evening, she and Laura, leaving the ladies' room to rejoin the men, found Jackson and Philippe in deep and serious conversation.

"Philippe, come on, it's just too good an idea to pass up!" Gaby heard him say.

"But, Jackson, I still do not approve of a designer being so . . . so . . . visible." Philippe was protesting.

"Then get old and ugly, my boy. You're a terrific model, a great partner. That you're the designer just makes it perfect—and unique."

"Gaby"—Philippe rose as the ladies approached, took Gaby's hand, and escorted her and Laura to the couches on which they were sitting—"Jackson has come up with an idea. I'd like to know what you think."

"The idea, my girl," Jackson was beaming, "is to use what I've shot tonight as part of a story sequence. We'll have you going all over New York, to the most fabulous places, wearing the new Valmont collection and accompanied by Valmont himself. Clearly, it's a genius concept, but Philippe is too modest to buy it.''

Deciding that to say nothing was the best course, Gaby smiled noncommittally, hoping with all her heart that Jackson's normally foolproof powers of persuasion would function up to expectation. For she wanted fame, badly, almost as much as she wanted to spend a week in the company of Philippe de Valmont.

A few days later Gaby learned that *Vogue* had flipped over the Studio 54 contact sheets and granted Jackson as many pages as he wanted for the full layout. Once he had *Vogue* behind him, Jackson could make an irrefutable case with Philippe that no designer, regardless of his cherished privacy, could afford to pass up such a golden showcase for his work. Overnight, the dresses Philippe had chosen for Gaby were on their way from Paris; overnight, Gaby's quiet past capitulated to her brilliant, glowing future.

So she left her job at the museum, sorry to see a simpler chapter of her existence come abruptly to a close but awed by the possibilities waiting ahead. The poor little rich girl had been transformed into a fairy-tale princess, complete with handsome prince, beautiful dresses, miraculous balls, and the willing and warm adoration of her court. She had friends who were devoted to her, who made her life so easy that she need do nothing but look lovely. Gaby Blake was too exclusive even to need an agency, for, since she was working only with Jackson and Philippe, she could be represented by her cousin and lawyer, Gerald Blake, who took a retainer but not a percentage. So tempestuous was the glittering storm that followed in her wake, she didn't even have time to contemplate that it was all too good to last; she was on a fabulous roll, and she felt it was her destiny to flow with it. In snow-white Romanov chiffon, she accompanied Philippe to Regine's. In gold paillette tunic and narrow plum satin trousers, she surveyed Manhattan from the dazzling heights of Windows on the World. In a cream-colored Regency shirt under floral brocade vest, with jeans, she stood beside him as the Circle Line boat sailed around Manhattan. In a little yellow batiste dress of schoolgirl innocence, she ran toward him as he held out his arms to greet her by the Rockefeller Center fountain. In a white tuxedo to match his black one, she applauded Bobby Short at the Carlyle, then strolled with Philippe down Park Avenue as the sun came up.

And it was in a Monroe-esque, tight pink satin sheath that she waltzed royally on his arm into Elaine's one night and ran right into Terry Barron, who muttered a curt hello and proceeded to walk out on both of them.

chapter six

CANNES,
May 1982

I SHOULDN'T have been surprised, certainly had no right to object, when Valmont entered Gaby's life, and, simultaneously, she disappeared from mine. I actually thought I was pleased by the turn of events, but as soon as Denise boarded the Concorde for a long stay abroad, my mood took a sharp turn for the worse.

At first, I attributed the doldrums to my concern for a buddy. Here Gaby was, clearly head over heels in love with a guy whose private life was veiled in mystery. Since everybody called him "the monk" and left it at that, I just couldn't figure out what he and Gaby were doing when they were alone, but I sensed that sooner or later she was going to get hurt.

I actually did a little sleuthing among the rich ladies I'd met through Denise, but nobody had any dirt on the guy, only nice stories and a lot of question marks. From what I was hearing, not only were the Philippe-Gaby photo sessions said to be fabulous, but the word around town was that Valmont was really taken with my old chum. Even I had to admit they looked great together, although it hurt me to do so. Finally, I decided to stay out of it. If Gaby was willing to risk the pain, it was her business.

So I did a lot of work on my novel, saw a lot of the Yankees, hung out at many watering holes, and stopped expecting her to get in touch. She was having the time of her life, and good sport that I was, I was going to swallow that bitter pill and be happy for her. And it worked. Like a charm. Until the night I watched them waltzing into Elaine's, looking like the couple of the century. And then I was forced to realize that the last thing I felt about Gaby Blake was happy.

chapter seven

NEW YORK,
October 1977

"TERRY Barron! My God! Where have you been? I've only left about three thousand messages on your machine."

Gaby had been forced, when the phone rang, to vacate grudgingly the decadent serenity of a long, languid soak in the tub, but now it seemed worth it. Terry's defection to Denise's side in East Hampton had really enfuriated her; he had behaved like a jerk, and she had no intention of letting his bad behavior pass unnoticed. Still, after the bizarre encounter at Elaine's, she realized she'd gone too far, that it hurt her to be snubbed by him; and starting the morning after the encounter, she'd been calling him on the average of twice a day. That he had never picked up the phone himself or called her back irritated her, but as the days and evenings with Philippe began to consume more and more of her thoughts, she'd shifted Terry's silence to the back burner. Feeling personally on top of the world, she was able, maybe for the first time in her life, to consider the rejection his problem and, actually, his loss. And yet, when she heard his slightly sheepish voice on the phone, she felt a wave of relief lap at her heart. He was her best friend, and she'd missed being able to share her new happiness with him.

In response to her demand to know where he'd been, he'd mumbled something about having been busy with a story, but his tone was unconvincing. They bantered for a couple of minutes before a strange, new silence fell between them, which he finally broke by gracelessly inviting her to a Giants game that night.

"Gee, Terry, I can't do it. Philippe and I have to go to the opening of a new musical."

"How about tomorrow, then?" he'd countered.

"Can't. We're doing a shooting in Wall Street."

"At night?"

"Yeah. Strictly black tie. Then Jackson's moving us over to the River Café."

"Well, then"—he sounded slightly surly—"when are you free?"

"God," she mused, "nights are going to be pretty tough for the next couple of weeks. Jackson's got to wrap the shooting before the twenty-eighth when Philippe goes back to Paris. He's already postponed his flight twice, and he can't do it again. His directress calls twice a day with problems; he's worried things will be beyond repair if he stays here much longer."

"Okay." He was clearly prepared to hang up. "Call me when you're free."

"Hey," she suggested quickly before she lost him, "how about lunch today?"

"Naw," he demurred, "you probably want to rest up for your big night."

"Don't be a creep. I've been resting for hours, and

I'm bored. Plus the fact that, for some peculiar reason, I'd really like to see you.''

''I don't know. I really should do some work.''

''Come on, Barron, be a sport. Pretty please.''

''Well . . .''

''Where are you? At Denise's?'' With great relief she realized that, for the first time, she could say it without the old tinge of resentment.

''No, I'm in Brooklyn.''

''Want me to meet you halfway? Chinatown? SoHo?''

''No, it's all right.'' He was sounding warmer. ''I've got an appointment at *New York*. Why don't I do that and then pick you up at your place?''

''What time?''

''Let's see. It's ten fifteen. If I get to *New York* by eleven thirty . . . hmmm . . . assuming Clay can see me fairly fast. . . . Why don't we aim for twelve thirty, give or take a half hour? Sound good?''

''Sounds great. I'll be here,'' she told him cheerfully.

''See you then.'' He signed off in spirits obviously much improved. Gaby didn't believe the *New York* Magazine appointment for a minute. It was Friday, and Terry had clearly forgotten that he'd mentioned that the editor he worked with always took Fridays off, but that only made it better. A real reconciliation attempt, by a closet gentleman. And it would be great to see him!

Ten fifteen. The bath water was cooling off, and anyway, her fingers were already shriveled from the hot water, so she let the tub drain, removed the towel she had hastily clasped around herself on her run to the phone, lotioned herself luxuriously, slipped into a sheer blue cotton caftan from Philippe's new ''Marrakesh'' collection of at-home wear, and settled back in bed with the *New Yorker*, turning first to the review of *Annie*

Hall. When the phone rang, she was so sure it was Terry canceling that her hello was practically barked.

"Gaby, my dear, whatever is the matter?" Philippe sounded amused by her aggression.

"Oh, Philippe." Her voice softened as it always did when she talked to him. "I thought it was somebody else."

"Undoubtedly an enemy, from your tone of voice. I can't imagine you have many of those," he joked lightly.

"Oh, no, not an enemy. Just a friend with whom I've had a . . . misunderstanding?"

"I see." He was too polite to make further inquiries. "And are you busy?"

"No, actually, I'm ashamed to say I am doing absolutely nothing today and enjoying it immensely."

"Then come out and join me for lunch."

"Oh, Philippe"—she was genuinely disappointed and momentarily considered canceling Terry, then chastised herself for the thought. "I can't. I've got a lunch date. With the misunderstanding friend. It would be just too rude to cancel."

"Of course, I would not want you to. It is unfortunate. Ours would be a celebratory lunch!"

"Why? What's happened?" she demanded.

"I would prefer to share it with you in person. Well"—he sounded wistful—"it can certainly wait until tonight."

"No!" she protested. "Philippe, I can't wait. Why don't you stop over here . . . now . . . if you're free. I make a relatively good cup of coffee."

He didn't hesitate. "Why not? I've just finished a breakfast meeting in my room"—he was staying at the Sherry Netherland—"and I've no appointments until later in the afternoon, so perhaps I'll stroll over. It is a beautiful morning. See you soon."

"And I can't wait to hear the news, Philippe. See you soon." Her voice always softened even more when they said good-bye to each other, as if, at the end of a conversation, she could express all the tenderness she'd tried to disguise as breezy charm while they talked.

Let's see. If he left the hotel at Fifty-ninth and Fifth in five minutes or so, he would be at her place in half an hour at the most. Deciding to keep on the caftan, she spent most of the time on her makeup, so lightly applied that it almost appeared natural, and gave her hair fifteen minutes with the hot rollers before combing it around her shoulders. By the time the doorbell rang, she complimented herself on looking like a grande-luxe houri.

In a blue pinstripe suit from his own menswear line, replete with snowy white shirt and exquisite paisley tie, Philippe de Valmont stood before her, a vision of manly elegance, brandishing a bottle of champagne. Kissing her warmly on the cheek, he placed his arm lightly around her shoulder, and together they walked to the couch.

"For us." He held out the champagne, a by-now almost priceless vintage, Krug '61. "I believe I secured the last bottle in New York. It's still cold," he added, "but why not give it several minutes in the freezer with the glasses?"

"Of course." She relieved him of the bottle and nestled it, along with two tulip stems, in a freezer that contained only six ice trays and the kohl eye pencils she was chilling so they would be firm enough to sharpen later. Running back to the living room, she demanded, "What's happened, Philippe? Don't torture me any longer!"

"Sit down, Gaby." He took her hand and pulled her

down next to him. "You are so adorable when you are excited"—he cupped her chin with his free hand—"like a delightful child."

"The delightful child will turn into a terrible brat if you don't tell me at once what's happened."

"Well, where to begin?" He was smiling with her, teasing her, making it better. "This morning several things happened at a meeting attended by me, a highly successful blue jean manufacturer, an account executive, and a friend of yours, Jackson Pendleton."

"And . . ."

"And, at the meeting, we first worked on the announcement to the press of Philippe de Valmont jeans, which will be in the stores by next spring. I have been courted by many manufacturers who want my label on a jean line, but this man, Ivan Solomon of Prestige Industries, shares my opinions on the quality and cut of the product. Next, we came to an agreement on an advertising compaign, budgeted at one million dollars, and, believe me, it is a brilliant plan."

"What is it?" she urged.

"Oh, not so fast, my girl. First, the champagne!"

"No!"

"Yes, little one, but you stay seated." He rose and returned shortly with the slightly chilled glasses and the bottle, which he proceeded to uncork with a minimal pop.

Once the champagne had been poured and both Gaby and Philippe held their glasses, he turned to her, his eyes twinkling. "We have decided to try something really revolutionary. Not only will we advertise in print, but we are going to bring the campaign to television. We will work with only one model in print and on TV, and both the ads and the spots will be shot and directed by one man, and that man is ——"

"Jackson?" she broke in.

"Yes," he nodded, "and that one model is——"

"Me?" she inquired, strangely uncertain.

"But who else?" He lifted his glass. "To Gaby, who will very soon be very, very famous indeed."

Automatically, unconsciously, she downed the champagne, following his lead in setting her glass on the table. "Gaby," he took her hand, "have you nothing to say?"

She sought for the words, but they were too far beneath her, down on earth. Instead, she squealed and threw her arms around him. "Philippe," she gasped, "Philippe, thank you!" For a second, she felt a strange resistance from him, the same resistance she had sensed so many times before, the same reticence that had kept them at a distance from each other, loving companions, but never lovers. Then, something happened; she felt him relax, felt him grasp her shoulders, saw him look at her with adoration and desire, sensed him making a decision not to turn back. Then, she was in his arms, clinging to him as he gracefully bent back her head and kissed her slowly, his hands exploring her with the strength of great passion long denied.

"Gaby," he murmured, "Gaby," and as he maneuvered her gently down upon the couch, her joy overshadowed any feeling she had ever known, and the downstairs buzzer rang.

The force of her frustration drove Gaby deeper into Philippe's arms, deeper into his lovemaking, away from the intruding drone of the bell. It was, of course, Philippe who drew back, gracefully regaining his poise enough to ask, with an exemplary grin, "Expecting someone?"

Jerked so radically out of entrancement, Gaby stumbled over her words like an embarrassed adolescent. ''Uhh . . . well . . . my lunch date. But he's not due for an hour.''

As the bell rang again, Philippe kissed her gently, and rose. ''Don't look so sad, my dear Gaby. There will be other times. But now I think your misunderstanding friend will in fact be your enemy if you do not answer the door. Come on, get up,'' and he took her hand and helped her up, smoothing her hair and arranging the caftan for her in a fashion so loving it made her dizzy. ''Remember,'' he hugged her one final time, ''to be a good sport.''

''I just cannot believe this.'' She laughed mirthlessly as she pushed the buzzer to admit Terry to the building. While they waited for him to climb the stairs, Philippe poured them more champagne and settled himself comfortably, formally back on the couch. By the time she admitted Terry, order had convincingly been restored.

Dressed in an exceedingly baggy, run-down pair of brown cords and a crew-neck sweater as blue as his eyes, Terry Barron looked good; only her desperate desire to slam the door in his face spoiled Gaby's pleasure at seeing him again.

''Hey''—he pecked her chummily on the cheek—''sorry I'm early. I got finished at *New York* faster than—'' Seeing the seated figure on the couch, he paused, then continued, ''Jesus! I'm not interrupting something?''

''Of course not.'' Gaby attempted an air of levity. ''Come help Philippe and me celebrate. Philippe, you remember Terry.''

''Yes, of course.'' Philippe gallantly rose and shook the proffered hand. ''Always a pleasure.''

''Champagne in the morning!'' Terry commented, in

a slightly too hearty tone. "This must be some celebration!"

"Indeed it is!" Philippe replied as Gaby went to the kitchen for another glass. When she returned, Philippe filled it, handed it to Terry, and suggested they raise their glasses.

"To Gaby," he toasted, "and to her ever more glorious future!" He flashed her a smile so dazzling that, had Gaby been able to look at Terry, she would have seen resentment coupled with embarrassment settle in his eyes. For Terry's benefit, Philippe repeated the good news, then went on to explain, "We'll be doing the TV spots in various cities—Paris, for instance, Mykonos, Venice, Kyoto, Amsterdam, places with histories extending centuries farther back in time than Levi Strauss's Dallas. We will be selling the truly classic jean, the jean with a provenance, a heritage. Quite a lavish campaign. And very glamorous. And the only model we will be using will be Gaby. She will be *the* woman of Valmont."

"And when will you start shooting?" asked Terry, with the slightest trace of surliness.

"Oh, I should think in a month or so. We may start in Venice. Once winter comes in, we'll move to Gstaad. The idea is to follow the season. Perhaps next we'll move on to Marrakesh. And end, of course, with April in Paris."

"Sounds terrific," Terry drawled with obviously artificial enthusiasm.

"More than terrific," Gaby said. "It's a dream. Philippe, I can't believe it!"

Patting her hand, Philippe told her, "But it is true. And it is hard work as well, but we will have a wonderful time despite that." Smiling brilliantly, he rose, announcing, "I must go. I only just dropped by to bring

Gaby the good news." He crossed to Terry's chair and shook his hand. "So good to see you again, Terry, and to have your company at our little celebration." Then he walked with Gaby to the door, kissed her hand lightly and murmured, "Till tonight, then," and was gone in a blaze of elegance, leaving Gaby aglow and Terry inexplicably pale.

chapter eight

CANNES,
May 1982

THE smoothness with which the De Lorean took the Riviera curves contrasted radically with my thoughts, which were careening recklessly back into the past. There are some things that you never confide to anyone, because they are things that never came to be. Because, even uncompleted, revealing them would cause pain or embarrassment or anger to the people who love you. If Denise had sensed, way back in the autumn of '77, that I was ready to leave her, she had never let on.

It happened in the couple of weeks after I'd behaved like a twelve-year-old and stalked out on Gaby and Philippe at Elaine's. Gaby had called me repeatedly, but I wanted to upset her at least as much as she'd upset me, so I kept my distance. And took a lot of walks, mused, brooded, refused to answer my phone, and let the machine do all the work. Denise was out of the country, so I hid out in Brooklyn, in so foul a temper that on a couple of occasions my own mother told me to get lost.

Nights, I'd walk around the Heights, mooning and remembering the easy, happy, feisty times I'd had with Gaby before she became *the* woman of Valmont, as the frog so possessively put it. She was my friend, goddamnit, and anybody who says you can't be hurt by a friend as much as by a lover is crazy. Or so I thought until the night I forced myself to face the fact that she wasn't a friend, not to me.

In the short time since Gaby and I had begun keeping company, my relationship with Denise was the one that had been shifting from romance into chumminess. Denise was a great and generous woman, glamorous, sexy, magnetic, but she was simply not capable of the kind of messing-around, sloppy intimacy that makes two people want to spend weekends and holidays together. With Denise, the distance between the heights on which she lived and everbody else's level was so huge that you always felt a little bereft, a little lonely, in her company. With Gaby, it was share and share alike—laughing, sparring, joking, making coffee to go with the brandy at 4:00 A.M., ferreting out Mission furniture in Columbus Avenue junk shops, sending out for Chinese food, watching *Saturday Night Live*, playing the same record four times in a row without feeling stupid. It was, let's face it, a down-home Manhattan courtship, and I had grown too used to its privileges not to miss it terribly. Without Gaby, I was lonely and lost, and even Denise's sparkling phone calls couldn't make that emptiness go away.

Seeing Gaby with Valmont had shocked me into recognition. If I loved her, and I knew I did, I would have to move fast before Valmont took her away. So one day, I picked up the phone and made plans to go rushing over, throw myself at her knees, and sue for her heart and her hand. Terry Barron, *boulevardier*, was good and ready to settle down; Denise would, in time, come to understand. It was all decided, so much so that I showed up at Gaby's early ,before my anxiety consumed me. And what I got for my trouble was the jolt of my large-egoed life. For all my past skills at sports, I'd somewhere along the way lost my timing; I showed up at Gaby's just in time to lose her to fame, to fortune, and to Philippe de Valmont.

BOOK II

chapter nine

MARRAKESH,
March 19, 1978

So, Barron . . .

Here we are in Marrakesh, dividing our time between the Mamounia (what a hotel!), where we're shooting, and Philippe's house, where we're all camping out. Don't retch when I tell you that, after spending months in hotels, even the best ones, it's a relief to be in somebody's house. And this is some house! You've probably seen it in some fancy magazine or other—real famous. Anyway, your letter caught up with me at Gstaad, and it was good to hear you sounding so jealous and mean-spirited. The old Terry! I almost miss your playful (?) insults. Everybody's treating me as if I'm golden, which I guess for the moment I am. Glad to know we're getting mentioned in the columns. But, from what I hear, so are you! How could you be dating all those famous women at once! Does this happen every time Denise ups and marries a tycoon? Jesus, where do you find the time to grind out that great, hard-hitting journalism? And which one do you really love? The baby tennis player? The best-selling novelist? The lady lawyer in the Justice Department? The film critic or the rich and glamorous divorcée? Come on, gimme a hint. Philippe's arriving any minute from Paris, and in the meanwhile we've been shooting preliminary stuff. I've been working my butt off all day, then lying around in the evening on cushions watching Jackson, the crew, the writer, and the account executive pig out on food as magical as the Arabian nights. I, of course, am not allowed to touch most of it. And when they pass the *kif* pipe, they always skip me. Ah, the high life! I keep telling Jackson that I want to become rich and famous so I can build myself a home in some secluded spot, install the world's greatest junk food collection, and retire there, where I'll do nothing but eat it all up. Pizza. Peanut butter. Doughnuts. Chili dogs. Jackson says that's all ka-ka, but what does he know? I'm the one who's hungry. But, admittedly, happy. And nervous. The first commercials are going to air in April. I think I'll plan to be in Tibet at the time. Very scary. Do you think I could find a zen monastery with a McDonald's concession? If so, you're invited to meditate over a Big Mac, far from the madding crowd.

Gaby suddenly found herself not knowing what to write next, so she put down the pen and gazed out the latticed window into the night shadows of the palm garden beyond. Terry's infrequent letters always came as a wonderful surprise, even when they made her worry.

All in all, he was a pretty tough guy. Either he had accepted Denise's latest precipitous marriage with the same graceful resignation as he'd taken the previous ones or he was relieved to be back in the saddle. Everything she knew about his love life, she obtained third or fourth hand from gossip or from magazines hastily chosen in airports and read while waiting for always delayed flights. Airports had, in fact, assumed an almost mystical significance in her life. It was in the airport in Geneva that she'd first spotted the *Vogue* with the New York series Jackson had done of her and Philippe. And it was really something. More than a shooting. A story. A love story in pictures. With a long, languid text. It was dynamite. Within weeks the international fashion press was describing them as the couple of the century. After that, the high rollers in Gstaad had begun to recognize Philippe and her.

More and more stories speculated that wedding bells might soon be ringing, that perhaps they were waiting until the commercials started to run. If it was true, the press knew more than she did.

She got up from the desk, opened the latticed doors, and walked out into the jewel of a garden. The fountains played an exquisite melody as the birds sang and the candlelight dusted the flowers and lush greenery with the lightest layer of gold. Immediately, silently, a white-caftaned servant appeared to inquire after her pleasure. She dismissed him, and sat alone by a particularly playful fountain.

In the months they'd been working together—in fact, since that day when Terry had interrupted them in her apartment—she and Philippe had somehow, through a combination of exhaustion and conflicting schedules, managed never to begin again what they had started that morning. After his momentary relaxation, she thought his reserve seemed to have increased, although that could have been her imagination, for he did have a lot on his mind, and business came first. Still, although he treated her with a combination of adoration and respect, kissed her and hugged her in public, filled her wine-glass and frequently led her onto the dance floor, he always dropped her at her room, then immediately departed.

Jackson, ever the protective coach, joked with her and played pranks, brightened her days and made light of Philippe's distance. She rarely mentioned it to him anymore, but as always, it nagged at her happiness. Clearly, she couldn't afford for professional reasons to be seen with other men, and she really didn't want to, anyway. But it was frustrating.

On the other hand, maybe the papers were right. Maybe Philippe did have serious intentions and was behaving so traditionally and honorably that he didn't want them to become lovers until they were married. But if that was so, why, goddamnit, didn't he ask her? All the presents in the world—and he was the most generous, thoughtful suitor she'd ever known—did little to disguise the fact that he was keeping her at arm's length.

There were moments, when she was seated in the world's most glamorous nightclubs, basking in the luxury of one of the world's greatest hotels, dancing in one of the world's most expensive dresses, when she wanted only to be back in New York, at Yankee Stadium with Terry, cheering for the team and cheating on her diet with hot dogs.

She didn't even know how much money she was making. Her cousin Gerald treated her like a simpleton, but made sure she had everything she wanted and handled the Beekman Place house so the rents kept coming in. The old rift with her family had never been mended, and if they knew about her new success, they hadn't bothered to contact her or Gerald.

Oh, come on, she told herself. For her to feel sorry for herself was absolutely disgusting. She had all the things any other woman in the world would do anything to get, so what was the problem? But the terrible loneliness, the nagging sense of estrangement, lingered.

With her eyes cast down, her fingers playing with the braid on her *djellabah*, she sensed, rather than saw, a figure towering above her. Assuming it was the solicitous servant, she glanced up, a dismissal already on her lips, and confronted Philippe. He had, apparently, just this moment arrived, for he still was wearing a business suit, and must have come directly to find her. His extraordinary presence erased, for the moment, the lingering doubts that had arisen in his absence.

In his hand he held a large, velvet Bulgari box. "Gaby," he sat beside her, embracing her warmly. "How I have missed you. And to show you how much, I have brought you a gift."

"Oh, Philippe," she said, smiling, "you didn't have to."

"Not only did I not have to," he said softly, "but I shouldn't have."

"Shouldn't have?" she mused. "What is it?" She made a grab for the box.

After the briefest of tussles, he allowed her to capture it. "You must tell no one," he cautioned her.

Slowly lifting the velvet top, Gaby gasped, for lying on a satin cushion was a box of Reese's Peanut Butter Cups. "Oh, Philippe!" She laughed aloud. "This is the best present anyone's ever given me."

"But you must not tell Jackson. Promise."

"Don't worry about that," and she kissed him lightly on the cheek.

"And now," he continued, "a little nothing that I thought might amuse you. Let me see. Where did I put it?" And he pretended to search his pockets, finally locating something wrapped in a handkerchief, which he extracted and handed to her. The little nothing was a pair of exquisitely understated emerald button earrings, circled by a border of diamonds. They were perfect.

"Philippe, my God!"

"You don't like them?"

"Like them? I adore them!" She clipped them immediately in place.

"And how they become you!" He glowed with delight. "How you make them shine! Now, come with me." He rose and took her hand. "Have you seen my quarters? No? Then let me show them to you."

As he led her through the lacquered halls, their footsteps echoing on the marble floors, she was aware that only they and the invisible servants were still awake. "My apartment." He indicated an elaborate inlaid wooden door and opened it for her.

"Oh!" she nearly gasped, as he swept her into a dream. She had seen pictures of the room in magazines, but like any other great beauty, the photographs did not do it justice. You had to be there, watching the stream of moonlight filtering through the latticed windows that comprised two walls, each one casting an exotic, patterned shadow onto the azure tile of the floor. The room was vast, white stone where it wasn't window, the only interior light supplied by real blazing torches in wall and standing sconces. Spartan as a monk's cell, its sensuality was, nonetheless, overwhelming. At the far fourth wall, which must have been glass, the latticework was replaced by a solid screen of hanging plants and trailing flowers, ostensibly growing wild, but actually planted in a gorgeously intricate design. Before this cascade was a huge, circular tub of azure and white mosaic, its gentle, gracefully rippling water moved by some hidden source.

Opposite it, against the stone wall, stood a huge, low bed, as understated as a cot and covered with unbleached cloth.

"Come." He took her hand and led her down the length of the room toward the bath. As they approached, she saw that resting on the mosaic border were a bottle of champagne in a mosaic bucket, two glasses, an intricately carved wooden box, and a long, brightly painted pipe with a small stone bowl. "Sit here." He indicated the unbleached muslin pillows arranged near the champagne. As she did so, she saw him push a button almost hidden in the elaborate mosaic design, and at once, strange, exotic music began softly to fill the room. He poured them each a glass of champagne.

"I shouldn't be doing this," she protested without force. "Jackson would kill me."

"But he will never know," Philippe promised her, then picked up the pipe, lit it with a match from inside the wooden box, drew deeply, and handed it to her.

"Ummm . . ." She savored the earthy taste as she felt the smoke make its way up to her head.

He didn't move toward her, just sat near her as they smoked and drank champagne. The moonlight began to dance before her eyes, and the music began slowly to enfold her. She thought she could see the plants and flowers sway under the graceful power of an invisible breeze, and as she was forming the thought of wanting a sweet, she looked up to see him bending over her, then placing a piece of the candy on her tongue. Its unbelievable richness lingered long after it had dissolved, in her mouth, in her head, in her body. She thought she was probably dizzy, maybe even semiconscious, but at the moment, she seemed to be in a dreamworld, a state of heightened sensual reality in which there were no prohibitions.

He was so close to her that she could feel his breath against her cheek, yet he made no move toward her, simply looked at her and said, "Let me undress you." He did it slowly, wonderfully, working the *djellabah* sensuously up her body and over her head. As she moved to take off the earrings, he stopped her. "No, leave them on. I want you to leave them on," and so she lay back on the cushions, wearing nothing except the jewels as she watched him remove his own clothes. His body, even in the darkness, glowed, caught the flame from the sconces, and became golden. He was more than manly; he was, at that drugged and fabulous moment, man, as he approached her, kneeling beside her, running his hands the length of her body, exploring, measuring, appraising, always to his delight. When she reached up to touch him, he drew her hand away, helped her up, and led her into the pool.

The water was both cool and warm, and the magic waves seemed to caress them both as they embraced, their bodies melding, touching at every place, inextricably bound together. At last, he kissed her, with elegant abandon, deep, long kisses that actually made her weak so that she clung to him for the strength to stand. As he moved his mouth from her lips to her breasts, taking in first one nipple, then the other, she felt a streak of ferocious desire shoot from her breasts to the place that his hand now reached to massage. Then she was floating, and he, still standing, was holding her as she relaxed into the wonderful water, her hair billowing out around her, and then he easily slipped into her as if they were meant to be lovers. And as she gave herself entirely to the night, the water, and the music, their mutual cries of delight and ecstasy rose from the pool and echoed in the lush and all-fulfilling night.

chapter ten

CANNES,
May 1982

THE winter of 1977, which somehow slouched into the early spring of 1978, was one of those vastly bad personal times that appear to have meaning above and beyond themselves. Either fate was teaching me a lesson for winning too much too often, or my luck had finally deserted me, and in spades.

I didn't have any justification for resenting Gaby's apparently effortless choice of somebody else over me; after all, I'd never offered myself as a serious option. Still, having at last come to grips with the sloppy, sentimental feelings I'd been masking under my hard-hitting cool, I felt as bereft as a child without its teddy. The afternoon I blew it, she and I rekindled the friendship that she seemed to value and I finally had to settle for. It was good to see her joyous, because I loved her, but it also made me want her even more. And resent her even more.

She did manage one final evening with me instead of

Philippe before they sped off for Venice. We went to a little Middle Eastern dump near Atlantic Avenue in Brooklyn, ate the fattening food she loved, then went for a long, memory-filled walk along the Promenade. She actually hugged me good-bye, and that was that.

After she split, Denise returned to lift my spirits and make me forget. Oh, at least, that's what I was counting on.

When I picked her up at the airport, flower-laden and well-groomed, she didn't even wait until we got into the limousine. As we strolled through the crowded lobby, she told me off-handedly that she was married. To a French industrialist who had made the cover of *Time*. Because of their mutual celebrity statuses, they'd married most quietly in a small town on the Riviera, weren't going to announce it until they were both ensconced in Jean-Louis's perfect little mansion in the sixteenth arrondissement. She'd just come back to get the things she'd really need, was taking the Concorde right back to her beloved, and would be out of the country indefinitely. I took this all with unusual graciousness, given the fact that my entire private life had just been declared M.I.A.

We had a cheery last fling, did an all-nighter the evening before she departed, and when I woke up the next morning in the very floral River House bedroom, she had gone. Had I been more liberated, I would have wept for myself. In those moments when I thought I'd landed Gaby, I had actually suffered over the prospect of giving Denise the heave-ho, but Denise hadn't even bothered with *my* tender feelings. As Gaby hadn't bothered to disguise her adoration for Philippe, although I'd always tried to soft-pedal my relationship with Denise. I had been burned. And scammed. And torn and frayed. Women!

Well, I was going to show them. If I had been a world-class ladies' man before, I was now going for the Grand Slam. And those two dames in Europe were certainly going to hear about it!

So I started dating a best-selling novelist, a cute, smart, feisty little number who regarded sex as a sport. Making love with her was like trying to keep up with an Olympic gymnast, but it was certainly diverting. We were quite a perky pair. Until she met a five-foot-four lawyer with an inquisitor's mentality and the instinctive knowledge of every position in the *Kama Sutra*. So I lost the novelist.

Then there was the baby tennis player, sweet, loving, only eighteen. She had turned pro at fourteen and now, given tournament prize money and endorsements, she was making about a million a year. I couldn't keep up with life in the fast track, and besides, we couldn't even go to F.A.O. Schwarz for a toy orgy (hers) without being besieged by autograph hunters and adoring fans. Anyway, she turned out to be in love with her coach, a gorgeous, Nordic old codger of thirty; if it hadn't been for me making him jealous, they never would have gotten together. And on and on.

I was dating, dining, and bedding the greatest bevy of famous, talented, desirable women ever assembled in one small black book, and I was losing every single one of them. I, who had once had to fight them off with a stick, couldn't keep them now if I'd chained them to a wall.

To make matters worse, every time I opened a paper or a magazine, flipped through a bedside *Vogue* at a girl's apartment, or eavesdropped at Elaine's, I kept running into Gaby. Gaby and Philippe. They were making international social headlines wherever they went, sometimes with Jackson following them with a camera through the back streets of Venice, sometimes alone and glowing, strolling down the curving byways of Gstaad, their radiance captured even in haste by the swarm of *paparazzi*. Only *Architectural Digest* held Denise's defection up to me; in its pages, I came across the house her husband had caused to be done over for her in Paris. That I could stand. The other stuff, the stuff with Gaby, the very mention of her name or snapshot of her face, made me feel like I'd taken one in the gut. I never wanted to hear about her—never wanted to hear anything good, at least. My fantasies always stopped short of ruin for her; I'd settle for a major disappointment. I didn't want her to be miserable. I just didn't want her to be happy. Which is why I surprised even myself by writing to her. And when no answer came, I had only myself to blame for feeling so lousy.

Round about March, I was boring even myself with my despair and had actually taken up with a girl who seemed to want me, a luminously lovely Japanese designer. It was her company that started me on the road back, that made me stop measuring a woman's every gesture against Gaby's. Suki was pretty swell, and I was beginning to forget, when Gaby's letter came—a letter so peculiarly joyous, so desperately, blindedly enthralled, that I realized, first, that I still cared about her and worried about her, and second—because I could read her so well—that she was in deep and serious trouble.

chapter eleven

PARIS,
April 1978

GABY strode boldly down the Boulevard St. Michel toward St. Germain. At nine o'clock, the lights sparkled on both sides of the wide expanse, and after the lull that followed the seven o'clock rush hour, the streets of the *rive gauche* were once again bustling with the evening crowds.

Paris in late April was beginning to become everything they always said about it. The trees were beginning to bloom, and people were beginning to risk spring clothing. Tonight, a light jacket would be enough protection against the night breezes, but Gaby was coatless, and a mild chill had seized her from the first minutes of shooting. Although she walked alone, an assemblage consisting of Jackson, a cameraman, and a man holding lights trailed in her wake. This was the fifth time she'd made this walk, and desperately she faced the fact that there might be five more tries before they got it right. Over and over. Along Boul' Mich to St. Germain, turn left, up the steps of the Cluny Museum, and into the Unicorn Room. So far, they'd just gotten to the turn-off.

Every time they started over, a makeup man checked her for needed repairs, a hairdresser made sure her hair was just so, and a script girl saw that she did not leave behind the burgundy satin mask she carried on a gilt stick.

This time she felt it was going well, that her stride was both bouncy and assertive, that the hideous ache produced by striding for an hour in four-inch heels didn't show in her walk, or in her expression, as Jackson and the camera operator danced around her, shooting her from all sides. "This is going to be one hell of a bitch to edit," she heard the American cameraman say to Jackson.

"Come on, Chris," Jackson parried, "this is the easy part!"

They had enough footage by now, Gaby speculated, to make a four-hour feature, but if the extravagent overuse of film didn't bother Jackson, who was she to complain? She remembered how, in the early days in New York, when Mark was trying to shoot the little horror movie on a shoestring, they had settled for less than perfect takes to save on overtime and film. She'd even been in a couple of crowd scenes in order to save money on the budget. Actually, now she was glad for the experience because it made doing the commercials a little easier. Mark! How strange that she could think of him without a pang, without a stab of desperation; at last, she'd come far enough to see him as a character in the film of her past, no longer as the man in her life. Everything was different—since Philippe.

Philippe! The thought that she would be seeing him once they reached the Cluny gave an extra bounce to her aching feet, causing Jackson to shout, "Way to go!" She was on target at last.

She was starting to cook, to give some kind of performance, and the glimpse of herself in a glass storefront gave her an idea. "Jackson," she called, not breaking stride, "why don't you shoot a sequence of me reflected in windows as I walk? The stores are lit enough to provide a good reflection, so why don't you give it a try? Me looking at myself as I walk?"

"Hey, baby, you're learning!" Jackson cheerily called back, and he and the cameraman began to devise a way to do just that. "Okay," he told her, "just start looking at yourself."

Every woman's dream! To be able to gaze at her reflection in windows without having to look away when someone passes. No embarrassment—just frank, open narcissism. And she had to admit, she looked good. The jeans of Valmont looked great on her—a perfect fit, smooth, sinuous, and clinging. The knee-high, tight-fitting boots, which had somehow made it over the straight, narrow legs of the jeans, were of a medium oxblood glove-leather polished till they glowed like the satin of her extraordinary shirt. Oh, that shirt. Absolutely Valmont. It was like a Renaissance bodice—burgundy velvet comprised the huge sleeves, caught at the elbows by a band of golden braid, only to billow out even more defiantly toward the narrower golden ring at the cuffs. That same gold traced the neckline, which flowed exquisitely from the very edge of the shoulders, curving downward toward a soft, deep vee of a décolletage. The bodice itself was contoured through the torso so that it clung to her form and slid easily into the jeans, which were encircled by a narrow gold belt fastened by a tiny, elegant gargoyle clasp. Her hair was piled high, also in the style of the Renaissance, and the heavy gold-and-amethyst earrings and necklaces made it all work together in a wonderful fantasy of fashion past and future. Hanging from one shoulder was a tiny square gold metal evening bag, suspended from a gold chain. In one hand, she carried the burgundy mask.

She was concentrating so hard on being a girl going to a ball that she was shocked to realize that she had made it all the way to the Cluny. She guessed that was what actors meant when they said that they were "really into it."

"Keep on going," Jackson shouted, as she mounted the steps, then made her way through the fabulous house of medieval treasures. From upstairs and down a corridor, the strange, haunting dance music of the Renaissance floated with a powerful allure, and her bootheels clicking across the marble floors played a counterpoint to it.

As she moved toward the music, she sped up her pace, anxious to arrive, dying to find Philippe. She was almost running as Jackson shouted, "Great! Go faster!" She had moved beyond the pain in her feet; she just wanted to reach the end of the corridor, fling open the heavy oak door, be stunned by the glamorous and gorgeous assembly masked and costumed in a seventies fantasy of a Renaissance costume ball. The crowd was arranged against the grandeur of the huge unicorn tapestry behind them, but her eyes did not linger over them or the works of art; instead, they moved until she saw, across the room, Philippe, masked but in evening dress, waiting for her. As she rushed to him, the crowd parted to allow her to pass, and then she was with him, mask held to her face, allowing him gently to push it aside, slowly, by degrees, until her full face was again revealed, wreathed in smiles, delighted by the sight of his hand on hers, while Jackson and the cameraman moved backward until both she and Philippe could be seen full-length, the most beautiful couple in the world.

"Okay!" Jackson yelled. "Great! Great!"

As the crowd stopped pretending to make conversation, Philippe announced in English, "All right, everyone. Now let's all really have a good time." He retained Gaby's hand just long enough to murmur, "I adore you."

Three glasses of champagne later, Gaby and Philippe made their escape.

"Philippe"—she bent toward him in the limousine that was bearing them across the river.

"Yes, my darling."

He nuzzled her neck as she murmured, "My feet are killing me!"

He laughed, then cradled her head on his shoulder and stroked her hair. "Let me take care of that," and he lovingly released her, allowing her to recline across the limousine seat as he took her left leg onto his knee and gently eased off the boot.

"Ummm," she cooed, "now the other one," and he obliged. She started to sit up, but he urged her to stay as she was, then proceeded to massage her feet. "Wow," Gaby sighed. "You could get a job doing that."

"Only for you," he responded, smiling. "I am not so gentle with anyone else."

"Like who?" Her eyes narrowed in mock jealousy.

"And that was beneath you," he chastened her, softening his words with a kiss on her left instep.

As the limousine pulled up before the magnificent grey stone building that housed Philippe's celebrated triplex, Gaby sighed and sat up. "Philippe?" She bent toward him conspiratorially. "If I go barefoot, will I ruin your reputation?"

"Probably," he whispered back. "Certainly, my driver will never again treat me with respect." He paused, then smiled broadly. "But I have an alternative plan."

"And just what would that be?"

"I will carry you, and my driver will follow with your boots," and before she could object, he had left the car, walked around it and opened the door, gathered her up in his arms, and lifted her, flailing with shock. "No, behave, *petite,*" he cautioned her, "unless you want to have me arrested for abduction."

She grinned shakily and threw her arms around his neck for support as he conveyed her into the building and toward the great curving staircase. "Philippe, the elevator's over there."

"The elevator! What bad form. When I convey ladies in my arms, I always take the stairs," and off they started as Gaby protested, "Philippe, I'm too heavy. You'll slip a disk or something."

"Be quiet," he told her firmly but warmly enough so that her embarrassment, her ever-present fear of losing control, capitulated to the sweet, silly celebration of surrender.

When they reached the second landing and approached the door, he asked, "Would you mind reaching out your hand and pressing the buzzer?" She did that, and in seconds, Jean-Claude, the ubiquitous houseman, admitted them, displaying not even a trace of surprise that Gaby was in Philippe's arms.

As Philippe brought her into the study, he called back to Jean-Claude for coffee and brandy. Having reached the white couch beneath the great windows that afforded a superb view of the Bois de Boulogne, he lovingly set her down, kneeling by her side and caressing her face. "You see, that was not so bad."

"It was wonderful." She covered his hand with hers. "Really wonderful."

"Now," he announced, rising to his feet, "I will return in a moment."

After he had left, Gaby decided to try walking, tentatively at first, for the soles of her feet were literally bruised, but the thick carpet soothed them, and she walked to the exquisite Second Empire desk that stood across the room, surrounded by ceiling-high dark wood bookshelves. On the desk rested a perfect brass table lamp, and she was reaching over to turn it on when she noticed, among a stack of mail, a postcard of elegant Japanese design—three cranes taking flight. Turning it over to see who had designed it, she could not help but read the message, and when she did, it took her an anxious moment to decipher the European handwritng, then to translate the French, which finally revealed itself as:

> *Darling Philippe, New York is so lonely without you.*
>
> *Dominique.*

In a heart-pounding moment, she willed herself to replace the card in the stack of mail just as she'd found it, then limped hurriedly back to the couch, arranging herself lanquidly despite the cold sweat that had broken out on her forehead.

When a knock on the door informed her that Jean-Claude had arrived with the coffee and brandy, she responded in a calm voice, even smiled at him as he placed the large tray on the coffee table then bowed and retreated, closing the door behind him.

She sat, staring out at the fairy-tale vista of the Bois, seeing none of it, understanding some things for the first time, horrified at that understanding. Now it was clear: the unexplained distance in New York, Philippe's public warmth and private aloofness. Of course, he couldn't have stayed with her, not with the mysterious Dominique around to seduce him away from her. Dominique. She wondered if her rival were younger or older, richer or poorer, simply more stunning or clearly more beautiful. She racked her memory for some luminous "Dominique" she'd seen in *Women's Wear Daily* or encountered at one of the chic restaurants or dinner parties to which Philippe had escorted her, but she could come up with no face to match the name.

Was she a model, the wife of a diplomat, an artist, a courtesan? Did she read the paper, the columns, listen to the conversation at the next table at Regine's or La Grenouille? If she did, she must know about Gaby, but the postcard didn't sound as if that knowledge had shaken her confidence so much as one iota. He had probably answered any of Dominique's accusations with the excuse that his relationship with Gaby was all business. And what if it was? No, that was the old Gaby responding that way, the Gaby who drew some kind of morbid satisfaction from the romantic paranoia of exploitation. You could tell, could really intuit, when somebody loved you, and she was sure Philippe did.

As sure as she was that the card would disappear from the pile of mail by tomorrow, that the name "Dominique" would never issue from his lips, that the secret of his strange, hidden relationship with the other woman would never be revealed.

"Ah, still awake?" Philippe entered the room and came to her, carrying the Moroccan pipe and the small wooden box. "I expected to find you asleep."

"No, just dreaming wide awake. Falling asleep in front of this view"—her hand swept toward the window—"would be a failure of the imagination," and she bent toward him, kissing the top of his head as he settled himself on the floor beside her.

He was so graceful, so loving, so expert as he poured the coffee, then the brandy, then prepared the pipe, lighting it, then offering it to her. As they drank and smoked, her panic began to dissipate, her limbs began to relax, her body began to warm to his. And as he urged her down beside him, initiating a dream of sensual bliss, the notion that they had never made love without the *kif* pipe beside them flitted through her mind, then danced from her thoughts, as passion overwhelmed them both.

chapter twelve

CANNES,
May 1982

ON an exquisite spring morning, which I'd been planning to sleep through, Suki woke me up, shouting, "Terry, here's that commercial."

Suki got up at six every morning so that she could run and still be in the office by nine, and with Oriental ingenuity, managed to shower and dress and breakfast without waking me up. Since the loft she lived in was one large space, she watched the *Today* show with the sound barely on so as not to disturb me.

"Terry,"—she shook me again—"here's your friend," and I came instantly awake to the glorious, disturbing sight of Gaby striding down some street in Paris, looking like a sexy angel from the Renaissance.

"Turn up the sound," I commanded, and she obliged just in time for me to watch Gaby, radiant with love, dash up some stairs with antique music playing beyond her, into a medieval ballroom and directly into the arms of the exquisite Philippe. As the camera drew back to reveal both their forms, Philippe's voice-over crooned, "The woman of Valmont. The jeans of Valmont. History-making." And then it was back to today's weather. I stifled an urge to puke.

"Terry,"—Suki sat down next to me—"isn't that fabulous? Everybody's talking about those spots. "Barry"—he was her boss, the Harvard-educated Seventh Avenue manufacturer—"says the spots are good enough to gross them a couple of million in sales the first year. They really look like they're in love. Are they?"

"How should I know?" I snapped back, reaching for the morning cigarette I'd promised Suki I'd forego.

"Well, she's your friend." My little designer was miffed.

"Hey, I'm sorry, kid." I drew her toward me with an affectionate little hug. "It's just . . . you know . . . that's the only thing people seem to care about. That I know her. I feel like Gaby's press agent."

"Well,"—Suki allowed me to nuzzle her just enough to show that all was forgiven, but not forgotten—"I just thought you'd want to see the spot."

"I did, darlin', but you know what a monster I am when I don't smoke."

That seemed to ease her. "Well, you're smoking now, and frankly, I'd rather have you cranky than have you killing yourself."

"And who didn't run this morning?" I inquired nastily as she picked up her stuff and headed to the door.

"Smart ass," she shot back. "I go to the gym at lunchtime on Wednesdays. So there."

"Dinner?" I relaxed with the cigarette.

"Sure, call me this afternoon and we'll decide where. Bye," and blowing me a kiss, she closed the door behind her.

It took me three cigarettes to stop replaying the commercial in my head. God, she looked wonderful. God, *he* looked wonderful. All right, *they* looked wonderful. The perfect lovers. The perfect relationship. Keep away, Barron, it's none of your affair! I'd heard they were both due in New York any day, were probably already here, but I'd decided to let her make the first move if she still remembered who I was. Whatever lingering doubts I'd had about her happiness were groundless, after all—just sour grapes. All I could do by calling her was take it on the chin and possibly disturb the best, most reciprocal relationship I'd had in a long time. So that was that. I'd conquered my self-destructive urge to contact her, and if it took three cigarettes to get there, it was worth it.

Deciding to catch a few more Zs, I got up to turn off the TV, proud of my rationality and self-control, then staggered back to bed, put out my last cigarette, pulled up the covers, picked up the phone, and called her.

chapter thirteen

NEW YORK,
May 1978

IN the roughly three minutes that it took her to get from the apartment to Billy's, where she was meeting Terry, Gaby sustained a shock halfway between a dream and a nightmare. Strolling up First Avenue in jeans, boots, a collarless man's shirt, and doeskin vest, she glimpsed herself captured in her peripheral vision, turned toward the street, and saw a bus lumbering up the boulevard with her photograph plastered to its torso. The ad, which read, "The woman of Valmont, The jeans of Valmont, History-making," was a still from the Marrakesh shooting, and she wore, in addition to the jeans, yellow curled-toe Moroccan slippers, all kinds of Berber jewelry, and a short, loose black-and-white woven jacket with the hood draped back. Behind her was the three-ring circus of the Djeema-el-Fna on the night that the Berbers showed their wares, and off to one side was Philippe, immaculately turned out in a dinner jacket.

"Wow!" she exclaimed to herself, then quickened

her step as she neared the restaurant. Almost directly in front of the entrance was the plastic shelter of the bus stop, where her image had momentarily paused with the vehicle. And as the passengers boarded the bus, she could see the large advertising panel at one end of the shelter: herself again, this time in the Renaissance costume of the Paris shooting. For a moment, the high sheen of the plastic panel caught the sun's rays in such a way that her watching image was superimposed on the panel, and as the bus started to move, its image of her, too, was caught in the mirror surface of the ad. Gad, the three faces of Gaby! It was totally unreal, and her mood leapt higher than it ever had, to a new level of something like ecstasy mixed with terror.

Suddenly, she saw another figure reflected in the shining panel, and a familiar voice inquired, "Haven't I seen you somewhere?"

Without turning away, she smiled into the reflection. "I can't imagine where," and whipped around to surrender herself to Terry Barron's hug.

"Hey, baby," he laughed, as he released her. "Did you plant this here?"

"No way," she said, giggling, "but I would've if I could've." She slipped her arm easily around his waist, as he did hers, and they casually kissed, then walked together into the restaurant.

She noticed several people at the bar obviously engaged in trying to figure out where they'd seen her before. Others, at the tables, had identified her, were telling their luncheon companions to look toward the door. As she and Terry walked through the wood- and mirror-paneled Irish bar for the affluent, she felt all eyes upon her, measuring her against her flawless media image, trying to remember her name.

When they reached the table, she mentioned to Terry,

"Boy, that was really like running the gauntlet. What do you think they all thought?"

"What I thought." He grinned, reaching for a salt roll. "That you're twice as beautiful in person!"

"Blarney," she muttered mockingly, "sheer Irish blarney," then paused as the waiter came by to take their drink order. "Since this is a kind of celebration, I'm going to splurge on a white wine," she announced, "to keep you company." He had ordered a beer.

"Where's Philippe?" Terry inquired casually. "I expected him to join us."

"Oh, no, he's at the hotel with Ivan, seeing some department store people from the Midwest. They're launching a huge promotion with the jeans. Plus he's working on the new fall *prêt-à-porter* line for the boutiques. God, he's busy."

"He's not staying with you?"

"No," she replied nonchalantly, over the wine. "It would be . . . I mean, he has appointments and breakfasts and lunches and drinks dates—you know. A lot of it he prefers to do out of the hotel—the personal touch—and neither of us wanted to turn my little retreat into an office, so. . . ." Her words trailed off, leaving only the slightest hint that she wasn't telling the whole story.

"Oh, sure." Terry smoothed over the uneasy silence. "God, you look gorgeous. All that fancy European living is turning you into a goddess."

"Yeah?" She looked up at him. "I'm so used to seeing myself I can't tell if I look better or worse."

"Take my word for it." He beamed, obviously delighted to see her. "Now"—he controlled the softness of his gaze by turning toward the menus posted high on the walls—"what'll it be?"

"Well," she mused, "I should be having shrimp with no dressing, but . . ." and her eyes began to dance with the fires of rebellion, "if you ordered me a rare bacon-cheeseburger, it would be bad manners to refuse."

Immediately, Terry got the waiter and ordered two rare bacon-cheeseburgers plus an order of potato skins and one of onion rings. "Another wine?" he asked.

"No. A draft, just like yours. Boy, am I being wicked. If this gets out, I'm——"

"Have no fear, stringbean." He patted her hand. "Your secret is safe with me!"

The beer came before the food, and she downed it fast, a taste as good in actuality as it had been in memory. When she went to the ladies' room, she returned to the table feeling the slightest bit dizzy, to find another round waiting for her along with the burger.

The beer and the food relaxed them, warmed them, making them giddy and easy and very much like the old days. "Barron"—she stopped eating, burger in hand, and shot him a grateful look—"how I've missed you! You're the best person in the world to pig out with."

He laughed. "What a thing to be loved for. Gluttony!"

"No," she countered, knowing he knew what she meant, "not that. It's . . . it's easy to have a glamorous time, a thrilling time, an extravagant time, but it's hard to just have fun. You know, good old, informal, slobby American fun."

"Well, thanks kid," he told her archly. "I'll be sure never to clean up the act!"

"I'm taking the last onion ring!" she announced.

"Be my guest. Want another order?" he asked.

"Oh, God, no!" she panted. "I'm so full, I feel sick."

"Then I guess you don't want another beer. . . ."

"I didn't say that!" she exclaimed. "Anyway, it's your decision. I've got to call Philippe to find out where we're supposed to meet tonight." And she rose and walked grandly, gracefully, dizzily to the phone.

It seemed to take forever for the Sherry operator to answer, then Gaby had to repeat, then spell Philippe's name several times before the operator got it. At last, the room number was established and the anticipatory buzz turned slowly mournful, as the operator rang and rang and rang. At last, even Gaby had to believe he wasn't there. She had to be content with leaving a message.

Maybe Philippe and Ivan had decided to take the buyers out to lunch. Maybe they were downstairs in the dining room. She should have had them page the dining room. No, why would they spend the money on a suite with a dining room if they were going to lunch out? But none of that was the real problem.

In Paris, Philippe had been constantly with her, and although she had retained the room at L'Hotel, she had stayed with him more often than not. And when she did spend a rare night at the hotel, he was either with her or constantly in touch. In New York, it was different. Of course, he had business to do, big-money business, but his distance came from another sphere. The sphere of Dominique. Whoever she was, Gaby was sure he was seeing her. There had been too many unexplained absences, missed phone calls, too many business evenings to which she was not invited. He was as gentle, as adoring as ever, faultless in his manners, but infrequent in his loving.

Once, left alone in his Paris apartment, she had gone through his address book, but had found no "Dominique." In her week in New York, she had checked out every woman at every party, including the members of the big French colonies on upper Madison and down in SoHo, but to no avail. Wherever, whoever Dominique was, she kept out of sight, out of mention, but to Gaby, she was constantly present, constantly driving her farther from Philippe.

Yet another beer was waiting for her at the table, but Terry had disappeared into the men's room. She sat down, sipping the beer and idly surveying the crowd, daydreaming, worrying, ignoring the appraising looks of the patrons.

It was sheer coincidence that she was looking toward the front doors when they opened and Philippe strolled in. Her heart thumped to her stomach with shock. He hadn't known where she was lunching. And he wasn't with Ivan or with any bunch of buyers; he was alone, looking elegantly casual in slate beige gabardine pants, blue Oxford-cloth shirt, and chocolate brown cashmere cardigan. Checking the bar first to see if his companion was waiting, he then scanned the room to see if his lunch date had been seated, and in the course of that, he saw Gaby. Immediately, he walked to her, as if this were the most natural encounter in the world.

''Darling, what a surprise.'' He bent over and kissed her sweetly.

''Philippe, what happened to Ivan and the buyers?''

''Oh,'' he smiled easily, ''we've changed it to dinner. In fact, there's a message on your answering machine about that. I'm sorry, darling, we'll have to postpone our dinner till tomorrow.''

She wanted to cry, to scream, to yell that he was a liar and a phony, but instead she invited him to join her and Terry until his luncheon partner—an old friend, he had said—arrived. ''All right, but just for a moment, I'm sure Terry would like you all to himself. . . . And what are you drinking? Beer! Gaby! You are a bad girl!''

Terry, returning to the table, was obviously confused

by the appearance of Philippe, who smoothed over the moment by greeting him warmly, then chastizing him for leading Gaby off her diet.

"Oh, you know, Philippe, I thought she deserved a celebration, now that she's visible all over this town!"

"Yes," Philippe agreed. "It is astonishing that the ad should appear just outside this restaurant."

Just then, the front doors opened again to reveal a distinguished man of about fifty, dressed in an elegant business suit, his silver hair combed back, his superb physique belying his age.

"Ah, here is my friend," said Philippe, rising and waving to catch the man's attention. "Over here!" he called to the man, who walked to their table. The stranger's smile was gracious, but as he looked at Gaby, she thought she could sense a certain coldness.

"Terry and Gaby"—Philippe remained standing to make the introduction, his manner as easy and elegant as ever—"I would like you to meet an old and dear friend of mine, Dominique Lefebvre."

And then she knew, and it all made sense, horrible sense, stupid sense, but she somehow managed to wait until they had seated themselves at a table across the room to excuse herself to the ladies' room and throw up.

The evening lumbered by, second by unbearable second, without the phone ringing once. Philippe hadn't called after the incident in the restaurant, and only the canceled dinner appointment on the answering machine gave substance to his presence in her life. Terry, after having uneasily offered to cancel his plans for the evening if she was sick, had been obviously grateful when she dismissed him in front of her door and sent him off to some other girl for the evening. He had promised to phone later, but he was out with somebody else, and she couldn't count on him to boost her plummeting spirits.

She dared not turn on the television, afraid of seeing herself in one of the commercials and of upsetting herself all over again. She tried to read, tried to pluck her eyebrows, do her nails, listen to the radio, call Jackson and Laura, who, of course, weren't home. In a childish attempt to hurt Philippe, she had ordered a pizza, hoping to consume the whole thing and blow up like a blimp by the next morning, but when it came, she tipped the guy five dollars, took one look at the baroque monstrosity, felt her stomach lurch, and threw it out.

A steaming bath and a hot shower, somehow upset her even more, and the one Valium she had left from an old prescription only slowed down her body, leaving her still-frazzled nerves to dance a frenzied tattoo on her raw feeling. The bath had been spent trying to devise a way to get out of the new three-year contract her cousin had just negotiated with Ivan. But Gerald was one hell of a lawyer, and he'd fought tooth and nail to hammer out a deal so generous, it was precedent-setting; there was just no way to walk away from it now.

At ten thirty, the phone rang, and stunned her. Rushing to answer it with a noncommittal but unshaken hello, she heard a teen-aged girl's voice ask for Valerie and slammed it down, finally bursting into the tears she'd been keeping back all evening. A year ago, without Mark, she'd suffered nights like these, but she hadn't imagined she could feel so lost, so lonely, with the whole world at her feet. So much for fame!

At midnight, having paced and grumbled and exhausted herself, she brushed her teeth, washed and creamed her face, took out her contact lenses, slipped into a nightshirt, turned off the lights, and came instantly awake. The silence of the room was now booming, coming in menacing waves perfectly synchronized with her misery.

When, at twelve fifteen, the phone rang again, it jarred her. Turning on the light before answering it, she talked herself into expecting another wrong number or, the perfect irony, an obscene phone call. ''Hello,'' she announced firmly.

''Hello, kid,'' came a slightly familiar male voice.

''Who is this?'' she demanded sharply.

''Gaby, baby,'' the voice continued merrily. ''I don't believe you don't know. Surprise, sweetheart, this is a blast from the past!''

''Who the hell is this?'' she shouted.

''Gaby, honey, it's me! It's Mark!''

chapter fourteen

CANNES,
May 1982

WENDING my way toward Mougins along roads that rolled and arced like my memories, I feared for the past. This friend of Gaby's, this Monsieur Corday, possessed the means to smash the fiction I'd fashioned out of my relationship with her. It occurred to me, as the De Lorean and I careered efficiently toward my karma, that I needed, wanted my version of Gaby to remain as pristine as a white shirt just back from the Chinese laundry.

If "my" Gaby was a concoction, only half-true, or rather, true to me only, well, so what, that half-truth comforted me. If I'd figured her wrong, I never wanted to know. If I could have saved her—worse yet, if I'd contributed to that destruction—what good would it do me to find out now? But then again, if part of the guilt was mine, godamnit, why should I be spared just because I was a great guy?

The guilt. It concerned me, because there had been

times with her when I'd decided against playing it straight, against coming clean with her, afraid that my mixed motives were leading me to misread Gaby's needs, or directing those needs to my own selfish ends.

I had been with her the day at Billy's when Philippe de Valmont's fatal flaw had announced itself to Gaby—and to me. The scene that day had required no interpretation; knowledge had simply come to her in the persons of Philippe and a man who was without doubt his lover—a lover some twenty years his senior, whom he resembled in the way that sexual protégés sometimes grow to resemble their masters. Philippe was an exquisitely fashioned copy of his friend, and had I not sensed Gaby's realizing the truth, I would have had to admire them. They were a stunning pair, almost father and son, but it was the "almost" that proclaimed the nature of their association.

Gaby clearly didn't want to talk about it, didn't suspect I'd seen what she had. Well, I'd felt that scene coming months before it arrived, but whatever satisfaction that provided gave way to more weighty confusion.

Should I walk her back to her apartment, settle her in as though I were her nanny, and let her cry on my shoulder? After she cried on my shoulder, should I confess that I had always loved her, take her in my arms, and make her mine? Should I call Suki and cancel dinner, pleading a friend in trouble, and let whatever happened come to pass? Should I keep the date with Suki and call Gaby every hour on the hour to assure her she wasn't alone?

But, suppose I was wrong? Suppose both Gaby and I had been wrong? Suppose Philippe were to appear at Gaby's that night when she and I were together? Maybe the best thing to do was just to let her go it alone, to let her recover, decide. I just didn't know, but by the time we got to her house, I had decided I couldn't leave Suki in the lurch; I respected her and loved her good cheer and generous company, and I couldn't hurt her—certainly not on an emotional flyer. In all fairness, Gaby never asked me to stay with her, never would have allowed me to alter my plans. Instead, we settled for a civilized farewell, and I told her I'd call her that night to check on her health.

When I phoned around midnight from Elaine's, the phone was busy. As it was at twelve twenty, twelve thirty, twelve forty-five, and one. By then, Suki wanted to split, and I was sort of worried that Gaby had done something desperate, but the operator who tried the number reported it was busy, not off the hook, so I got irrationally pissed that she'd gotten over her shock enough to blab to somebody for hours. Hurling her a silent "Screw you," I went home with Suki, where we spent a long and energetic night drowning my anger.

In the morning, my feelings still a little bruised, I refused to call Gaby, but when I checked in with my answering machine, I heard her voice, cheerful as a lark, urging me to contact her "asap" and receive, as she so gaily put it, "an offer you can't refuse."

chapter fifteen

NEW YORK,
May 1978

GABY, navigating around the islands of lunchtime strollers at the corner of Fifty-fifth and Sixth, spotted Terry by the entrance to the MGM building and ran toward him.

"Hi," she called eagerly, as she bestowed a hasty peck on his cheek, then caught his expression of mild perturbation.

"Jesus Christ," he grumbled. "Fame hasn't done a thing to improve your tardiness record. I thought the screening started at two thirty. It's two fifty-five!"

"Oh," she brushed off the remark as they entered the lobby, "you know they never start on time."

"Lah-di-dah!" he shot back, aware that Gaby was a little too animated, a little too flushed. As they crossed the lobby and headed toward the rear first-floor entrance to the screening room, he asked her, "Why didn't you ever mention you knew Mark Groseman?"

"Dunno, just never came up," but her smile held a

hint of an enigma. Mark. In seconds, she was going to see Mark. That awareness made her want to run away, although no force of man or nature could have kept her from the other side of that screening room door. For two days, ever since Mark's call, the prospect of seeing him had helped reduce to life-size her diminished dreams of Philippe. Now, with Terry by her side, she'd be able to show Mark the new Gaby: famous, glamorous, desirable, *secure*. She'd been dutifully rehearsing that role, pulling it off even with Philippe, who'd called the day after the Billy's incident. She'd been the one to beg off a dinner invitation, pleading previous plans, but had graciously accepted his invitation for a chic little supper tonight at Lutèce with Ivan and his wife and Jackson and Laura. Philippe had greeted her declining of his first invitation with grace; he had been as charming and warm and, she had realized, as distant as always, but for the first time, she'd sensed the strain beneath the elegance, and it occurred to her that perhaps he did care for her and that her begging off had injured him, and that made her a little sad.

She'd chosen to take Terry with her to the screening—Terry, well-known, well-liked, a good guy to be seen with, a real guardian angel and great moral support. Even Mark had been pleased that Terry Barron would be present to spread the word if he liked the film, had even expressed satisfaction that she wasn't bringing "the frog," so Terry was by her side, not even bothering to comment on how wonderful she looked in the buff-colored linen smock with the buff boots and the little braids in her hair. Philippe would have praised her, but Philippe was not there, might never be there, and it was Terry who was subtly dragging her toward the door, refusing to acknowledge, if he noticed it, that she was feeling totally stupid, scared, faint, embarrassed, terrified. Like Sidney Carton, she allowed herself to be led bravely into the huge, cavernous room. She was shocked that the room was almost filled; for some reason, she'd expected maybe ten or fifteen people at the most, but there was a crowd of about forty seated there, chatting with each other, smoking, and calling playful insults to each other as they waited for the screening to start. A quick survey of the crowd didn't produce so much as a glimpse of Mark, nor of anyone else she knew, just a bunch of people dressed in the casual denim-and-khaki uniforms that all creative types, famous or no, affected in daytime Manhattan.

"Wanna sit down?" Terry's voice made her conscious of the fact that they'd been standing in the back of the room.

"Yes, I guess so," she murmured, but as they started down the side aisle, a smart-looking redhead disengaged herself from a group she'd been bantering with and made her way toward them.

"Hello," she greeted them with studied warmth. "I'm Gloria Weston, Mr. Groseman's administrative assistant, and you are . . ." She either hadn't recognized Gaby or else a model just didn't rate in this strange, impenetrable hierarchy.

"I'm Gaby Blake," Gaby offered, crushed at her reduction to anonymity, "and this is Terry Barron. We're Mr. Groseman's——"

"Oh, Mr. Barron!" Gloria stepped decisively on Gaby's remark. "How nice to see you here!" She checked a clipboard that she held in her hand, "Oh, yes, here's your name, Ms. . . . Blake," then, flashing Terry another dazzling smile, she addressed him. "Make yourself at home. We're going to start in about three minutes."

"What a sweetheart," Gaby muttered as they made

their way to the second row, where, mysteriously enough, a pair of empty seats seemed to be waiting for them.

"Hey, Barron!" a hearty voice bellowed, and Terry wheeled around, shouted "Hamill! How goes it?"

Gaby glanced back and suddenly realized there were some very famous faces in this crowd—Dustin Hoffman, Bob Fosse, Norman Mailer, Faye Dunaway, Liza Minnelli, and Mikhail Baryshnikov were scattered throughout the audience, all dressed like real people. Everybody but Mark. Where was he? Maybe he had got cold feet and ducked out at the last minute. That wasn't like him, though; he was too gluttonous an egotist to miss such a casually star-studded moment, but as the lights began to dim, he was still nowhere to be seen.

The jolt of the anticlimax thrust Gaby to the brink of tears; without Mark, without the *intime* scene she'd envisioned, had rehearsed to the last detail, how was she going to sit through anybody's movie, especially his? Particularly when *Ikon* was being touted in all the columns as the film of the decade? Once again, he'd set her up and disappointed her, and for reasons she couldn't even imagine. The credits began, but she didn't even see them; they could have been a TV weather report for all she could concentrate on the big screen before her.

"Hey, looks good," Terry whispered, "*Twilight Zone* with a twenty-million-dollar budget," he predicted as she politely nodded.

"Can I have a cigarette?" she asked, and he looked puzzled.

"You don't smoke."

"Just give me the cigarette," she hissed, and as he responded, lighting it for her, he asked, "What the hell is wrong with you, Gaby?" to which she snapped back, "Why don't you talk a little louder so the whole audience can share in our conversation?"

"Jesus!" he shot back, then gave up and returned to the movie. When various actors' names appeared in the credits, their friends applauded, and when Mark's name crawled up the screen, the whole audience burst into cheers. Clearly, this was a private viewing for Mark's fifty most intimate friends. The creep.

The film began, totally engaging the attention of everyone in the audience but Gaby. The whispering around her ceased, and the click of cigarette lighters signaled the beginning of serious film watching. In the deep dark of the screening room, Gaby permitted herself a tear or two of tremendous disappointment, then attempted to concentrate on the movie, but its immediately apparent excellence made her flinch and want to escape.

Checking her watch, she saw that only five minutes had elapsed, that she had two more hours of sitting here, heartsick. And to top it off, somebody who had come in late was clumping into the row behind her, causing some kind of minor disruption. Whoever it was sat right down behind her in a flurry of rustling papers and hissed hellos. Then, when quiet had finally been restored, when she was just about resigned to the two-hour imprisonment, she felt a hand on her head, followed by a quick but serious peck on the back of her neck.

She was just about to whirl around and tell the jerk to stop when she heard a soft whisper in her ear. "Hey, baby. Let's get together after this thing, okay? Gotta go," and by the time Gaby collected herself to turn to the aisle, Mark Groseman was only a dim figure, fleeing through the blackness toward the exit sign.

chapter sixteen

CANNES,
May 1982

MARK Groseman. His very presence could light up a room—even a darkened screening room—like a nuclear explosion. And it wasn't until much later that you found out about the fallout and the poison clouds, and by then it was too late. Mark "Whizkid" Groseman. Under thirty and a power. No, more than a power. An energy source. Short, dark, and intense. Bearded, bespectacled, baseball-capped and t-shirted. Still a kid but already smoked Romeo & Juliettas. Never lettered in any sport, but played a snappy game of tennis. Golfed with the moneymen, roller-skated with the hot screenwriters, could do up a line as neat as any of the rock idols and movie stars he hung out with in his beach shack at Malibu. So unstruck by success that he hid away his private little screening room in the basement of his casual, unpretentious jewel of a house nestled at the apex of the Bel Air Hills. You never even noticed the interior design, it was that subtle. Or the fact that the wine was always a collector's item and the women were always tens with good conversation and at least the impression of a career.

Mark Groseman. So gifted, so witty, so down-to-earth. A regular guy with a manic streak of genius. And the prick of the age. The first time I experienced him, I experienced simultaneously an almost irresistible desire to deck him. Not since my salad days in the boisterous bars of Boston had I wanted to slug anybody as badly as I wanted to go for him. Because whatever else Mark Groseman may have been, he was, first and foremost, trouble.

We first met, after one of the early screenings of the undeniably brilliant *Ikon*, and from the initial moment of contact, Gaby stood between us. He greeted her playfully, and she melted. Just melted. My tough-and-tender girl had just divested herself of tough. Her capitulation was almost enchantment, as if Groseman had hypnotized her, but instinct told me there was more to it than that. Between them was a long, byzantine history of some kind about which I had been—and might continue to be—kept in the dark. So the momentary relief I'd nastily felt when I gathered Philippe was phase-outable was instantly replaced by a disappointment as strong as my sense of dread. Gaby had just moved farther out of my reach, but this time the waters were shark-infested.

chapter seventeen

NEW YORK,
May 1978

AFTER the post-lunchtime calm, the Russian Tea Room was working its way back up to frenzy. Theatergoers, queuing up for an early dinner, were vocal in their anxiety that they would miss the curtain, but no one made a move to go elsewhere. The bar, which had been filling up since fivish, was now packed solid, and the little half-moon banquettes at the front of the room, although meant for two, were jammed with three or more, including the table-hoppers, many of them recognizable Hollywood stars, the others their agents kibitzing and joking amidst the red and gold old-world splendor of the room.

It was to this bastion of Hollywood away from home that Gaby had been whisked by Mark after the unbelievable triumph of the screening. That it had been a success, and that word in New York spread laser fast, was evidenced by the fact that a steady stream of the famous and the near-famous, some from the screening, were heading for Mark's banquette, the women proffering their cheeks for a kiss, the men solemnly shaking hands.

"Gee, baby"—Mark crinkled a smile and took her hand—"I'm real sorry for all this interruption. I just didn't expect it."

"Oh, Mark," she said, smiling back, "yes, you did. You did expect it. That's why we're here. But it's all right. It's fine. God, I'm getting recognized, too."

"Ah, yes." He kept her hand as, with the other, he gestured toward the waiter for another round of drinks, "You're a great girl to be seen with. How did it all happen?"

"Karma," she said, laughing. Like your calling on one of the worst nights of my life, she added silently.

"Karma, yeah. Here's to karma," he raised his wine glass and clinked it to hers, then added, "To karma two."

Since they'd met after the screening, when Terry had begged off from joining them for a drink, Mark and she had been keeping up a fast-paced, quippy conversation loaded with smiles, secure glances, and neutral questions about their time apart. You would have thought we were just old friends meeting again after traveling round the world, she thought—glad to be back, pleased to be together.

"Karma two?" she allowed herself a leading question. "What's that supposed to mean?"

His gaze softened, his hand pressed hers; good old Mark was moving in for the kill. "It just means that . . . God . . . Gaby, when I look at you I don't feel like a success."

"Thanks a lot."

"No, no . . . I mean that . . . well . . . you know, I really missed you. A lot."

She shouldn't be saying it, but she did. "You could have called."

"No, no, darling," he began, pausing a minute to wave at Dustin Hoffman. "I couldn't. Because of the way you make me feel. You make me feel like I need you to be good. And I had to prove to myself that I could do it alone . . . that I wanted to be with you because I *want* you, not because I need you."

The old Groseman bullshit, and it still worked like a charm. "And did you prove that?" she couldn't stop herself from asking.

"Yeah. Yeah, I did. Gaby, let's see each other again." He moved fast, ostensibly to block a protest they both knew would never come. "I mean, I know you're involved with that frog. Sorry. And with your career. I'm not asking you to give anything up. I just want us to be able to *see* each other . . . at least for now. I mean, you travel and I travel." He went so far as to remove his dark glasses for emphasis, and looked at her lovingly. "It doesn't have to be heavy. It just has to be. Agreed?"

"Ummmm," Gaby replied, sipping her wine.

"Hey, babe, is that a yes or no?"

And he finally forced a yes from her, as she turned her head to notice that the restaurant had cleared out. "Mark, what time is it?"

"Why? It's eight thirty."

"Because"—she went cold with fear—"because I was supposed to be at Lutèce an hour ago."

"You'd better call." He reached in his jeans pocket for a dime.

"No, no, I'd better just go." She collected her purse and rose.

"Wait a second till I pay this, and I'll drop you!" he insisted. "A coupla minutes won't matter."

"That's what you think. The fashion business isn't the movie business."

"Okay. This should cover it." He reached back in his pocket, extracted a fifty, left it on the table, jumped up, grabbed her hand, and raced her out of the door.

Miraculously, an empty Checker cab appeared, cruising slowly east across Fifty-seventh. Mark would have dashed into its path to halt it, but a wave of the hand sufficed. The cab pulled to a stop, and soon they were on their way, heading due east. It wasn't until they had crossed Fifth that the crosstown traffic began to build up. "Oh, God!" Gaby gasped. "It's Thursday! The stores are open till nine. That's why the traffic's so bad!"

"Relax," cautioned Mark, grinning calmly. "It just looks bad. See, we're already at Park." But the closer they got to Bloomingdale's, the worse the congestion became. It seemed as though they had been in the taxi for half an hour by the time they got to the bottleneck at Lexington and Fifty-seventh, but Gaby didn't look at her watch because she couldn't face it.

"Oh, God! Mark, this is terrible. It must be nearly nine. No, don't look! I don't want to know."

They tried to make small talk, but Gaby couldn't concentrate. Her heart raced with the anxiety of the perennially tardy caught in a genuine time crisis. "The traffic's not moving at all," she moaned, noting that it was taking two lights to make one block down Lexington. "And I'm not even dressed right."

"You look swell, babe," he cooed, all California casualness. "You'll wow 'em."

"If they're still there." She glanced at the street sign, which announced they had reached Fifty-third. "Listen, Mark," she said suddenly, "I can't stand this. I'm going to walk."

''Gaby, we're almost there.'' His hand on hers urged her to stay.

''No, I can't. Really, I can walk it faster!'' Commanding the driver to pull over, she prepared to make a fast exit when, all of a sudden, Mark grabbed her and kissed her, harder than he had any right to.

''Call you tomorrow,'' he murmured, and for a moment too long, she stayed in his arms. ''Gaby,'' was what he said instead of good-bye, as she broke away and began her flight for the remaining blocks, realizing, as she half walked, half ran east that she was drunk, terrified, and happier than she'd been in much too long. Mark was magic, maybe black magic, but any magic was better than no magic at all, she thought, giggling as she sped toward Lutèce, with the lights of Manhattan twinkling and glowing, the lovely May breeze tenderly stroking, full of infinite promise.

As she rounded the corner of Fiftieth and Third and hurried down the block toward Lutèce, Gaby's euphoria receded before a tempest of panic. It had to be at least nine; she was marginally, but not really, dressed for dinner. They had probably stalled over drinks for an hour, then ordered. Since she hadn't called, it occurred to her, they might not have ordered at all because they might actually be worried. Did people worry when you were an hour late for dinner? Maybe they'd gotten over being worried and left. But why would they leave? They had to be there, waiting, fuming, expecting a valid excuse for her inexcusable behavior. And she had none. No excuse. What could she say? A last minute appointment? An old friend in trouble? A taxi accident? A heel broken off a boot? Nothing that would have prohibited her from calling. And, Jesus, this was a business dinner, and Ivan Solomon was all business. She dared not plead irresponsibility. Damn! Half stumbling over a crack in the pavement, she retrieved her balance just in time to avoid plunging to the ground and perhaps tearing her stocking or bruising her knee. Maybe a bruise or two would have been a hint of an excuse. She wanted to turn around and flee. She wanted to get there. She wanted them not to be angry, worried, or perplexed. She wanted them to be anything except stunned that, quite simply, she'd forgotten.

And then, she was there, standing before Lutèce, running down the couple of steps to the wooden door, pushing it open, shocked, when it didn't give, into thinking it was so late the place was closed, then remembering the door gave outward.

As soon as she burst into the tiny bar, she was greeted by Madame, who recognized her. "Oh, Miss Blake! Here you are!" Was Gaby mistaken, or did the woman's exceedingly polite voice broadcast just a hint of condemnation? "Your party has been waiting for you!"

"Oh, yes, a slight mistake," Gaby apologized to the woman, smiling desperately. "Where are they?"

"Jean!" The woman called to the maître d', "Miss Blake has arrived!" Worse than her expectations! The whole restaurant had been alerted to her shame.

"Miss Blake! At last!" The maître d' was as charming as ever, but she could sense in him, too, that same disapproval that she would dare to offend not only her party, but the restaurant. "Please come with me," and he escorted her straight back down the narrow hall leading to an area of tables that fronted a glassed-in greenhouse beyond. "Here they are!"

She saw them all from a distance, Ivan and his wife, Doris, Jackson and Laura, Philippe and the empty chair that was to be hers. When she came into view, no one rose; they all looked as if they were seeing a mirage.

They were in the midst of their hors d'oeuvres, and their forks seem to freeze in midair. Finally, as the maître d' conducted her toward them, Philippe got up.

"Gaby! Where have you been? We have been so concerned!" She allowed herself to be seated, smiling with a manufactured concern she hoped was touching to them all.

"Oh, God, I'm so sorry," she murmured, her eyes cast down, then, placing her hand lightly over Philippe's, she cooed, "I'm just so glad that I'm finally here!"

And that was that. She said no more in explanation, but charmingly accepted the white wine that was being poured for her and, at the head waiter's urging, consulted with him on her choice of entree, having decided, in the interest of time, to skip the first course. The conversation retained a certain stiffness for the next twenty minutes, then settled into a fair imitation of relaxed dinner talk. By the time they had gotten to coffee and business, Gaby, with a slowly growing amazement, realized the reason she had been so easily forgiven: They needed her. As much, perhaps more, than she needed them. She was the woman of Valmont, publicly if not privately. Without her, the campaign would suffer a severe setback, and the projected new set of commercials would have to be scrapped. They had to humor her. If she had shown up three hours late, they couldn't have afforded to get mad enough to fire her. She, Gaby Blake, was an asset, and a major one.

What she had interpreted as condemnation when she entered the restaurant was actually a multimillion-dollar anxiety so profound that even the restaurant staff had caught it. What if the woman of Valmont had, in fact, sustained some defacing accident? How would the moneymakers cope with the financial tragedy of a star model with a broken nose? A prominent scar? A broken leg? They needed her, and they needed her in perfect shape.

As she pondered this over the brandy and the talk, she felt her confidence growing to a peak that came close to arrogance. She didn't have to be afraid. She was famous. She was a necessity; she could honestly value her worth to them in seven figures, had even gotten Ivan to negotiate. She was a star. Smiling a dazzling, condescending smile at Philippe, she allowed him to help her up from her chair after the check had been paid and to escort her through the restaurant. On the sidewalk, everybody kissed everybody else, a sign that the business discussions had proceeded smoothly and that the new series of commercials was set, then Ivan and his wife hailed a cab and, followed soon by the Pendletons, disappeared into the night. Philippe, his arm sweetly around Gaby's shoulder, waved them off, the perfect picture of the attendant swain, then, as their cabs receded in the distance, began to walk her east, his arm still around her, toward her apartment.

When they were almost to First Avenue, Gaby, caught up in the euphoria of newfound power, realized that Philippe had shifted his hand from her shoulder to her arm, which he was now grasping with considerable strength, and that he wasn't talking. His pace had speeded up, and she felt the pressure on her arm increasing.

"Philippe," she said, "you're walking too fast." To which he said nothing. "Can't we stroll for a few minutes?" she implored, smiling a little drunkenly. "Let's walk by the river. It's a beautiful night." But her murmured words and her adorable smile seemed to have eluded him, for he continued to rush her toward her doorstep, saying nothing.

"Well, thanks for the lovely dinner," she said, drawing her key from her purse. "See you tomorrow?"

"Open the door, Gaby," he ordered, and for the first time, she felt a hint of menace. "I'm coming up."

"Oh, Philippe," she demurred, "I'm so tired. It's been some day!"

"Open the door," he ordered in a voice that made her do it without delay. He made sure she preceded him up the stairs, as if to be sure there was no chance for her to escape, then stepped back while she opened the door and admitted him.

Not knowing what to do, she threw her purse down on the couch and asked cheerfully, "Would you like a brandy?" she turned to head for the kitchen before he could answer, but his hands grabbed her arms in midstep and whirled her around to face him. He was furious, all trace of sweetness gone from his handsome features; his countenance bore the stern immobility of a warrior's statue, and his voice, when he spoke, chilled her.

"Where were you?"

"I—I . . ." Her fear stunned and silenced her.

"Where the hell were you? What were you doing?"

"Philippe——" she started to protest, but he interrupted her.

"Do you realize what you risked? Do you know what you could have done?"

Suddenly, her fear began to turn to anger, to memories of the awful shock at Billy's, of the desperation of those nights when he had begged off, of the lies, the exploitation, the hypocrisy of what he had dared let her believe was a love affair. And that anger made her strong enough to twist out of his grasp.

"Yes, Philippe," she said calmly, "I know what I could have done. I could have cost you money. Quite a lot of money. I could have shown your associates that the woman of Valmont is *not* the woman of Valmont."

She watched the shock spring to his eyes, saw his

hands drop to his sides and his fists clench. ''What do you mean? What are you saying?'' he demanded tonelessly.

Gaby turned away and walked across the room, opened a window, then turned back to face him. ''Do you really want to talk about this?'' When he nodded, she continued, ''I know, Philippe. I know.''

He took a step toward her, then stopped. ''Know? What do you know?''

She sensed the fear in him, saw him tense for the truth he must have known was coming, wanted to end the conversation right now, but knew it was too late not to go on. ''I know about Dominique.''

It seemed to take a minute for her words to register. It seemed to take that long before the strength, the rage, in him dissipated, before something in him seemed to collapse although he made no move. Then, slowly, he raised a hand to his face and drew it across his eyes as if to quell a pain, or to erase a moment. ''Oh,'' was all his acknowledgment, but it was enough. He would never ask her how or from whom she knew, or exactly what she knew; he was too much of an aristocrat to ask a *paparazzo's* sneering questions. And he was too much of a gentleman to protest. Instead, he presented her with the affirmation of his silence. She knew, too, that he would never storm out or sneak out or creep out in defeat or embarrassment; he would stand there, wearing his shame, until she dismissed him. And, for the first time, out of nowhere, it occurred to her that his anger had not been only about the money; there was a disappointment in him as abject as her own—his grief for the loss of a hope he had treasured just as she had.

When, at last, she crossed the room to him, she seemed to move through air still crackling with the anger of their words.

"Philippe," she said solemnly, taking up one of his hands. "I'm sorry I behaved so badly, showing up so late at the restaurant. I think I must have been very angry at you, but I didn't know it."

"Yes." He raised his free hand and placed it over theirs. "Yes, I understand. And you must know how I regret my words, my actions, to you."

"Let's forgive each other, then." She smiled up at him.

"Yes, some time, we must." He looked to her for a direction, then, receiving none and taking it as a dismissal, disengaged his hands from hers and began to turn to the door.

"Oh, please don't leave," she urged. "I mean, not unless you want to." He seemed relieved at that. "Come, sit down, let's have that brandy." When she returned with the glasses and the bottle, he was sitting quietly, his head lowered, thinking. Looking quickly up at her, he watched her pour the brandy, set the glasses down in front of them, and slip down next to him.

"I don't, of course, know what you know, Gaby," he told her, "but I feel perhaps you should hear my story . . . from me, yes?"

She nodded, then let him take her hand as he slowly made her his confidante. He told her how he had met Dominique when he himself was thirteen and Dominique, an aristocrat and international financier of some renown, often away from France but this once, this Noël, visiting Philippe's family in the country. Dominique Lefebvre, twenty years ago, at thirty-five or so, had been more than urbane and sophisticated; he had been a glowing physical and mental presence that, especially in a boy Philippe's age, inspired a profound desire for imitation. Philippe, who was too tall, too thin, too quiet, too uncompetitive, too sensitive, found, in this perfect gentleman, the man he wished above all to be. When, to Philippe's amazement, Dominique seemed to find in the awkward, solitary boy some spark of which Philippe himself dreamed, their mutual attraction was decided. And so it had been, for the past twenty years, in which Dominique had been Philippe's teacher, his psychiatrist, his advisor, his best friend, his lover. They had never lived together, rarely resided even in the same country at the same time, and as Philippe's extraordinary design talent began to emerge from the first halting sketches he had dared show only to Dominique, they buried their relationship deep in the background of their lives. Neither had ever felt the urge for a new partner, for new adventures, for a more conventional kind of domesticity. Despite distances they were inseparable, and as the years passed, Philippe had become convinced they would be lovers until death.

''So,'' Philippe continued, over more brandy as the night grew later, ''passion, or rather, the kind of passion most young men seek in their lives, was something I sacrificed, or disregarded. Dominique had devoted his life to me, and I was happy with him when we were together. We wrote, we telephoned, we vacationed together. Besides, I had the passion of my work, the romance of my success, to enchant me. So many beautiful women, so many parties, houses, everything. It all came quite easy. When women flirted, I flirted back, but politely. There was always gossip about me and someone, which I never denied or confirmed, and soon it died out. They began to call me the monk, and for all they knew, I was.''

He had loosened his tie and unbuttoned his suit jacket. Reclining casually, elegantly against the couch, he struck Gaby as the most beautiful man she would ever know. The brandy and the emotions of the story had flushed his face with a semblance of color like Carrara marble; the softness of his voice caressed, lingered over her, calming them both.

"That day in East Hampton," he continued, his eyes glowing with the remembered pleasure, "was something . . . something . . . *unusual* for me. The sight of you pleased me; you made me happy. It was a great surprise." He laughed at the thought and took her hand. "You were so lovely, so warm, but so . . . so human . . . angry, spoiled, disappointed, stubborn. Not like a mannequin. Not like a rich matron. Still surprised . . . delightful. Like a little girl, but very alluring. I saw, of course, what Jackson saw in you, what will make you a great star, and I wanted it."

He lifted his hand and lightly let it graze her cheek, while she sat perfectly silent, struck by the joy of the memories and the sadness of their passing.

"You must know," he continued, moving his hand gently to smooth her hair, "it was not for business that I craved to be with you. I fought Jackson on that, but he won, and then I was glad. I hoped, you know, that our . . . our . . . affair . . . had transformed me—a fairy tale, of course. I pretended to myself that when the time came Dominique would understand, would not be hurt or jealous, but. . . ." She looked at him, wondering, and he answered the unarticulated question. "But . . . I lied to Dominique. For the first time. No, not lied, allowed him to deceive himself. Let him think my . . . *tendre* . . . for you was for the house of Valmont. . . ."

"Philippe." She moved toward him, seeing the distress in his eyes, but he waved away her solace.

"No, Gaby, I do not deserve to be comforted. I was foolish to think. . . . Oh, Dominique is not a young man. That day in the restaurant, I realized that I could hurt him, that I can never tell him. It would kill him if I left him.

"I must be frank with myself, as you must with yourself. All I can offer you is some part of my life." He cast down his eyes, then, taking her hands, looked at her, sadly. "And that is not enough to give you, not enough. . . ." His voice trailed off, and he smiled regretfully. "But know that I love you and that, profoundly, I wish that things had been different with us."

"Philippe." Surprising herself, she put her arms around him, holding him, soothing him. "Philippe."

"Do you think, Gaby," he murmured, "do you think that . . . that there is some way that we can continue together? Some way?"

She drew back to face him. "There must be! I do love you, Philippe."

"Gaby." He kissed her lightly. "I love you, too. It is too late to change that. And you must know that I will always be your servant, your—how do you say? —your swain?" He wiped away the tears she hadn't even realized were there. "If ever you need me, ever, for anything, no matter how big, no matter where, you must always be sure I will be there for you. Trust me for that. For always."

In response, she nodded, worrying for him, loving him, as they sat, mourning the passing of an evening and a magic time, and the birth of a future together they could never ever begin to imagine.

chapter eighteen

CANNES,
May 1982

AFTER the *Ikon* screening, Gaby changed again. What shocked me was how the difference in her produced differences in me. Involuntarily, my mood slowly blackened as each day produced a brand, spanking-new disappointment. For one thing, instead of being her customary hard-to-get-hold-of, she was now totally unreachable. Either she wasn't home—or wasn't picking up—for days at a time, or else the line was busy for hours—maybe she'd taken the phone off the hook.

My jealous fantasies, which in the days of Philippe were at least emotionally containable by a sort of calm predictability, now, in the summer of my obsession, rushed at me in tidal waves, like a disco lighting effect: too much sensation, too many images, knocking me off balance, working me up to a frenzy, then sending me crashing with an intensity that made me impossible to be around.

When I did, eventually, catch up with her, she was either busy with someone or on her way out. There were times when my paranoia mushroomed into the certainty that she was actually spending a quiet evening at home and had just plain written me off. When the delirium subsided, I was always forced to admit to myself that that was what I wanted to believe because it made me more important in her life than I knew I was.

Every so often, she'd consent to meet me for lunch or a drink, but something always interfered. Either she had a shooting or, wreathed in the most intense apologies, she bemoaned the fact that something absolutely crucial had come up. Man, was I pissed! And hurt. And haunted with suspicions.

Camc thc day I strolled early into 21 for a lunch interview with George Steinbrenner, and at the bar ran right into her, merry as hell, bound by the simian grip of Mark Groseman and standing amid a group of pretty dour-looking top brass from Warners. I attempted to walk right past her, but she saw me, screamed my name, and dashed into my embrace with the solid-gold wantonness of someone so secure she dared to make a scene at 21. Her seemingly genuine pleasure at running into me brought, for some reason, the hot ball of childhood tears to my throat; I wanted to weep, I guess, because her insouciance assured me that my five million calls hadn't even registered in her consciousness. She quickly ran down what seemed like a prepared list of excuses: the new commercials, the business evenings and parties with Philippe, hairdressers, fittings, facials, benefits, interviews—all garbage. She was a different person, some kind of changeling, and I knew instantly that no matter what the ads proclaimed, Gaby was no longer the woman of Valmont. She had, off camera, lost that pouty, little-girl ebullience. Now, she was hyper, nervous, almost fevered, worn down in ways a camera couldn't pick up but I could. Her attention was elsewhere, somewhere behind her, specifically on the spot where Mark Groseman bandied points with the Warner brass. No, Gaby was no longer the woman of Valmont; she was the woman of Mark Groseman, or if she wasn't, she was trying to be with all she had. And it hadn't done a thing for her peace of mind.

In the course of her litany, Groseman called to her, and, breaking off in midsentence with a breathless, "I'll call you," she ran to his side. With a wave to me, he escorted her and the movie execs inside to lunch. She never looked back.

That night was the occasion of my first major set-to with Suki. Over pasta at Bruno's, she asked me what was bugging me. I demanded to know why she thought anything was bugging me. She pointed out that I was drinking martinis, which I never did, in a quantity I'd not in her experience equaled with Bourbon or beer. Whereupon I accused her of accusing me of being drunk. At which she smiled demurely. In response, I requested she remove that shit-eating, self-righteous grin from her face. To which she thrust at me the charge that I was becoming a monster. And I parried with the fact that monsters are made, not born. When she asked if that meant it was all her fault, I matched her previous demure grin with a malicious one. To my surprise, she burst into tears, fought to regain control, and remembered to throw down her fork like a challenge to duel before grabbing her purse and walking out, leaving me feeling like a complete jerk, which, of course, I was. It took an hour before I got her to answer the door that night, but when she did, she found me touchingly penitential, my arms laden with about fifty bucks worth of flowers, my vow never again to drink gin moving even me to tears.

So that was round one. The next time, after I'd seen Gaby and Groseman holding hands on West Broadway, I'd arrived at Suki's loft in so abusive and foul a mood that she quickly informed me she felt we should split for a while. I informed her how good it was that she was expressing something I'd been feeling. Intending to wound, I had practically murdered, and coolly taking my leave with a couple of shirts I'd left there, I could almost physically feel the intensity of her pain relieving my own. It wasn't that I didn't care about hurting her; it was worse. It gave me pleasure. So I walked back down West Broadway, following the phantom Gaby and Mark into thc night, as my life again faded to black.

chapter nineteen

NEW YORK,
June 1978

WHEN the phone rang, Gaby, still deeply asleep, reached instinctively for it, anxious to stop its shrilling before it awakened Mark. "Yes?" Her mind commanded her voice to broadcast alertness to the caller.

"Gaby, where are you? It's ten thirty." It was Jackson's voice, and he was not happy.

"Ten thirty?" she mused groggily, forcing her gaze to focus on the clock, whose configuration brought her instantly awake. "Ten thirty! Oh, God, Jackson, I'm sorry. I don't know why, but the alarm didn't go off." She was hissing in a half-whisper, despite the knowledge that nothing woke Mark before noon and never had; in fact, his only motion was to turn away from her and grab a pillow, incorporating it into his dreams.

"That's hardly the point, Gaby," he announced icily. "Just get your ass down to this studio—and fast. You're really not my only account, dear."

"Uh . . . okay," she murmured, hurt as much by

his dismissal of her importance to him as by his slamming down the phone without saying good-bye. She managed to roll out of bed and place her feet firmly on the floor before the hangover hit. On her perilous way to the bathroom, as the waves of nausea and headache washed continuously over her, she tried to reconstruct last night. She had wanted to split early from that music mogul's townhouse because of the morning shooting, but there had been just enough champagne and cocaine to keep Mark bound into innumerable conversations until five thirty in the morning.

Even in the old days at New York University, he'd been a star talker. She'd first sighted him at a film school grass-and-kultur-klatsch, where he'd been talking, wildly, brilliantly, surrounded by a hypnotized and adoring crowd who lapped up his energy, enthusiasm, and dazzle. Even then, Mark Groseman was hot, this Great-Neck-born son of a wealthy Seventh Avenue manufacturer. Spoiled rotten, Mark had never enjoyed a moment of self-doubt despite his less than awe-inspiring physical appearance. Women—first his mother, then his sisters, then his teachers, then his plural girlfriends—fed off his high-spirited sensuality; men, off his boundless but merry ambition. Mark Groseman was born to lead because the greediness of his bonhomie passed as a generosity that promised to take all who fell under his sway along on the joyride to the stars.

Gaby, made shy by her height and cynical by her shyness, instantly doubted everything about him—his excessive flash seemed liable at any moment to short circuit, his feistiness masked belligerence, his enthusiasm suggested irresponsibility clothed in the innocence of the guiltlessly narcissistic. So Gaby had put him down to her friends who raved about him, refused to bathe in his aura, turned silent and sarcastic in his presence, and of course, attracted him because of her exotic indifference. In time, it became obvious to her that if Mark Groseman could show any girl a good time, what made an ice princess from Louisburg Square immune? Groseman might be trouble, but what a way to go!

Given the ordinariness of the men she'd grown up with, Mark's mercurial quality was miraculously exciting. The Boston boys offered security; Mark offered emotional suspense. He would show up unexpectedly, stay for two days, then not call at all for a week and a half. At the end of the week and a half, Gaby was convinced that whatever lucky streak had brought this dangerous yet thrilling presence into her life and her arms had ended. Mark was gone, and his departure would always be as mysterious to her as his advent. She was crushed, she was furious, she was dazed. Had he found a more exciting woman? Was he working on a script with somebody else, so hyped on speed and creativity that he just forgot about her? Had he driven to Cape Cod with one of his buddies to scout locations for a short they had been talking about? What did it matter? It was over. Then, when three weeks or so had passed, he would appear at her door, proffering no excuses, just eighteen hours of high-energy love. After a year of this erotic torture, she found she was getting too attached, that, although she had always been a good student, the Art Institute was too tough a school to allow for obsessing over a man twenty hours a day and studying once a week. It took her months of practice, but finally she informed Mark that she couldn't stand his inconsistent behavior a moment longer. To her surprise, he suggested that he move in with her. So, at last, she had him. In spades. He was her life; she let her own alliances fade away in favor of his, and since her place was always filled with his "associates," as he liked to refer to his friends, she ended up studying at the library, in flight from the endless progression of story conferences, all-night raps, and football games.

But it had all been worth it. Even her mother and stepfather's horror at her shocking, bohemian cohabitation with a man whose pedigree and aspirations were as unacceptable as Mark's hadn't shaken her resolve to make a go of the relationship. With Mark's support, or pressure, she stood firm in the face of her mother's insistence that she terminate the affair. Since her father's early death, she'd always felt unworthy in her mother's eyes, though she had never been clear on exactly why she was so suspect; but now, with Mark's commitment filling the emptiness her dad had left behind, she gathered the strength to say no. Her private life was her private life, and since she had never managed to please her mother anyway, it seemed ridiculous to sacrifice actual happiness to that puritan, snobbish status quo, which she had been rebelling against as long as she could remember. So, by the time it all came to a head, when her mother insisted that Gaby choose between Mark and the family, it was hardly a choice. She had always taken the threats of disinheritance and estrangement literally, so the letter from her mother's lawyer had come as no surprise.

After that, there was no turning back. She hadn't needed the financial support, anyway, since her father had left his only child an enormous, income-producing trust fund and, in addition, an even then priceless piece of Manhattan real estate. As for emotional support, her mother had never done much to make her feel secure, so what did she need her family for? Mark lectured her: *he* was her family. And he had been, through graduation and the years after until, abruptly, without explanation or warning, Mark Groseman had simply picked up and moved on.

But, even in the best of their time together, Gaby had always lived in terror of the parties, when his eyes darted wildly around the room, scouting for action, and she was sure that, if he found it, he would rush off, never to return, on a whim that could last the rest of their lives. Even now, years later, her own celebrity took a backseat to his, and as the night dragged on till morning in the music mogul's townhouse, she'd saddened at the realization that things hadn't changed. Her next day's shooting should have been a higher priority than Mark's social compulsion, but it wasn't. At one point she'd considered leaving the party by herself, but the chronic terror that, if she did, he would never again show up at the apartment kept her close to his side, despite the fact that she knew even then how awful she would look for the shooting.

Now, one glance in the mirror confirmed her worst fears. Even though she'd declined the cocaine, all that alcohol and the lack of sleep had made her skin terribly dry and distinctly lined. As if Jackson weren't angry enough already. Gad, when he saw her skin . . . and the circles under her eyes and the puffiness. She went to work on the puffiness with a strong astringent, hoping it wouldn't worsen the dryness. Dressing as fast as she could, she tried to push away the awful regret she always felt when she had to leave Mark, the nagging fear that she would never see him again. That was just plain silly girl's paranoia, she told herself, listing as evidence the fact that she had either seen or talked to Mark every day for the last three weeks. True to his word, he'd called her the day after the screening, all bounce and solicitude, inquiring about the Lutèce debacle, and her heart had leapt when she heard his voice.

When he asked her to join him for dinner the first night she was free, she contemplated canceling all her existing plans, then decided to play it cool. So they'd met two nights later at a Mexican restaurant where they used to eat often when they lived together. The meal was heavy on margaritas and memories, but he'd not pushed her, just talked about what fame was like, made some hilarious jokes, told cynical stories of the Hollywood cognoscenti, looked at her both with love and with a cool, professional appreciation of her beauty. From the world's newest hot movie director, the flattery acted like brandy on her tanked-up feelings, and by the time they began the ten-block walk to her apartment, she was in a whirl of happiness. In the restaurant, gazing at him across the table, she'd longed to plunge her fingers into that dark, shiny, thick hair, had let herself be lost in the almost slanted hazel eyes behind the wide-rimmed glasses, had remembered those thick, sensual lips on hers and ached to know how the encircling beard would feel against her skin. Walking home next to him, she could almost feel the heat, the excitement, from that short and stubby body, which radiated an irresistible combination of teddy-bear huggability and fantastic sexuality. Deciding that this time she would not capitulate when he wanted to come up, she knew, despite the decision, that the choice was his. So, it was with something between dismay and confusion that she accepted his innocent good-night kiss at her doorstep, accompanied by his promise to call her . . . "soon". Her spirits sank as she realized he hadn't changed at all. Their relationship could exist, but only on his terms. She was still the one who had to wait.

She tried to be out of the house the next day to avoid the waiting, and still, when she got home from shopping for things she neither needed nor particularly wanted, there was no message on the machine. But, at six thirty, as she was dressing for an evening with Philippe, Mark called. It seemed, then, so natural to be talking to him that she wondered why she'd ever assumed he wouldn't call. And he was in top seduction form. When she told him she was rushing out, he inquired gloomily if she was seeing "the frog," and her heart thrilled. Once she admitted she was seeing Philippe, he changed the subject, urging her, cajoling her, to see him the following night. When she said she didn't think she could alter her plans, he begged her to try, besieging her will with the firepower of his enthusiasm, and told her he'd call her early the next afternoon.

And unlike the old days, he had kept his word. When the phone rang at three, she had already canceled her evening with Philippe. Ever the gentleman, he had let her off the hook so quickly that she assumed he felt some relief at being able to spend time with Dominique.

Still, just in case Philippe did call to check on her welfare, she told Mark that she was sick of getting dressed up and going out and being recognized and just wanted to laze around the apartment in old jeans and send out for Chinese, if that was all right with him. Not only did he heartily agree, he volunteered to pick up food on the way. He didn't even ask what she wanted, just arrived on time—another startling change—in a Dodgers t-shirt and jeans, bearing a huge brown bag. The bag contained, of course, all their favorite dishes from long ago, and the gesture, the remembering, so moved her that she decided on the spot to forego any attempt at dieting. As he relinquished the bag into her arms, he told her to take it upstairs, then made a beeline for the kitchen and soon appeared in the bedroom with a huge tray of forks, spoons, plates, beer cans, napkins, all of which he could find fast, since this had been his home, too. Gaby sat on the bed and watched him turn on the TV, thinking she had never, ever been so happy. Mark was back.

Ninotchka—a mutual favorite—just happened to be on at eight, and they laughed and giggled and thrilled as they consumed masses of cold noodles with sesame sauce, moo shu pork with pancakes, dumplings, spare ribs, lobster Cantonese, double-sauteed dry beef, fried rice, shrimp egg foo yung. The beer flowed like their laughter, and when they both fell back, sated, it was into each other's arms. As he kissed her, just as she'd remembered, just as she'd missed, her last civilized thought was that she'd have to get up at five and run at least four miles to work off the food. Then she had given herself up to absolute, joyous abandon.

But in the morning, in the middle of her run along the river, her happiness pushing her merrily along, she was suddenly struck by the cold, terrible fear that when she got back Mark would be gone, gone again, perhaps finally, from her life. She considered any *faux pas* she might have made. Had she come on too strong? Been too desperately attentive? Drunk too much? Revealed her hunger for affection? Did he find her, after his great success, simply boring? Neurotic? Frenzied? Superficial? The catalogue went on and on as her anxiety pounded with her every step, building to such a pitch that by the time she raced back to the apartment, she was convinced he would be gone. But he was there, sleeping like an infant, dead to the world, just like in the old days. It would be hours before he woke, hours in which, if she lay down beside him, he would not so much as reach out for her in his sleep. When Mark Groseman slept, he slept alone. His genius, his specialness, gave him the privilege of setting the rules of the game. That hadn't changed, but at least this time, the rules were more humane. If he was distracted, he was distracted in her company. If he overlooked her social needs in favor of his own, he now remembered her before his neglect reached crisis point. Mark, she had to admit, was trying in his own self-centered way to please her, to provide her with some justification for lavishing love on him.

That first morning, watching him sleep, she could feel that love, that hunger, welling up in her. In the beginning, she had taken her confidence from the fact that such brilliance would choose her for its consort, but even though she now had her own recent celebrity and the pleasing public acknowledgment of her desirability, it could never begin to ignite her as her need for Mark did. Even today, while chastizing herself for humoring him at the expense of Jackson's shooting, she knew she might do the same thing again. Even today, she couldn't quite define the cause of her adolescent and foolish misordering of priorities. The closest she could come to identifying the source of Mark's almost mystical allure was his extraordinary ability to be cared about. Only Mark demanded that she give to him so fully, and the enormity of his demands transmuted her shyness and reserve into the fever of romantic passion. What he brought out in her was her wanting, her needing, to bestow love—more, even, than she wanted to receive it. He couldn't get enough, as she couldn't give enough, and she felt blessed by his allowing her to adore him.

His thrilling frenzy pierced the heart of her reserve and vanquished it. Through him, she could translate her girlish dreams of passion into reality, and that was good—so long as he was there. When he wasn't, she always paid for her vulnerability in fear. Whenever he went out without her, she was sure he had met someone and fallen instantly in love. She feared the phone would never ring, the call would never be from him; and when it was, she practically cried with relief.

But what scared her the most, what woke her in the middle of the night, was the knowledge that *Ikon* was scored and edited and ready to go and that some time in the foreseeable future Mark would be heading back to the Coast. He hadn't said when, hadn't even mentioned it, but that was how it would be. And as their times together grew sweeter, sillier, more casual, and more like the old days, just when they were once again becoming a couple, it was all going to have to end.

Unimaginably sad, unimaginably happy, she grabbed her big leather shoulder sack and dashed out the door. It was only when she'd run to First, gotten a cab, and arrived at Jackson's that she dug into the purse for her wallet and came up, instead, with an envelope she'd never seen before. It contained a first-class airplane ticket bearing her name and a note in the famous Groseman scrawl, which proclaimed:

Come to LA, and I'll make you a star.

chapter twenty

CANNES,
May 1982

THERE'S a jewel of a Deco residential hotel on Forty-ninth and First called the Beekman Towers. It's nestled right in the turn where an estuary of First Avenue, fancifully called Mitchell Place, wends its way up to the stately, movie-set perfection of that short block known as Beekman Place. Little of the original design remains in the plastic-marble style of the small lobby or the always empty elevator, which, despite its renovation to self-service, cries for the return of the elevator man. Such an attendant would check out the smartness of your officer's uniform and the platinum pageboy and seamed gams of your date, then convey you, without being asked, to the very pinnacle of the building, the Beekman Roof. In only moments, the doors would be drawn back, and like the officer and gentleman that you are, you would hand your date out onto a scene of Gotham splendor. It would seem to be in black and white like a forties movie, but actually it would be brightly colored by the ruby lips and nails of the ladies who languidly swayed, handbags nestled between inner arm and torso, toward the powder room to refurbish makeup and compare dates; by the gold of the Scotch and the rainbow highlights of the martinis being carried to and from the smoked glass bar. The tart and naughty strains of Cole Porter would issue from a piano camouflaged behind some palmlike potted foliage. But, seductive as the scene is, your eyes would be drawn to the periphery, as the headwaiter greets you and, smiling with approval at the beauty you've come home to, escorts you out to the Beekman Roof. The month is June and the night is mild; it's 1945, and you're feeling victorious and bullish on the future. With your dream girl by your side, you know that you can take New York. It's here for the taking, right here, beyond the Roof, stretching out around you, twinkling and glowing and bustling, just on the other side of the railing next to which your tiny wrought-iron table is nestled. The gentle night breeze selects a few strands of your girl's hair and fox-trots briefly with them as the gin competes for intoxication with the music from within and the glamorous conversations at other tables. At the Beekman, who could be anything other than young and golden?

All that, of course, is a dream. It's been years since the roof officially became the Top of the Beekman, since they glassed it in, crowded in more tables, and accepted the fact that its heyday had passed. Still, it's a good place to go with a girl who likes to pretend, and in the old days, Gaby and I used to stroll over for a nightcap. It had become, for us, a sanctuary, a place of significant privacy where we never ran into anyone we knew.

So, when, after weeks of total neglect, Gaby called me and urgently asked me if I could meet her for a drink at the Beekman, I knew I wasn't in for just a casual good time. Given that, plus what I could only construe as her total rejection, I wanted to tell her sweetly, warmly, to stick it, and then hang up. Instead, I practically jumped at the chance to see her. So anxious was I that, having gone back to Brooklyn after my breakup with Suki, I decided to revoke my own ironclad rule and forego the subway for a cab. When I said half an hour, I meant it. She, of course, living all of two blocks away, wasn't there yet. The vigil began at 8:53 P.M., as I gazed out alone over the East River, nursing my martini and feeling like a sixteen-year-old who's been stood up. After fifteen minutes had passed, I was sure she wasn't going to show, and as my fury built, so did my nervousness. I was chain-smoking cigarettes I didn't even want. Sloshing back martinis I couldn't even handle. All to calm myself down so I could be Spencer Tracy. It didn't seem to be working.

After twenty-five minutes, I actually called her, but got only the answering machine. Did that mean she was on her way over or that she had changed her mind and was en route somewhere else? Choosing the latter explanation, I grumbled to myself as I ascended the stairs, crossed the main room, and headed out to the table. And there she was, standing against the railing, waiting for me, absolutely radiant in some light blue silk *shmatte* that billowed in the night breeze. And next to her, the unmistakable form of the neon gnome, Mark Groseman. That she had actually dared to bring him to one of our places did nothing to improve my mood, but I did manage a fair amount of good cheer when I greeted them and even more Irish ingenuity in inducing the waiter to squeeze in an extra chair at the table.

"Terry," Groseman said with sickening good cheer, "I hope you don't mind my horning in on you guys like this." I indicated with a wave of my hand that the thought existed only to be brushed off. "But I'm just here for the first round," he added, taking his beer directly from the waiter's hand and quaffing it. "Got a meeting at the Park Lane at ten." He set down the glass and threw me a crinkly smile replete with the old locker-room camaraderie. "But Gaby's told me so much about you—*most* of it good"—he caught Gaby's eye, and they both chuckled politely—"and I did want a chance to at least get to know you."

"Ummmm," I mumbled graciously, signaling the waiter for another drink.

It took me less than three belts of my third martini to admit to myself, painfully, that Mark Groseman was a star. Granted, he talked too much, too fast, skipped from subject to subject with such grace that, by the time you came up with the flaw in his otherwise dazzling argument, he had moved on. He gabbed and gesticulated and squirmed and hurled himself into the conversation, even resorting to slapping me five when we found ourselves in agreement over some sports point. He jumped up to make a phone call at least three times, but his presence remained at the table, reducing Gaby and me to staring at his empty chair as if he were still there talking. And why not? No one in the vicinity could follow his act. I had to face it: The man was brilliant.

When Groseman rapped, Gaby hardly spoke, mainly listened with all the intensity of her soul, occasionally throwing him a perfectly timed question set up, of course, to make him look even more like a genius. They were a real team, and that made me sad because it eliminated me from her intimate awareness. When she had been with Philippe—and I had to assume that was over privately, if not publicly—she had always retained a part of her attention exclusively for me, but to Groseman she gave her entire being.

It wasn't until after he split at ten fifteen, following a flurry of phone calls, that I realized Gaby was upset about something. So absolutely was she his that she toned down all her feelings, even anger, so as not to overshadow his performance. Talk about sacrifice.

So Gaby Blake was Mark Groseman's creature. So I was a sore loser. No, that wasn't all that was bothering me about Groseman. There was something else, something weird, for, even though he left me with a warmth that almost convinced me he was my friend, I couldn't like him back.

Maybe it was simply the awareness that he took too much from everything he encountered. His intensity, which was the source of his glamor, drained people. Like Count Dracula, he brought out the vitality in a person, but having extracted it, he never gave it back. It was as if, instead of borrowing Gaby's love for however long their relationship might last, he had bought it outright. If he was, indeed, her first love, he had made it a term of the deal that he would be her last, because he was the one who retained her power to love.

And it didn't stop with Gaby. He had secured even my sympathy, by effusively complimenting me only on pieces of mine that deserved such praise—not the most widely read, not those from the tonier rags, but the best by my own measure. He had bought my ability to be profoundly flattered. No one else would ever make me melt so intelligently as he. I loved the praise, but I didn't like it. He had somehow robbed me of my sense of privacy, and I missed it already.

Yep, Mark Groseman was a star, a simply irresistible presence, and, woe is me, I could see what Gaby saw in him. How that man could consume love—he just ate it all up and ordered some more. It didn't seem to me that being involved with a guy like that would be a picnic, so I wasn't surprised that Gaby was upset. When I inquired as to the cause, she claimed nothing was wrong, then let it slip fast. Over a sticky green margarita, she told me, when I asked what all the phone calls were about, that Groseman had been trying to make a cocaine connection. The last call had to have been successful because he had instantly proceeded to plunge off into the night. She went on to tell me, less casually, as the one margarita turned to two, that once he got to the hotel and the coke arrived and they all sat around and got high, Mark and the scriptwriters wouldn't get down to work until way after midnight. That meant that they'd be going all night, probably well into tomorrow, and that Mark wouldn't be back at the apartment until midafternoon, when he would head straight for the bedroom and sleep for fourteen hours.

"Listen, I shouldn't complain." She seemed suddenly to hear herself. "He's fabulous, isn't he?" I smiled agreement. "But, oh, these *artistes*!" she went on. "Oh, well. . . ." She let the words drift off into a silence we shared for a long moment.

"Hey, Gaby." Instinctively, drunkenly, I took her hand, leaning earnestly across the table in what I realized midreach was a Groseman gesture. "What's the matter? Why the emergency call?"

"Ummm." She gazed at me seriously, as if she were having trouble knowing how to start. "Ummm," again, then, "Another drink?"

"Margarita?"

She nodded.

"Sure? They look disgusting."

"Yes, I'm sure. I sort of like them." And she smiled wistfully, as I indicated another round to the waiter.

''Okay, shoot.'' I retracted both my hands, folded them, and sat forward, all business. Spencer Tracy.

''Well, listen. First I want to say I know I have no right to presume on you like this. I mean, after I've been so scarce, you know.''

''I sure do.'' I allowed myself that.

''But, see, I've got to make this big decision. Major decision.'' For the first time, the margaritas were showing in the flush of her face and the informality of her conversation. ''And, Terry, listen: You're the only person I can really talk to about this. Because—'' She paused and turned her head to catch a view of the East River, then turned back. ''—because you're the only person I can trust. Because you . . . you can't make any money off me.''

''Hey, thanks. Sorry everybody else was busy.''

''No.'' Now it was she who took my hand. ''That's not what I mean. What I mean is that our relationship is probably the only relationship in my life that exists just because we care about each other, not because of what we can do for each other. That's rare.''

''Okay, I'll buy that. It is rare. So?''

''So, okay. I haven't mentioned this to anyone. . . .''

''My lips are sealed.'' I emphasized my trustworthiness by a smile that outcrinkled Groseman *and* Tracy.

''All right. Here it goes.'' With perfect timing the waiter arrived with the drinks, allowing her one sip before breaking the news. ''Mark wants me to do a movie with him.''

''What?'' I took back my hand and used it to hoist my martini. ''What do you mean?''

''He wants to make a movie with me . . . ummm . . . in it.'' She smiled feebly.

''But you're not an actress. You're a model. And you're under exclusive contract.''

"Well, I don't think I'm an actress, either. But Mark does. He says even if he hadn't known me, he would have been interested in me from the commercials. He says he wants to do a small picture after *Ikon*, a romantic comedy, a little picture like *Roman Holiday*. He's got the script, at least a first draft—that's what they're working on tonight—and he says if *Ikon* is as big as they think it's going to be, he'll have no trouble raising money."

"Okay, maybe," I conceded, "but what about the exclusive contract?"

"Mark says that, of course, we have to discuss it with Ivan, but that he feels he can persuade him that I can still do the commercials, since they're shot in groups. He wants Philippe to do my costumes, anyway, and he'll have me wear jeans in one scene and we'll give them a credit in the end titles. It'll be good for the corporation."

"All right. So far so good. What about Philippe?"

"Oh, well . . ." A trace of regret passed over her face. "I . . . well . . . there are problems. Personally, I mean. I guess you sensed that. And he knows about Mark, even though we never talk about it. He would never try to stop me from doing what I wanted."

"Jackson?"

"I can't see what difference it could make to him. Lauren Hutton—hell, even Audrey Hepburn—a lot of actresses do fashion photography. I'd certainly be available. In fact, Mark thinks the fashion stuff'll be good for the movie, and he'd want Jackson to do the publicity shots, in any case."

"Wow," was the sum total of my judgment.

"Wow? Say more than wow." She was looking at me with concern.

"Wow, golly," I suggested archly, then got serious,

or as serious as you can get when you're drunk as a skunk on gin. "What do you want, Gaby, advice?"

She nodded, eyes wide in anticipation.

"Jesus Christ, Gaby." My own anger surprised me. "Why the hell are you asking me? I don't know what to tell you. I haven't even seen you for a month."

"I know, I know." She cast her eyes down toward her drink. "But——"

"But what? Be straight with yourself, kid. It doesn't matter what I tell you. It doesn't even matter if you want to leave New York or modeling or anything. You're going to do it, and you know it. So why are you asking me?"

"I don't know why." She was playing with a matchbook, not meeting my glance. "I guess . . . I guess I don't really want my life to be any different than it is now. . . . I'm afraid—" She paused and looked up. "I'm afraid I won't be the same, but . . ."

I was afire with fury. "Gaby. You seem to be asking for my sympathy, if not my outright pity. And, frankly, I find that hard to grant you. It's just real difficult to see you as one of the needy. Especially now." I was reaching in my pocket for my wallet, then changed my mind, as I looked around for the waiter and realized that the place was totally empty except for one obviously adulterous, drunken couple making out at the south end of the balcony.

Gaby was startled by my vehemence, and somehow that only increased my rage. I wasn't about to hold anything back. "And let me make this clear. You made a slight miscalculation in your definition of friendship. The only people you can count on to be there for you after you've treated them like shit *are* the people who make money off you. The others, the ones who love you, take just so much, and then they bail out."

I found myself rising to my feet, grabbing her shoulders as I rose until we both stood, the tiny table between us. "So I guess I'm bailing out."

"Terry, please. . . ." She sounded really upset.

Before I walked away, the gin turned me back toward her. I walked the half-step around the table, grabbed her and kissed her, hard, harshly, so fast she didn't have time to resist. For one instant I drew her to me, let my hands roam over the back I'd never explored, let my tongue trace the curves of the mouth I've never made love to, felt her relax under the persuasiveness of my passion. Then, just as suddenly, I broke away, murmured an oh-so-cool, "See you in the movies," walked to the door, turned back for one last gaze, called softly to her, standing there alone, "Your treat," and strolled suavely out of her life.

BOOK III

chapter twenty-one

CANNES,
May 1982

ALL of a sudden, it was night. The De Lorean was continuing to negotiate the curves and I was still behind the wheel, but so far away had my thoughts taken me that it had grown dark without my even taking note. I had sped through the Riviera dusk, rushing toward a town that now lay a mere ten kilometers ahead, but the driving time had compressed into an instant. I had even, at some point, turned on the lights, totally unaware of doing it. It was like waking up, the journey back from my memories, so much so that the shock of my reentry made me blink my eyes and try to shake the past out of my head. But it didn't work. As I banked for a particularly elaborate curve, my mind, slowly, gracefully, eased away from the unsettled anxieties of the immediate future and onto the other road, safe, secure, unlike the present, a road of turns already taken. . . .

Waking up in Brooklyn late in the morning following

my brutal dismissal of Gaby, I actually moaned—partially from the massive hangover, but mainly from the strain of confronting the finality of my parting from her. I regretted doing it more than anything I'd ever done, and I'd done worse. A future absolutely without Gaby was a dreary prospect, and I had to consider some compromise on the assumption that an occasional snippet of Gaby would be better than no Gaby at all. I wanted to call her, almost did many times that morning, but I always stopped myself. And what stayed my hand was the unavoidable truth of it all: that I couldn't accept just a snippet of Gaby; she took up too much emotional space in my life, making me happy when she wandered by, miserable when she didn't. For whatever quirk of fate and time, Gaby was a temptation I had to make myself resist, even if I didn't want to.

That she was in thrall to a man who wasn't good enough for her stymied and disappointed me. In basic, honest, human terms, she was light years beyond Mark Groseman, and I was infuriated even more by her underselling herself than by her rejection of me in favor of a living, breathing special effect. Whatever deep-seated insecurity kept her scurrying back to the razor's edge would always mystify me, but I couldn't stay around any longer, watching her wreck her life. So I left it all the way it was meant to be left. If I lived to be ninety, I would greet every day with the sad assurance that I was not going to see her again. I had whited her out. Like a beautiful sentence that didn't fit in a paragraph, Gaby no longer existed for me.

But I was fooling myself, once again, as fate was to fool us both. There was just no way I could untie all those karmic knots and drift free of Gaby Blake. No earthly way . . .

chapter twenty-two

PARIS,
June 1979

THE best part of being a celebrity, Gaby thought as the limousine languidly snaked toward Charles de Gaulle Airport, is that they hold the plane for you, hold the screening, the dinner, the shooting, or the showing for you. For someone who was habitually late, who lived in dread of missing things, being famous was unbelievably reassuring. And the second best thing, it occurred to her as the publicity guy's Dupont lighter flashed to the ready before she had even extracted the cigarette from her purse, is the twenty-four-hour service. That you were rarely alone was compensated for by the fact that all you had to do was be you, and that an endless staff of flunkies, lackies, panderers, and babysitters—all experts, some under salary, some not—were always on hand to make sure you always gave your best performance as yourself.

Jack Burton, the studio publicity guy on the Continent, hadn't allowed her one second of anxiety or inconvenience all morning. He had arrived at the hotel two hours before the flight, obviously coerced the maids into "helping" with Gaby's packing, briefed her on the plane schedule as she played at arranging her underwear—the maids would do it over, and perfectly, but she had to do something—made sure the tickets were in his pocket, along with her passport, that the limousine was on its way, that the hotel help was tipped and the bill covered.

She suspected that he was carrying at least two packs of her brand of cigarettes now that she smoked again, her favorite flavor of mints in case she decided to stop, uppers in case she was sluggish, a tranquilizer if she was edgy, a pain-killer in case of a twinge. Jack's intimate knowledge of her was almost terrifying; obviously, he'd memorized some awesomely complete dossier supplied by the studio, but his ability to anticipate her habits kept her always on edge. Somewhere between a duenna and a prison guard, Jack Burton covered her like a basketball guard who even made peripherally pertinent small talk.

She'd found him waiting at L'Hotel when she'd flown over from London, and he'd hovered in the background while she'd squeezed in three days of intensive *Vogue* shootings of Philippe's new collection with Jackson. If she went out to dinner with Jackson and Philippe, Jack would drift off to indulge whatever private social urges he felt, but regardless, he was always at the ready early the next morning, refreshed, refreshing, and absolutely impersonal. Mark Groseman was now priceless to the studio, and she was priceless to Mark Groseman; hence, she was a property worth protecting.

Sometimes, Jack even became a Mark proxy. Mark had been so caught up in the tempest of publicity surrounding the London triumph of *Ikon* that it fell to

Jack to explain that Mark sent his love but hadn't had a minute to call her, that he was eagerly awaiting her return to London, and that he missed her and adored her. It wasn't Gaby's idea of romance, but she accepted it as part of the wages of celebrity. It was she, not Mark, who had balked at the Paris detour. She was still afraid to leave him, although he urged her, graciously, to be her own person. So she'd gone, against her better judgment, to Paris, determined to survive without Mark for the first time in a year. When they had taken off for LA the summer before, her fear of breaking the news to Jackson and Philippe had turned out to be disappointingly groundless; in fact, they'd seemed almost relieved, and Ivan, as Mark had predicted, had been clearly overjoyed by the prospect of a movie career for a model he owned exclusively for the next several years.

Terry, of course, had totally disappeared from her life, causing in her a lingering sort of regret that had surprising staying power. During the hyper California months, as she'd smiled blandly through too many identical dinner parties, she'd wished for a little Barron sharpness to cut through the Hollywood mush, but what was over was over. There were nights in the house in the hills, when Mark was attending an all-night production meeting, when she actually picked up the phone to call Terry but never made it to the dialing stage. He had made it clear she had no place in his life, a life that, since her absence, was blossoming. Denise, once more divorced, was back in the States and in Terry's company, according to Liz Smith's column. Her return seemed to have stirred up Terry's creative juices, for he'd quickly tossed off a brilliant novel, just published to great acclaim.

Seeing him on the talk shows made Gaby homesick for New York and lonesome for Terry's loyalty; it had taken time before she could bring herself to read the novel, which turned out to be brilliant, evocative, tough, and romantic, but distressingly, among the female characters, she could find not even the smallest hint of herself. She simply no longer existed for him. As the weeks passed in a haze of hype and *Ikon* opened to huge business, as the little script of the romantic comedy kept not being put into production, Gaby forced herself to ignore the hurt of Terry's defection and the disappointment of not being able to share his success and submerged herself completely in the tidal wave of Mark's manic celebrity.

"Hey, lady. Return to earth!" Jack's perfectly accentless voice startled her out of her reverie. Looking up, she saw they had arrived at the entrance to the Air France terminal.

"Sorry for being such a lousy conversationalist," she said jauntily.

"Think nothing of it," Jack retorted. "I've never known a lady not to clam up on the way to the airport. Something to do with fear of flying, right?" And he chuckled as he added, "All you girls are the same. Am I right?"

Her look of shocked horror seemed to elude him. Where had he spent the last fifteen years? In Victorian England? The necessity to reply was quickly canceled out as he handed her out of the limousine, took care of her luggage, and escorted her through the bustle, away from the line at the ticket counter and toward the security check.

"How are we doing on time?" she asked tensely, surprised by the enormous queue that had formed on the far side of the security checkpoint.

"Fine, fine. Don't give it a thought," he assured her. "Your first-class seat is waiting for you."

"Okay," she responded, still tense, still afraid of missing things. Ten minutes later, when the line had snaked forward only slightly and a line of comparable length had formed in back of them, Gaby was even jumpier. In order not to have to stand there, killing time and growing tenser, Gaby, spotting a café stand off to the right, told Jack that she was going to run to get coffee.

"Fine," he commented pleasantly, not in the least bothered or surprised by her defection from the line. "Take your time. Look around. I'd say we've got another ten minutes before we get to the check."

"Okay, I'm just running over there. Can I get you something? Coffee? How do you take it?"

He looked surprised at her generosity. "Why, thanks. Black. I always drink frog coffee black."

Smiling wickedly she announced, "One black frog coming up," and took off, glad to be able to move at her own pace.

The airport was humming, despite the relatively early morning hour, and she took advantage of the modicum of free time to compare perfume prices in the duty-free shops—no bargains—then made her way back to the food stand, ordered the coffees, paid, and was just picking up the two paper cups when a commotion off to her left caused her to look up. A crowd was flocking around a group of people slowly making their way toward the security queue. Through the barricade of excited passersby, she could see that the group was composed of an extremely tall middle-aged man, a young blond woman, and two blond young men.

In the next second, two things happened simultaneously. At the exact moment when she realized that the first young man was Bjorn Borg and the second was Terry Barron, one of the coffee cups seemed to take on a life of its own and dive from her hand, showering scalding black liquid all over the front of her brand-new lilac silk Valmont.

Even the impact of hot, wet silk against her body wasn't enough to uproot Gaby from the spot on which she stood, transfixed. That it hadn't actually been Terry didn't even enter her mind; it was him, all right—the steely novocain sensation spreading through her chest was identification enough. That she was happy or sad or dismayed, those exquisite details would come in a second. At the moment, she was simply stunned.

"Madame," the voice of the woman who had sold her the coffee penetrated her trance. "Madame," she continued, "would you like a *serviette* for your dress?"

"What?" Gaby, shaken back into life, turned back toward the woman and, at that moment, realized she was dripping wet. "Oh, my God!" she moaned, then, "Yes, thanks so much." Placing the full cup back on the counter, then retrieving the fallen one, she gratefully accepted the towel and did a hit-or-miss job of soaking up some of the coffee.

"Such a beautiful dress, madame," the woman commiserated.

"Yes, it was," Gaby replied mournfully.

"Do not say that, madame, perhaps a dry cleaner . . ."

"Yes, perhaps. Thanks again," and handing back the coffee-stained towel, she began the long, humiliating walk back to her place in the queue. "Don't let him see me," she prayed to fate, then, realizing the crowd surrounding the Borg party was bound to cut off Terry's view of idle passersby, she felt disappointed that she wouldn't get one more look at him. Strolling gracefully, pretending her dress was perfectly intact, Gaby approached Jack to find him looking around anxiously.

"Oh, there you are!" He was accompanied by an Air

France official. ''We've been waiting for you! Listen''—he grabbed her arm, noticing, as he did, the mess that had been her dress—''what happened to you?'' Then, without waiting for an answer, he told her, ''Listen, this kind gentleman has been assigned to walk the VIPs through security.''

''Mademoiselle Blake.'' The Air France guy made a half-bow. ''If you will just step out of the line, over here, I will be right back,'' and before her startled eyes, she saw him head straight for the Borg party, extract them from the press, and begin to lead them over to where she and Jack stood.

Terry looked good. His hair was shorter, he had a tan, and he was dressed in a safari jacket, polo shirt, jeans, and loafers. He was a good two or so inches taller than Borg and had inclined his head slightly to make some joking remark to the tennis player. She knew that because both he and Borg were beginning to laugh at the precise moment when he saw Gaby, and in that instant, Terry Barron definitely stopped smiling.

chapter twenty-three

CANNES,
May 1982

IT was a dream of a Parisian day, so splendid you could imbibe it even in the terminal of Charles de Gaulle. It was that magically suspended time between the French Open and Wimbledon, and I strode through the throng at the side of a champion so young, so perfectly mannered, that it was as if I walked with a prince in a fairy tale. I was doing a piece for *Sports Illustrated* on Bjorn Borg, a young man who had twice won the French Open and was heading for England to take Wimbledon for the fourth time. At the tender age of twenty-three he was an ultra-world-class tennis star, a multimillionaire, the ideal of graceful success to the crowds who always sought him out. It was a great assignment; I'd interviewed him before, and he seemed to like me—I could make him laugh and banter, and he, famous for his silence, was talking, even joking. The piece, whether he won or lost Wimbledon, was going to be aces, for sure, and walking across the airport I felt, for the first time in my life, a feeling it took only seconds to identify as satisfaction.

My last year had been incredibly productive. I was even the author of a best-seller, and an odds-off best-seller: *Sirens' Song*, a small novel that made it big. Some TV critics had said, "Not since *Love Story* . . ." and although to my mind it was more a matter of "Not since *The Sorrows of Young Werther*," I had to admit that mass praise and an influx of capital (the paperback rights had gone for a cool three-quarters of a million) made it considerably easier to sleep through the night.

If bad things happen in threes, good things happen in twos, and my literary success had been preceded in the upswing by the return of Denise. Whatever had happened with the Frenchman must have been pretty mortifying because she came back bruised as hell. And I didn't feel much better. We were like two beaten fighters; all we wanted before we thought of winning or losing again was to heal. For more than a couple of seasons we had done just that, and the fact that each of us was responsible for the other's improvement bound us together on a whole new level—you've got to love someone who helps you to survive. At last, the past was receding; old loves had finally given way to new expectations. And then, straight in my path, looking scared and vulnerable and gorgeous and soaked in wet coffee, stood the statement that proved me wrong.

I couldn't draw back. I couldn't make a run for it. I couldn't blend into the crowd. And I certainly couldn't hide behind Bjorn. I was a successful adult, and I could easily control a thundering heart, a dry mouth, a mental refusal to give my muscles the command to advance. And, in fact, when my party finally reached her party, I was enough in control to treat her like an acquaintance. I said her name—"Gaby"—as if it were a rather pleasant concept, then drew her lightly to me and gave her a peck on the cheek. She didn't move or talk, but when I drew back to introduce her to Bjorn, his girlfriend Mariana, and his trainer, she did manage an utterly beautiful smile, but when she introduced the studio guy, she got his first name wrong, then breathlessly corrected herself. Anyway, we all made it through security in a state of absolute politesse. She congratulated me on my book; I mentioned the success of *Ikon*. She asked after my mother and sisters; I, after Groseman. We were distant as Alaska and Mexico, but we managed to stay on the same continent. Looking back on the encounter, I realize it never occurred to me to wonder how she felt about seeing me; just getting through the meeting was taking all my energy. It took every bit of willpower I had not to lunge at her throat or take her in my arms. So it was with a mixture of relief and cataclysmic disappointment that I parted from her on the plane, since, I explained, I had to work with Bjorn. Luckily our seats were so far apart we couldn't distract one another.

After we lightly kissed good-bye, I followed Bjorn to our seats, then, my heart still thumping, turned my attention back to my assignment. As we rapped, I inwardly congratulated myself on my expert handling of the scene. It was only after takeoff, when I'd allowed my eyes to dart around First Class in an unsuccessful attempt to locate Gaby, that I turned back to Bjorn and saw the mixture of compassion and commiseration glowing in his steel blue eyes. And then I had to face the terrible truth that the only person I'd managed to fool was myself.

chapter twenty-four

LONDON,
June 1979

"MARK! How could you do this to an innocent hotel suite!"

The stately rooms of the Connaught, home for more than a century to the great, the important, and the organized, appeared to have been ransacked. The sunlight streaming in from Carlos Place played lightly over half-eaten food on room service trolleys, fine wood tables laboring under the weight of abandoned cups of coffee and tea, dirty ashtrays stacked on top of one another, dozens of crumpled telephone messages, all blanketed with the lightest dusting of loose marijuana. The once-proud carpet had been humbled under layers of telephones, newspapers, magazines, scripts left randomly open in their multicolored binders, legal tablets, an occasional glass, the odd shoe or sock, and a couple of derelict tea pots.

In the midst of the melee stood a pajama-clad Mark Groseman, phone in hand, gesticulating emphatically to the person on the other end of the line. At Gaby's entrance, he paused, blew her a kiss without interrupting himself, motioned her to approach, still without stopping his diatribe to someone or other, attempted to brush layers of papers off half of a couch, watched her step daintily around the piles of debris, looked away, then, mischievously, surprised her with an abrupt hug. She play-fought him, pretending to beat his chest with her fists, as he talked on, then suddenly, he shouted, "I can't take this anymore. I'll call you later," banged down the phone and grabbed her for real, wrestling her down onto the cleared-off couch and kissing her deeply as his hands roamed all over her. Pulling back his head, he looked at her cheerfully and said, "You're a great feel, kid!"

"Ah, Groseman," she sighed, drawing away and sitting up, "you always make a broad feel like a lady!" But it was a comfort to see him and to have him touch her with the intimate rudeness of ownership.

"Hey, what happened to your dress? Some love-crazed frog hurl you into an espresso machine?"

"No," she giggled, "it's Philippe's new idea. If you buy them dirty, you save on dry cleaning bills. . . . And, speaking of cleaning, I thought this hotel was famous for its service. How could they let the room get like this?"

"Oh, that." Mark bent to nuzzle her neck. "I told 'em not to touch anything. Paid 'em a fortune not to spill the beans downstairs. Lot of important stuff on this floor. They could throw away a future Academy Award winner." He inclined his head to a particular pile of scripts.

"Has plague broken out in the bathroom yet?" she inquired jauntily, rising and heading for the door to the bedroom.

"Not that I know of, but be careful of the broken glass," he added. "And the knives in the bed."

"Oh, Mark, for Christ's sake, did your parents board up your room when you went off to college . . . or just send the contents to the National Center for Disease Control?" She had reached her luggage and was picking up a small Vuitton suitcase.

"Are you going in there?" he asked with some anxiety.

"Shouldn't I? What's in there?" She looked at him, her eyes wide.

Instead of answering, he simply shrugged his shoulders in resignation and told her dejectedly, "Oh, what the hell. Go ahead!"

With trepidation, she approached the closed door to the bedroom, vaguely aware that Mark was making another phone call, as if to dissociate himself from the nightmare on the other side of the bedroom door. "Well, here goes. But," she called as she turned the knob, "this place is going to be clean by tonig—"

She stopped dead. The large, Victorian room was awash in flowers, gigantic arrangements far surpassing those created for any conventional function such as a royal wedding or Mafia funeral. Great standing bouquets carpeted the floor, spilled off windowsills, covered dresser tops, were suspended from every available light fixture. Red, yellow, purple, white, golden, pink, green-leaved, lilac, in baskets, pots, and divine bunches, and the entire bed was strewn with roses—hundreds of them, almost obscuring the coverlet. And above the bed, attached miraculously to the wall, was a huge arrangement of every color of flower and ribbon in the world, spelling out "Gaby, I missed you."

"Mark!" she shrieked, but his only response was a terse, "I'm on the *phone*, Gaby!"

She couldn't find a place to put down the suitcase without damaging the flowers, so she made her way through the meadow to the bathroom, where, of course, there were more flowers, thousands more, and resting grandly on a small bathroom chair stood a glass keg, filled with something close to a gallon of a golden-colored liquor. Dropping the suitcase, she approached the keg, trying to figure out what it was, then, turning it around, she finally arrived at the label—Joy. Joy! Her perfume, her only perfume, and a gallon of it. A gallon of Joy! "Oh, my God!" she murmured, thrilled by this wild and delightful expression of his love. "Oh, my!" she repeated as, suddenly, she was gently seized from behind, turned around, and nestled in his arms.

"Hey, babe," was all he said as he held her, then, "Let's get you out of that *schmutsesche* rag." It was off before they hit the bed, as was everything else they were both wearing by the time they fell back upon the hundreds of roses, crushing them with abandon.

"Mark," she murmured, as their lips briefly parted. "Mark, I feel so good."

"Not as good as you're going to feel by nine o'clock tonight." And he grinned mysteriously.

"What do you mean?" She pulled back to look at him.

"Sorry, sweetkins, you're going to have to wait till dinner."

"Mark. You can't do that to me!"

"Not only can I do that to you, but I can also do this to you." He attacked her navel with a hot and eloquent tongue.

"Mark, no, stop! Come on, Mark, tell me."

And Mark, his voice muffled in her warm and willing flesh, said only, "Trust me, woman. By nine o'clock tonight, you'll be the happiest girl in the world!"

* * *

When the waiter arrived with the tea at five, Gaby had jumped out of bed and run into their bathroom, leaving the door slightly ajar to see if the inscrutable Connaught demeanor collapsed under the impact of flower-covered chaos. Naturally, he didn't so much as narrow his eyes, nor did he wait for Mark to get out of bed, just calmly walked over to him, held out the bill for signing, and asked whether the cart should be set up or simply drawn up next to the bed. Choosing the latter, Mark had signed the check, and the waiter, a study in excellent service and impassivity, wished Mark good-day and took his leave. Gaby had just opened the bathroom door, all giggles, when they both heard the crash from the adjoining room, indicating plainly that the waiter had fallen victim to a minefield of paper and dirty china. The clatter that accompanied the man's collecting himself made them both want to break up, but staring at each other across the flowers, they breathlessly managed to contain their laughter, like sixth graders, until they heard the sound of the front door quietly closing. Then Gaby ran from the bathroom, hooting, made a dive for the bed, and they had collapsed in hysterics, in each others arms.

Now, at eight-thirty, she eased the black silk dinner dress over her just-done hair, Mark grumbling in the background over having to wear a tie in the Grill, and wondered about the grand surprise he had planned.

As she drew up the zipper, fastened the necklace of tiniest pearls, almost invisible against the base of her long neck, and eased a couple of small, single pearls attached to gold hairpins into her hair, she stared at herself in the mirror and hoped. She looked great: makeup all alabaster and rose, fabulous little nothing of a boat-necked, short-sleeved, small-waisted, and flare-skirted black Valmont masterpiece, dark stockings and low-heeled, tuxedo pumps, hair floating perfectly like an auburn pre-Raphaelite crown. No bracelets, no rings, nothing that would detract from the glory of the ring she was praying he would present to her. That very night.

She could feel it. Sense it. Maybe going to Paris had been a stroke of genius. Maybe her absence had made him realize how much he needed her. Maybe being without her had made a dent on that maniacal streak of independence that made him leap away from even the hint of a suggestion of marriage. Maybe his great international success with *Ikon* had given him the security he seemed, paradoxically, to lack totally. Maybe he was ready for a household, for kids, for emotional fidelity, for the state of family comfort he'd always professed to fear as middle-aged.

His lovemaking that afternoon had been so warm, so jolly, so relaxed, really different from the torrential passion that had always excited her like a roller-coaster; today, it had been smooth sailing in mellow, blessedly familiar waters. She smiled one last radiant smile at herself, then, turning from the mirror to look for her purse, she noticed Mark at a side table tapping a small pile of cocaine out onto the shining marble surface. Separating it into tiny lines with an American Express card, he extracted a bill from his wallet, rolled it up, bent down and snorted the lines. "Want some?" he asked, as if by rote, because she never did, then threw back his head, inhaled deeply, and moaned, "Ahhhh!" Then, "God, you look gorgeous," and she did, but not as radiant as she'd looked moments before, when she gazed in the mirror and dreamed of the proposal. Mark only used cocaine when he was doing business; it made him even sharper, more persuasive, more insistent, but it certainly never made him more romantic. Just the opposite. So tonight was all business. Her first impulse was to cry, but she held back.

Boy, are you middle-class, she chastened herself as she located the purse and began shifting key articles into the tiny, black lacquer evening bag. Marriage, yukkkk; engagement rings, arggh. Jesus, you gave all that up years ago. Is success making you so soft in the head that you want what your mother did? Is fame too much for you? Mark loved her, she was sure of that. After all those years, he would have to. And there was plenty of time to have kids. As Mark would have said, what's the hurry? Tired of great hotels and superb clothes and total luxury and absolute freedom to go anywhere, anytime, and being photographed and recognized and made love to? It'll come, he would say, it'll come in time. And he would be right, and she would be, as he always accused her, just showing how terrified of success she still was.

In the background, Mark was doing a nonstop rap about the bitch of having to dress for dinner, about telling the floor concierge to have the place cleaned up by the time they came back upstairs, about what time it was in LA, about every little thing except the mystery evening.

As she checked herself in the mirror one final time she could see Mark grudgingly, irritably, struggling into a suit jacket, his tie hideously malformed as if in defiance. "Mark," she turned toward him, "let me do the tie for you!"

"Oh, shit, Gaby," he grumbled, then mellowed. "All right. If it makes *you* feel better."

So she undid his tie, thinking as she stood close to Mark and struggled against his will, that Terry Barron, of all the men she'd known, was the only one who could carefully and elegantly make a tie look as if it were tied perfectly though wrong—the way the silk emerged from the knot in a half-turn, aimed for a flip-flop, the way the knot was loosened just enough to give the impression that he couldn't stand wearing this ridiculous, respectable costume one second longer. Terry had elegance, weird elegance, but elegance all the same.

"Mark!" she reprimanded him, "Stop fighting me. It'll just take longer. Stop pulling back, I'm not going to strangle you. . . . Oh, you are such a child. . . . There." She drew back to look at her handiwork. "Not perfect"—she was thinking of Terry—"but not bad. . . ."

"Okay, one more line for the road, and then we're off," Mark strode to the table, put down a little more cocaine, snorted it, then dropped the tiny vial into his jacket pocket. "Okay, let's go."

As they carefully made their way across the living room, the image of Terry in a tie evolved into Terry at the airport. Seeing him again, even under strained and surprising circumstances, had seemed like a piece of enormous luck. There had been moments over the last year when she thought she'd never see him again, and this chance meeting seemed a miracle, a harbinger of certain good fortune. Even if she never saw him again. . . .

In the hall the floor concierge lay in wait. Mark beat her to the punch by demanding that the suite be put in order immediately, which caused her first confusion, since he had paid not to have it touched, then something akin to joy. "Of course, sir." She drew herself up to her full height. "It'll be taken care of immediately.'' Gratified to have order restored, she disappeared down the hall, no doubt to summon the cleaning team who had probably been poised for days to attack.

''Let's take the stairs,'' Mark grabbed Gaby's hand and together they walked through the glass doors to the great, central staircase of the Connaught. Dark burnished wood paneling shone in the glow of chandeliers, and looking down the elegant symmetry of squares winding beneath her, Gaby felt as if she had slipped into a time warp. It could have been 1879; to gaze down on dark wood, carpeted stairs, and glowing lamps was to feel time slip away.

''Come on, gotta hurry.'' Mark's urgent, excited voice brought her back to 1979. He grabbed her hand and they raced together, silently on thick carpet, down the six floors to the lobby. On the far side of the glass enclosures at several floors, guests and servants looked aghast, never having considered the possibility of running down those august stairs.

''Hey,'' Gaby cried, ''this is fun.''

''But we gotta slow down now,'' Mark cautioned her, doing just that. ''We're getting close to the lobby.'' And in seconds, they stood next to the front desk. ''This way.'' Mark placed one hand on her back and turned her around, back toward the elevators, then to the right. ''We're going in there.'' He pointed to a doorway directly ahead of them. ''The Grill's supposed to be the best dining room in London.''

''So I've heard,'' she said, then, ''Will I get the surprise right away?''

''You'll just have to wait and see. Come on,'' and again he took her hand and escorted her into dark-paneled, consummate British splendor, and gave his name to the maître d'.

"Ah, yes, Mr. Groseman, your party has already arrived," and with a smile, he escorted them through the busy dining room to a table near a window, where the surprise Mark had promised instantly manifested itself as overwhelming, mind-blowing shock.

chapter twenty-five

Cannes, *May 1982*

WITHOUT encountering Gaby at the baggage check or in the customs line at Heathrow, I'd arranged to meet with Bjorn the next morning in Hampstead where he practiced, then grabbed a huge London cab and raced off to the modest but exquisite little Regency townhouse in Belgravia where Denise awaited me. The house was hers—a good-bye present, it seemed, from some ex-husband or a souvenir from some past *grand amour*. Madame answered the door herself, dressed in a simple yet lascivious negligee, and I quickly took the hint. The afternoon passed rapidly, and only every once in a while, midpassion, did my thoughts slip guiltily back to Gaby. At half-time, Denise disappeared, then returned to the flowery, China-trade bedroom bearing a silver tray of caviar and champagne. As we picnicked in the great, canopied bed, I playfully grabbed her ass, nuzzling her neck as I murmured, "This is some lunch!"

"If you think lunch is something, just you wait until

dinner, my boy.'' She chuckled in that husky, little-girl, star's voice.

''Hey, not so fast, you witch. By tonight, I might not have the stamina.''

''No, silly,'' she said, grinning, ''I don't mean that. We're dining out.''

''Okay. So?''

''So. You'll just have to wait and see. It's what's termed a surprise.'' As I started to inquire as to the nature of said surprise, she cut me off with a firm, ''And no asking questions. You'll just have to wait. Let's see if we can make the time pass faster,'' and, guiding her hand down the length of me, she announced her strategy in no uncertain terms.

By eight thirty that night, we were stepping into a limousine, dressed to the nines. Denise, in some $3,000 sea green thing, I in my multiseasonal wedding-funeral-and-talk-show costume—blue pinstripe suit, white shirt, $2-million Sulka tie. ''Terry''—she stayed my hand as I reached into my inside pocket for a cigarette—''you're smoking too much.''

''Surprises always make me nervous.'' I grinned, playfully attacking her knee with a warm squeeze.

Although she wouldn't tell me our destination, I could see the limo was heading past the Palace and along Park Lane. ''Mayfair, hmmm?''

Making a short circle off Park Lane, the limo approached Carlos Place, where sat the solid, Victorian structure that is the Connaught. I'd been to the Connaught, but not often; for one thing, its rigid dress code turned me off, and its high level of formality made me class shy. When I'd been at Oxford, I'd taken various holiday meals there, hosted by the moneyed parents of chums, but I always felt the staff were looking down their noses at me. Even now, as I handed Denise out of the limo and took her arm to lead her up the front steps of the hotel, the knowledge that I was with a world-famous figure, that I was no small success in my own right, contributed nothing toward quelling my anxiety. I still felt like a Boston Irish kid who wasn't wanted within those hallowed, snobbish English halls. And then there was the business of the surprise. Denise was one of the most generous women I'd ever known, but every once in a while, her generosity bordered on the sadistic. There had been times when, in a self-involved attempt to please me wildly, she'd thrown me radically off-guard—with presents too overwhelming to be reciprocated, with company so exalted and so indifferent that I felt like a gigolo.

As we entered the stiff and stunning Victorian lobby, I had an instinctual flash that this surprise might be one in the torture series, then pushed back the fear as we entered the Grill. Denise dashed to the maître d', murmured to him under her breath, and by the time I caught up to her, I'd lost my chance to catch the name under which the reservation had been made. The maître d' was already enveloped in the special pleasure—even in this bastion of the rich and famous—of escorting a movie star to her table.

The surprise guests—or hosts—hadn't yet shown, so we sat for ten minutes or so, me over a martini, she a sherry, attempting and failing at making small talk, so galvanized were we both by expectation. I had just begun silently praying for a no-show when I saw Denise's face light up to star level and wave. So my eyes followed in the direction of the wave, and stopped as my worst fears of danger were solidly confirmed—by the advancing forms of the teeny *terror* Groseman and the woman I guessed I would always love.

chapter twenty-six

LONDON,
June 1979

TERRY'S amazement was as obvious as her own, if only by contrast to the knowing look that Mark was exchanging with Denise. Whatever was going on had been planned, or at least discussed, between them, and they both beamed with the one-up confidence of people who have all the answers.

"No introductions necessary, right? We all know each other." Mark motioned Gaby to a seat between him and Terry, shook hands with him, then sat down, leaving Terry to jump up quickly to seat her. The brief look he and Gaby traded suggested first veiled accusation, then confusion, then, finally, mutual mystification.

"Gaby"—Denise was addressing her with deliberate gaiety—"we haven't actually met for so long . . . not since . . . since. . . . But I've heard so much about you"—she cast Mark a heavily significant glance—"I really do feel I know you." Yeah, thought Gaby, the last time we met at the Pendleton's you didn't *want* to know me, you hypocritical bitch! "And, Terry darling"—Denise patted his hand as if it were a lap dog's head—"you and Gaby haven't met in ever so long, either."

"No, we haven't." Terry responded fast, obviously having decided, as had Gaby, that the airport meeting should pass unmentioned. They hadn't even spoken to each other, certainly weren't up to telling shared travel anecdotes, especially ones that could become either an amusing anecdote or an embarrassing memory, depending on future developments.

"What're you drinking, Barron?" Mark demanded jovially, shifting into old boy last-name gear.

"Martini," Terry told him.

"And, Denise, white wine?" She nodded, and Mark signaled the waiter for another round, a kir for Gaby, and a martini for himself. Mark rarely drank, and certainly not gin; whatever this dinner was about, it was super important. Suddenly, Gaby realized that Mark was extremely nervous and that Denise's nonstop chattering meant that she, too, was on edge. In contrast, she and Terry just sat there, and when Denise paused in her chatter and Mark ceased quizzing Terry on his picks for the '79 Series, Wimbledon, the Super Bowl, and the Stanley Cup, silence fell over the table like a lead cloud.

The jolly bustle of a busy, elegant restaurant at the peak dinner hour seemed not to extend to their table, as if the lead cloud had sealed all of them off from the surrounding conviviality. Gaby, acutely aware of the idiocy of formal manners in extreme situations, was tempted to demand to know what was going on, but was stayed by the arrival of their drinks.

"Wait, not yet!" Mark stopped them before they could raise their glasses to their lips. Turning to Gaby and Terry, he grinned, "I suppose you're wondering why we brought you here tonight?'' After smiling at Denise in amiable complicity, he announced, ''Well, I'm about to explain. And, let me tell you, it calls for a toast!'' He raised his glass first, then waited for the others to join him. ''Okay, I'd like to propose a toast to the 1981 Academy Award winner for best picture, best director, best adaptation, best actress''—he bowed his head slightly toward Denise—''and,'' he said, smiling at Gaby, ''best supporting actress.'' Gaby and Terry looked at each other, baffled, as Mark and Denise laughed heartily.

''Yes, indeed,'' Denise chimed in, and together they chanted, ''Here's to *Sirens' Song*.''

''*Sirens' Song*? My novel, *Sirens' Song*? What do you mean? What's going on?'' Terry looked at Denise, who looked to Mark.

''Well, kids,'' Mark sat back, all expansiveness, on the large armed chair. ''To make it perfectly clear: Once upon a time, maybe six months ago, a very beautiful and smart lady''—he took Gaby's hand—''read a very wonderful story, which she showed to her beau''—he smiled modestly—''who was looking for just such a wonderful story to make into a wonderful movie. In time, the beau read the very wonderful story and decided it would, in fact, make a very wonderful movie. All right, so far?'' He directed his penetrating gaze toward Terry, who nodded noncommittally. ''So, as he dreamed of the very wonderful movie, he saw that there were two terrific female parts. In one, he saw only the very beautiful lady. He could see her in the story when he read it—it was as if it had been written about her, the part of Karen had to be hers.'' He was building up steam, talking so rapidly that he didn't see the dismay in Terry's eyes or the astonishment in Gaby's, since she hadn't recognized any part of herself in the Karen character. "And for the part of Suzanne—the ageless temptress, the glamorous but soft-hearted seductress—I just *knew* . . . I had to have Denise." He smiled across the table and took a hefty hit of his martini. "Wanna take up the story here, luv?"

"You bet, maestro," Denise bantered back. "So Mark called me in New York a few weeks ago and broached the subject of my doing *Sirens' Song*. At first, well, I was hesitant. I haven't done a picture in a couple of years, but, of course, I *adore* the property." She placed her hand on Terry's arm. "And it is an Oscar shot. And, of course, I was extremely interested in working with the cream of the *new* Hollywood, a genius like Mark Groseman."

"Ah, Denise——" Mark protested coyly, as she ran over his line.

"So, when we discovered we were both going to be in London at the same time, Mark and I agreed to take a meeting or two. And, well, we really hit it off!"

Abruptly, Mark changed the subject. "What say we think about ordering a little something to start, okay? Venison pâté with Cumberland sauce sings to me. All right for four?" And, without consulting them, he called over the captain and ordered the first course. The maître d' inquired if they would like to consider ordering the rest of the dinner and handed them menus, which neither Terry nor Gaby even bothered to open. As it turned out, it wasn't necessary, for Mark ordered for all of them. Even at the time, Gaby had the distinct feeling that the last thing she would remember from this evening was what she ate.

"And a bottle of Roederer Cristal," Mark said to the captain, who acknowledged the order and drifted away.

"From here on, we drink only champagne, agreed?"

He beamed at them. ''Hey, guys, would you excuse me for a second?'' He bounded up and out, and Gaby knew he was headed for the men's room and the privacy of a couple more hits of the coke that was causing him to seethe and bubble.

''Denise.'' Terry managed to speak as Mark's dynamic figure receded. ''What is this? A joke?''

''Oh, darling, far from it.'' She made sure to include Gaby in her warm regard. ''We wanted to keep it from both of you until Mark had talked to your agent and, of course, gotten the studio go-ahead. That's what he's been doing for the last week. Oh, nothing's been signed, but Sandy's very bullish on the idea. In fact, he wants you to call him first thing tomorrow to discuss it. Mark even wants you to do the screenplay, dear, to make sure he doesn't violate the spirit of the book. And Gaby''—she couldn't have been more like a loving older sister Gaby thought—''Mark's right. The part is just written for you. It'll make a wonderful, wonderful debut piece. And Mark's praised you so highly, and, of course, Terry's always thought the world of you. . . . Terry . . . what do you think?''

''In football, they call this a blitz,'' Terry muttered, lighting a cigarette and brooding.

''But why aren't you jumping up and down, darling—both of you? Mark and I thought this would be the most joyous surprise for——''

''Jesus, Denise, you could have prepared me. I feel like five three-hundred-pound guys have run me down and thrown themselves on top of me in order to tell me I just won the Irish sweepstakes. It's a great way to get my attention if I survive long enough to collect.''

''Terry, I have no idea what you're trying to say. And you, Gaby, so silent. . . .''

''I'm just . . . I mean, this is so unexpected,'' was

all she managed to choke out before Mark returned, consummately effervescent.

"So? Are they happy?" He met Denise's eyes just as the food began to arrive. Gaby played with the Cumberland sauce, Denise consumed the luscious pâté in polite, minuscule bites. Terry, totally blown away, ate steadily as if under posthypnotic suggestion, and Mark didn't even touch the plate, but attacked the champagne, when it came, with gusto.

"By the way, Terry, when you talk to your agent—Sandy? . . . yah—I think you'll be extremely pleased with the deal we're offering. I don't want to talk money tonight, but believe me, you won't ever have to take a subway again!"

The remark provoked in Terry feelings that called for combat, but he let it pass. When Mark motioned to a waiter to remove the plates, three of them practically untouched, the man looked personally crushed, as if he had failed them. Gaby attempted a smile to soothe the insult of the uneaten food, but failed to brighten his gloom.

Somehow, they got through dinner, which was fabulous but almost extraneous. Mark, in highest gear, convinced Terry that he saw just how to bring *Sirens' Song* alive for millions of people. "But it's a tiny little story," Terry protested, "about three people."

"I see it as being *the* major work of the sixties and seventies," Mark assured him. "It's really about how this guy goes through Woodstock, Vietnam, the college riots, drug blow-outs, the whole big social scene, totally separately from his private life, which tells a parallel story, if you see what I mean," and Terry had nodded, yes, although he didn't see at all. "So what I said to the studio—and they loved it—is, let's do a sort of sixties *Dr. Zhivago*, you know, real big and romantic. We're talking—to start—maybe, ummmm, fifteen, twenty million."

"Twenty million," Terry had gasped. "That's big money."

"Right on, we all see this as big, like *Dr. Zhivago*, for now, right? Everybody's just freaking out over the concept."

"But it's still a little love story." Gaby had paused over her partridge, which she was too rattled to dissect in any case.

"Wrong!" Mark had insisted. "It's the story of an entire generation!"

"I don't know," Terry mused, eating his beef as automatically as he had consumed the hors d'oeuvre. "Don't you think you'll lose the human drama if you blow it up too big?"

"Absolutely not!" Mark had insisted, "Remember, kid, I'm the director, and you gotta trust me. You writers have to learn to let go of your material sooner or later."

And so it had gone, back and forth, with oodles of hemming and hawing and heavy, heavy persuasion. By the time they got to the Château d'Yquem, the puddings, and the fabulous candied fresh fruits, everyone was drunk and/or exhausted, everyone except Mark. Another trip to the men's room had sent him speeding through the galaxy. Gaby just sat, her head spinning, knowing, half sadly, that somehow Mark's irrepressibly strong will had prevailed over all of them, that now they were in his pocket, and God help them. She had stopped actually listening to him half an hour before; long ago, she had taught herself to tune out the speed raps when they got unbearable. She just gazed down into the sparkling gold of her wine and occasionally sneaked a glance at Terry. It was only when she saw an expression of something close to horror on his face that she looked up at Mark and demanded, ''What did you say?''

He grabbed her hand. ''Yes, darling, you heard right. The best surprise of all. I'm giving the production of *Sirens' Song* to the most wonderful, irreplaceable girl I've ever known . . . as a very special kind of present. A wedding present,'' and, in front of the entire Connaught Grill, he took both her hands and said, ''unless she turns me down. . . .''

chapter twenty-seven

CANNES,
May 1982

On the evening of February 16, 1980, principal photography commenced on the *Dr. Zhivago* version of *Sirens' Song*. It was eleven o'clock—the coldest night of the winter so far—and even the masses of klieg lights, which turned the burned-out, nighttime Second Avenue and Eighth Street of 1980 into the carnival East Village of 1968, didn't do much to raise the temperature. I had tried to stay away, but I couldn't, and surprisingly enough, Mark had greeted me fairly heartily. He was shooting a scene in which Gaby, the heroine, and Chuck Garson, a newcomer who'd emerged hot from the soaps to play my protagonist, meet by accident coming out of a Janis Joplin concert at the Fillmore East. It was a great scene, with just a touch of *The Way We Were*, but it wasn't from the book, and it certainly wasn't from my screenplay. Just one of those increasingly frequent little flashes of Groseman genius that had reconstructed the physiognomy of my story so that I probably wouldn't have recognized it. But what did I know? Groseman was the movie director, as well as the producer, and the most dazzling of all the baby directors who were making epics seven years out of film school. The studio sure seemed to think they had a super-prize. They gave him everything he wanted, including a British cinematographer who was shuttling between two assignments, one here and one in England which meant that a lot of the big stuff had to be shot at his convenience. For the interiors, the intimate scenes, Mark had decided to use a second cinematographer, an American. And as long as he was using two different guys, his brilliant idea was to contrast visually the hero's intimate life with his epic, big-event public existence. Two different styles. Sounded *meshugge* to me, but, here again, what did I know? Anyway, when Groseman demanded not one but two of the industry's most expensive professionals, he had only to call the Coast to get his way. As I'd long suspected, Mark Groseman always got his way. It was never a true contest of wills because Mark always wanted whatever was at stake more than the other person didn't want to give it to him. Take my screenplay, for instance. It had taken me three months to do a first draft, which Gaby, for one, thought was excellent. Mark thought so, too, but that didn't keep him from totally rewriting it. After a while, I stopped bothering to argue point by point and settled for an occasional pang of extraordinary gratitude when he actually retained one of my ideas.

The dread I'd felt when the project was first broached at the Connaught Grill hadn't eased, but I'd gotten used to it—a chronic ache. And, at least, it brought Gaby and me back into a place where we could relate to each other. Since we'd been railroaded simultaneously, we had perfect, mirror compassion for each other. And it was through my realizing that I didn't want to be a screenwriter, but, rather, that others wanted it for me, that I came to understand Gaby's similar fears. She had a career, just as I did, which she'd largely been responsible for. Now, all of a sudden, she was risking being catapulted to great stardom or great humiliation, in a role she never would have chosen for herself. She was doing it all for Mark, according to Mark's design, and although she tended not to express any qualms at all, I could sense she felt them.

In the months of story conferences, production meetings, and casting sessions ad infinitum, everyone had managed to behave rather well, given our myriad shared memories. Word of Gaby's impending marriage to Mark had made all the columns, but it never quite came off. I wondered why, but I never found out. Gaby and I simply didn't discuss it, although I'd heard Rona Barrett say on TV that there had been talk of a last-minute wedding in Paris, where they'd gone to scout locations for the Paris riot scenes. The Paris wedding was a romantic idea, but it never materialized, ostensibly due to their not being French citizens or some other arcane international prohibition.

After a while, the press ceased to care whether they were actually married or not, but continued to cover the courtship with *brio*, thereby guaranteeing that *Sirens' Song*, even in pre-production, was getting an inordinate amount of media attention. Gaby was a very famous face, and Mark was Hollywood's foremost baby mogul. Undeniably, they made good copy; I couldn't have written it better myself, and there were moments when I wondered if Mark, master exploiter that he was, hadn't coldly and cynically sized up the many benefits of hooking up with Gaby before the fact. But, then again, I was generally sore with the way things were going, and I had a right to be. Second only to Gaby and Mark, Denise was also right back up in the gossip columnists' bold type. She was, after all, deigning to return to the movies after a few years of relative retirement. Even Chuck Garson, the stud from the soaps, was being touted as the new Brando.

Me, on the other hand, the press could do without. When *The New York Times* did a piece on the filming, the writer spent days with Gaby and Mark. Me, she covered in a ten-minute phone interview, of which one whole sentence actually appeared in the article. And she wasn't the only one who made me feel extraneous. At first, when I attended a preproduction meeting, I'd sensed that Mark didn't need me. After a while, I'd sensed that he didn't want me. So I followed his lead and largely steered clear of the whole *megillah*, went back to journalism with a vengeance, and even began steady work on a second novel. Still, in the middle of an intense hockey game or a rip-roaring chapter, I'd find my mind wandering. Confusion over my fallen state was killing my concentration. I was feeling guilt for vile behavior when I hadn't even figured out how I'd erred. Only later did I understand I was just being treated like a screenwriter.

There must be a special circle of hell reserved for screenwriters in which you spend eternity yelling, "But it was my idea!" into a void bearing an uncanny resemblance to an empty movie theater, where the echo of your futile, anguished cries boomerangs back at you in Dolby sound. But the unique torture in this form of damnation is that you're never informed as to how you actually sinned. Of course, I'd always heard that writers can be trouble on a movie set, but I hadn't been. I hadn't forced my way into meetings, thrown tantrums over reconstructed story edits, or insisted on any kind of final approval. Still, everyone, from Mark down to the crew, handled me like super-trouble. Even Denise appeared to view me as an interloper from time to time. Only Gaby, probably because she was so new at the movie game that she hadn't yet bowed to the pecking order, didn't treat me as if I were a leprous child molester.

She treated me, in fact, as if I were the person I used to be before I became successful, well-off, and dispensable. She still laughed at my wisecracks, still put me down good-humoredly for being a smart ass. Yes, I did have that to make me feel better about myself: Gaby and I were friends again. Well, not exactly friends. More accurately, acquaintances who shared an intimate past, scores of painful, embarrassing, occasionally wonderful memories, all of which were assumed, but never acknowledged. I never pried into the vagaries of her relationship with Mark; she never quizzed me about Denise. Luckily, despite the shield of amiable formality that protected us from full disclosure, we could still joke and chatter a blue streak—about movies we'd seen, books we wanted to read, celebrities we'd met. As long as the subject under discussion was neutral, we were as fun a couple as we'd ever been. And it was a genuine relief to have fun with somebody again, even if it was such a guarded kind of fun. Our occasional lunches graduated over the months to infrequent dinners when Mark or Denise were otherwise engaged. I always anticipated those dinners with a mixture of exhilaration and anxiety and came to regard each session as something between an ordeal and an event, conducted with the forced casualness of a business meal until the coffee comes and the real discussion begins. Looking back, I see our times together actually as meetings—in the business sense. We just never got to the coffee; maybe we never would.

When we met for a Christmas lunch at Le Relais, she seemed in good shape, busy, excited about starting the movie. She'd just come back from Paris after a double-headed shooting both of some new jeans ads and of Philippe's latest collection of ball gowns. Everybody was happy with the job, and she'd even brought back her favorite dress, along with Philippe. He was escorting her to a chi-chi opening at the Metropolitan Museum, which was going to be the object of a big fashion and media blitz. Her wearing the dress, Gaby explained, would be great publicity for the whole Valmont line, and that was worth infinitely more to the house than the mere $10,000 price tag.

"You mean you aren't paying for the gown?" I noted my shock in the great mirror above the brown velvet banquette on which Gaby sat across from me.

"No, I never do."

"You're joking. Those rags are freebies?"

"It's worth it to them," she explained, as if to a child. "I represent the house. It's like a sports endorsement. It's like your friend Bjorn Borg not paying for his tennis rackets."

"Hmmm. Yeah, I see your point," I mused.

She then went on to explain that Philippe was really in town for some fairly confidential meetings with Gaby and her lawyer-manager-cousin Gerald. Valmont was launching a new perfume, *Cygne*, and they wanted Gaby for exclusive use in the advertising. At this point, they were negotiating the endorsement fee and perks like stock options in the perfume company, an American-based corporation that manufactured in Europe and of which Philippe had just acquired 47 percent of the stock. They were asking Gaby for a three-year commitment, but Gerald was insisting on two with a 25 percent increase on a base endorsement fee of $500,000 annually. His thinking was that, since *Sirens' Song* should be in successful release within two years, they could renegotiate at substantially better terms, without tying her to a third year at what would then be a bargain price.

"So that means, in a couple of years, you're going to be rolling in dough. But you're rolling in dough now, aren't you?"

She looked at me with total candor. "I guess so."

"If this isn't too personal"—I grinned sheepishly—"what are you worth?"

"I honestly don't know." She grinned back. "Gerald doesn't like to talk money with me. He'd be shocked if he ever found out I occasionally turn the pages of *The Wall Street Journal* with my teeny, ladylike fingers. Philippe explained what was happening with the deal; he actually gives me credit for having a fully developed mind that can add and subtract, and even do fractions."

"Hey." I actually took her hand in mine. "Wanna be my agent? My bookie? How about being my patron? Every artist needs a rich patron. And there's nobody I'd rather be patronized by than you, you killer tycoon. Whatever happened to the poor little rich girl I used to know?"

"Gone with the wind." She laughed merrily, dismissing the very idea, but I saw in her, for the first time, a new sort of toughness, a new self-confidence. And that's why, on that chill night in the East Village, I was shocked to see Gaby, after twenty-five takes of the same scene, walk calmly over to me, take me aside, and burst into tears.

chapter twenty-eight

NEW YORK,
February 1980

SHE was furious at herself for throwing a tantrum, but she was sobbing too hard to explain that to Terry. "Take me home, huh?" She fought for restraint, fought to quell the shaking, which came from anger and exhaustion as much as from the cold. Terry, comfort that he was, didn't ask any questions, just took off his down jacket and draped it around her muslin-clad shoulders. "Cab?" he asked, directing her toward the street.

"No, car's over there," and pulling herself together, she gestured toward a black limousine parked down the street, beyond the trucks and the kleig lights.

"Ready to go, Ms. Blake?" The driver, who was waiting by the curb, pitched his cigarette into the street and opened the door for her.

She attempted a smile, said, "Sure thing, Michael," and allowed Terry to hand her into the back seat as the driver started up the engine. Once inside, she shrugged off Terry's jacket and returned it to him as he climbed in beside her, then arranged the black mink coat, which had lain ready on the seat, over her shoulders.

As the limousine headed east and onto the FDR Drive, Terry chuckled, "You make one weird hippie." He indicated the long, straight hair, Indian shirt, jeans, and sandals, all blanketed by the luxurious mink.

"Yeah. What becomes a flower child most?" she joked bitterly, reaching under the fur collar to free her hair, which fanned out over the collar and around her face. "Styles change, even if people don't," she muttered.

"Hey"—he lit a cigarette and inhaled slowly, studying her—"who pissed you off?"

"Who pissed me off? Who didn't! Oh, Christ, who knows!" Reaching into her purse, she extracted a mirror and checked to see the extent of the damage done by her outburst. "How the hell do I do it? My mascara isn't even running! I even weep neat!" She slammed the mirror shut and hurled it back into the open sack. "What time is it?" She looked up at him abruptly, dry-eyed now and surprisingly fierce.

"Three. Hungry?"

"How'd you know?" The ferocity mellowed to surprise.

"Just know."

"But that is truly strange," she said, shaking her head in astonishment, and as she bent toward him, the mink slipped back from her shoulders, revealing her as their shared vision of the girl in his book—so young, so spoiled, so utterly irresistible. "Because"—she was giggling, moving closer to him—"the same second you were asking me if I was hungry, I was thinking of——"

"Ice cream," he suggested casually.

"Terry Barron! How did you know?"

He shrugged. "Just knew. No, to be honest I recall several occasions when we were young and foolish, and I learned the only way to calm you down when you were sore was to take you to an ice cream place and let you pig out."

"Oh, no!" Her hands shot to her mouth in embarrassed recollection. "That afternoon when—" She looked at him, catching his eyes and breaking into gales of laughter when she knew they were sharing the same memory. "The Palm Court!"

"Right," he took her hand, teasing her with the details. "You were so wrought up about some problem with Philippe."

"Hmmmm," she mused, waiting the proper amount of time before saying slowly, "Sure. Philippe was . . . let's see . . . flying off a day early or something. . . ." He nodded in agreement, but as she pulled the coat back around her shoulders, she remembered what had really infuriated her that late December afternoon. It hadn't been Philippe at all, although she'd blamed him to mask her anger at the man who even at that moment had been soothing her with fifty dollars worth of ice cream. Her dear friend Terry! Who had just canceled their date for New Year's Eve. Denise had been in Europe, and Philippe had to fly back to Paris on December twenty-ninth, and when she and Terry had discovered they were both on the loose, they'd been delighted at the opportunity to spend a down-home evening—no fancy parties, nightclubs, or discos. Just a Chinese dinner, maybe a movie, a late drink to see the new year in, then home before two. Maybe she'd even stay over in Brooklyn, just like the old days. She knew she'd been looking forward to it, but not how much until, on December twenty-eighth, when she'd gone with him to return a Christmas present at Saks, she'd asked him where he wanted to have dinner on New Year's Eve. Without blinking an eye, he'd casually told her that he was going to be out of town on December thirty-first. When she calmly asked him why, he told her he was being flown out to LA to do a cover story for *Sports Illustrated* on Vince Ferragamo. She wanted to demand angrily if he had intended to tell her at all or just not show up on New Year's Eve, but she hadn't. Instead, she had shrugged it off and steered them from Saks to the Palm Court, where she'd spent two hours bitching about Philippe and downing one and a half banana splits.

It amazed her now that he even remembered that tempestuous afternoon, and for a second, she wondered if he'd known at the time that it was he she was really mad at. No, of course not. Men weren't that sensitive.

"What?" She came out of her reverie with a start, aware that he'd asked her something. "I'm sorry." She smiled, turning to face him. "Thinking of past desserts. . . ."

"Making a movie about the sixties will do it to you every time," he quipped, and she laughed back, although she had no idea what he meant. "But," he continued, grabbing her hand, "we're going to forget all our woes and drown ourselves in a tidal wave of ice cream!"

"Where?" she inquired innocently.

"While you were dreaming, I was giving directions. We've arrived." The limousine had, although she hadn't noticed, been speeding west across the city, then up the outerspatial cathedrals of Sixth Avenue, and was pulling to a stop before a large, pseudo-Victorian storefront.

"Twenty-four-hour banana splits. And perfect service." Terry patted Gaby on the knee, then climbed out of the car, calling, "Wait right here!"

Ten minutes later, the doors of the restaurant opened to reveal brown-gowned waitresses with white aprons and caps, the very essence of *Upstairs, Downstairs*, each bearing a tray on which were displayed elaborate concoctions snuggling in crystal goblets, sheltered by silver bowls of ice, accompanied by spoons, straws, and napkins. Terry, burdened down with an armful of crested gold paper boxes, directed the women to the driver, who transferred the treasures to the bar in the back seat. Seemingly within seconds, the car had been transformed into a museum of multi-colored ice creams and sauces, in both white and ebony chocolate, topped by fruits, berries, and exotic candies and biscuits, by whipped cream, millions of nuts, bagatelles of candied fruit, and fat chestnuts swimming in their own honey-colored pools atop peaks of snowy white meringue. There was no end to the colors, the shapes, the combinations, all so alluring that the very idea of satiation seemed impossible.

The waitresses departed and Terry climbed into the back seat, turned to a stunned Gaby, and asked, "Where to?"

Lost in the rapture of deciding what to consume first, Gaby absently murmured, "Anywhere."

Shrugging one arm innocently around her, Terry called to the driver, "Anywhere, Michael, and make it snappy."

And off they set. To the bliss of a woven-sugar basketful of butter-Brazil-nut and butterscotch supreme, with a vein of chestnut sorbet to cut the sweetness, wreathed in marzipan blossoms, and slivered chocolate raindrops, they glided over to Fifth, past Tiffany's, past St. Patrick's, past Saks, and down to the library. As they attacked a cinnamon persimmon ice *au chocolat*, they cut over to Park.

Zooming up the approach to the Park Avenue overpass, they thrilled at, but couldn't identify, a lavish, luscious beige and green creation, studded with candied fruit. They soared past the upper levels of the new Grand Hyatt and the Pan Am building as if they were the only humans in Manhattan, for this sky-high route, packed during the day, was glamorously empty now, allowing the glow of Manhattan to light their way, like a trail of celestial cookie crumbs left by Astaire and Rodgers. As they took the last curve and headed into the underpass of the Grand Central Tower, he was feeding her a spoonful of lychee and blood orange parfait, sculpted like a lotus blossom.

By the time they had headed back uptown, cruised past the Waldorf and into the glorious seventies, the baked Alaska was but a memory. At Terry's insistence, they cut west and entered Central Park, oohing and aahing over the skyline, and all too soon they found themselves at Central Park South, having slowed down over a banana split. "Michael, go over to Madison," Terry called to the driver, and they proceeded east past the Plaza and up Madison into the high sixties.

"Feel like walking?" Terry asked her as he bunched up a napkin and caught a fleck of ice cream on her upper lip.

"But of course," she dared, sure that the mink plus the calories from the ice cream would keep her warm as August. "But I don't have gloves."

"Don't worry, I do. Michael," he called to the driver, "we're going to walk for a while. Want to follow us?"

"Sure thing," the driver replied and drew the limo to the curb. "And I'll just clean up the back seat if you're all through."

''Great! Okay, here goes,'' and Terry jumped from the car and, the perfect gentleman, handed her out, one of the gold boxes securely tucked under his arm.

''What's that?'' she inquired, the cold air stunning her face and eyes, but exquisitely refreshing.

''Candy,'' he told her, sliding the box into a jacket pocket. ''In case you get upset again.''

''I have no intention of getting upset again. Once a night is enough! Hey, isn't that a great shoe!'' She was urging him toward a window in which one ice blue satin evening pump shone like the priceless jewel that it was.

''Not bad,'' he decided, ''but I thought they sold them by the pair.''

''Peasant!'' she hurled at him, as she hurried ahead toward the windows of Rive Gauche. Blue-jeaned, besandled, and beminked, she caught her reflection in the window and liked what she saw, then liked it even more as he appeared behind her, tall and ski-jacketed.

''Hey,'' she told his reflection, ''I feel much better!''

''But of course,'' he replied in his best Charles Boyer accent. He put his hands on her shoulders, and she turned and smiled up at him, sweetly, and he took her chin in his hand.

''God, you really do look just like Karen, just like I pictured when I wrote . . .'' For a split second, she felt him wanting her, knew he was on the verge of taking her in his arms, but something, some inexplicable fear, made her step back and start walking again.

''I wish you hadn't mentioned Karen.'' She realized she was being bratty, but she didn't want to stop herself. ''I'd forgotten all about that scene tonight. . . . Oh, Terry, I'm sorry.''

''Hey,'' he caught up with her and took her arm,

"it's all right. I just can't figure out if you want to talk about what happened or not. Do you?"

"Oh, I don't know. Yes, I guess I do. Give me some candy," and she stretched her palm out toward him.

"Truffle? Chocolate-covered cherry? White chocolate fudge? What's your pleasure?"

"Fudge," she announced firmly. "Aren't you having any?"

"Yeah, think I'll work on a truffle."

They both chewed in silence until Terry lit a cigarette and suggested, "Now, don't bite my head off, but what happened?"

"Oh," she groaned, "Mark and I had a horrible fight. In front of everybody. I mean, we weren't screaming or anything, but it was obvious."

"Why? What happened?" He took her ungloved hand, the one without the candy, and placed it, already enclosed in his, inside a jacket pocket for mutual warmth.

"Well, we kept shooting the same scene over and over because Mark felt we weren't there yet. Up to a point, he was right. But then we really started hitting, and on the twentieth take, we got it!" She was striding fiercely on, quickening both their paces, her body still inclined toward his, one hand still resting in his, deep in his pocket. "It felt good to me. Good to Chuck. Good to the cameraman. But it didn't feel good to Mark." Her anger made her pause in the recounting. "Can I have a drag of that cigarette?" She withdrew her hand from his, accepted the half-smoked Camel, took a puff and returned it.

"How can you not inhale?" he asked her.

"I don't know. Never could do it right."

"You smoke like a girl."

"Screw you."

"Anyway . . ."

"Anyway"—unconsciously, her hand again sought his—"we kept on shooting. By the time I got mad, we'd peaked, and everybody was exhausted and stale. I mean, human actors aren't special effects—can't he tell the difference? Anyway, he wouldn't stop making us do it over, and finally, I just broke down and told him I couldn't go on. Jesus Christ, it's such an unnecessary waste of money. At this rate, we'll be over budget in three weeks. If he expects that kind of perfection he should get an animator to *draw* us!"

They crossed Seventy-second Street slowly, the spacious boulevard as empty as Central Park. "But you know the thing that bothers me the most?" she said as she felt the tears catch again in her throat. "He hasn't got any faith in my work. I'm a very good, very professional model."

"You'll get no disagreement from me." Extracting both their hands from his pocket, he placed his arm around her so that they swaggered slightly, as couples do.

"You know, Jackson always talks about 'feel.' And what he means is that combination of instinct, intuition, and taste that tells you when you've got it right. I'm good at that. I've got great feel and great concentration. I'm good enough for Jackson Pendleton, but I'm not good enough for Mark Groseman!" She spat it out. "Mark says I don't know what I'm doing, that I'm an amateur and a baby. It's just too much," and she burst into tears. "Goddamnit!" She turned toward him and impulsively threw herself into his arms, sobbing with frustration. "I'm good, Terry, I really am. I'm not dumb. I'm not simple minded. I'm a professional, but he's making me feel like nothing . . . like *nothing* . . ."

They were standing in front of the Whitney, in the middle of the sidewalk, as he held her close and stroked her hair. "Gaby, you're good," he crooned. "You're actually becoming my character. You're turning into Karen. Or you were before you walked off that set tonight. I was astonished. But"—he released her from his embrace so he could look at her—"but I thought my script was great, and Mark didn't agree. And he's the boss. Look, we put ourselves in his hands. We trusted our talent to him, just like the studio trusted him with the money to make the movie. And you love the man, right? You're the one who thinks he's a genius, right? So let's just hope that we're wrong and that his opinion counts more than ours. Okay?"

"Okay," she murmured with downcast eyes. "And I guess it's hard to work with someone you're . . . you're involved with."

"Sure it is, but it'll get easier," he told her, although she didn't for an instant believe him. "But what I primarily think," he smiled down at her, "is that you should go home and get some sleep."

Suddenly, she didn't want him to leave her, wanted to roll time back to that moment when they had almost kissed. Peace would be to hide out in his arms; calm would be his telling her it was all right. As they walked to the limo, she asked lightly, "Want to come over? Mark won't be back for hours."

"I want to," he smiled, his fingers sweetly grazing her temple. "I want to, but I think I won't." He helped her into the limousine, then leaned in far enough to lift her chin and kiss her gently on the forehead, then fleetingly on the lips. "Gaby," he told her solemnly, "I don't think you should do anything to make Mark any madder. But listen, my girl. Despite everything, tonight was a great one."

"Yes, it was." She smiled, disappointed, but in a way, relieved.

"Far superior to that time at the Palm Court," he told her before he disappeared into the night, "when you were so pissed off at me about New Year's Eve."

chapter twenty-nine

CANNES,
May 1982

NINETEEN-EIGHTY trudged along like a Napoleonic soldier on the retreat from Moscow. The seventies, whatever they had meant to be, were beaten, and everybody was exhausted with the prospect of adjusting to a new decade, to a whole new set of problems, and a whole new style to have to learn to fit into. And, keeping pace with the slow and painful progress of this particular year, *Sirens' Song* ground on and on, big and bold, not quite half-finished although it was four months past the projected completion date, and, it was rumored, mythologically over budget.

Even the columnists were speculating about when the studio execs would start questioning the exploits of Mark Groseman and his merry band. Time was flying to the tune of massive financial overcalls, requested by the producers and granted by the studio, based, it seemed, largely on the director's way with words rather than on actual footage, for no one except Mark and the editor was even permitted to see the rushes. And maybe Gaby. But she wasn't talking. When she was around.

For, in addition to being the longest and costliest movie ever made, *Sirens' Song* was shot almost entirely on location: Thailand for the Danang at Tet battle scene, huge and spectacular; Kathmandu for hippie drug festivals; Paris for the student revolts; Woodstock for Woodstock; Burma for war ruins; Kent State and Columbia playing themselves; etc., etc. It was back-breaking work for all concerned, but what amazed me was that even a *grande dame* type like Denise loved every minute of it.

In the rare times when she wasn't shooting the Peace Corps sequence in West Africa or the San Francisco love-in stuff, she would dance into town, looking ten years younger and acting very feisty. She proclaimed Mark a genius, as well as a magician. Even in bed, she talked about him.

"Jesus, Ter," she veritably purred, Academy-Award-winning smoke rings issuing from the fabulous rosebud mouth, which had so recently applied itself to me. "I really do feel a good ten years younger. It's his energy. Phenomenal. I've worked with the great ones, the grand masters, including Hitchcock, Zinnemann, and Truffaut, but Mark is so . . . so . . . *thrilling*. You just never want a shooting to stop. He's just so exciting to interact with——"

"*Interact*? God, Denise"—I tweaked her gently—"*interact*! You really do sound like you went to film school."

"Oh, you're just jealous." She pushed my fingers away from her breast in irritation. "Cut it out. I'm talking about my *work*. . . ."

"Denise, gimme a break! Just a little breather from encomiums about the teeny tyrant."

"That's hateful." She jerked her head away from me and angrily stabbed out her cigarette. "And petty."

"Where to next?" I politely steered the conversation back her way.

"Amsterdam, for the whore hallucination scene."

"The what?" I started to ask, since I hadn't written such a scene, then I decided I didn't want to know. "And after that?"

"Chicago. In three weeks."

"So when will I get to see you?"

"I don't know." Suddenly turning back toward me, she seemed to see me for the first time. "Oh, darling." She stretched her torso against mine and hugged me. "I'm sorry I've been so . . . negligent. It's just, you know, a movie this big, it's so . . . so overwhelming. I'm sorry. Hey"—her eyes lit up with a good-idea glow—"come to Chicago for the convention stuff. We're all booked into loads of suites at the Whitehall . . . it'll be great. And I'm not needed in a lot of the scenes, so we can vacation gloriously—just the two of us—without leaving the room." To reinforce her argument, she touched me in a most provocative place in a most provocative manner. "Won't that be fun?"

"You bet, lady." My hand urged her hand to continue, but she demurred. "Can't. Got to get dressed. The cast and crew always have dinner with Mark on Sundays. Come. Please. We just sit around and eat deli and drink beer or Perrier and just, you know, noodle . . ."

"Denise, your artistry may be rising, but your vocabulary's shot to shit! Where're you eating?"

"At Gaby's. Mark likes take-out."

"Well, it's close."

"Sure, half a block. Come on."

Against my better judgment, I returned to the scene of several crimes, but this time, the whole duplex was floor-to-ceiling Mark fans. The twenty or so people who lounged on chairs, stretched out on the floor, and more or less hung from the rafters to hang on every one of the master's words, belonged to him. They were in his pocket. The last supper as a picnic. The liturgical drone of the Sunday afternoon football game wasn't even a close second in the ratings to Mark's conversation. Except to Mark, who, media wizard that he was, could concentrate on two things at once and would, in midsentence, whip around to catch a great play in the offing. He missed nothing, and he was wild—coked, I suspect, to the gills—running amok with words and caresses and commands, a mad monk, worshipped by all.

Only Gaby hung back, and that so subtly that I must have been the only person, including Mark, who noticed her reticence. The fact that this love fest was being held in her grass-and-smoke-filled house gave her a good excuse to keep emptying ashtrays, cleaning glasses, and making constant, increasingly lengthy forays into the kitchen. At one point, I followed her in on the pretense of asking for a beer.

"Does this happen all the time?" I asked her.

"All the time," she responded dully. "All the time. I don't think I've been alone with him for a year. At one time it used to make me cry. Now I'm beginning to think I'm lucky."

"Hey, whaddya mean?" I demanded. She was leaning against the refrigerator, with one foot propped up on the counter opposite—graceful as a gazelle, prettier than ever, and mad as hell.

I jumped on the counter and sat facing her, with one hand placed loosely on her raised calf, and sipped my beer.

"I mean, this is reminding me of the emperor's new

clothes,'' she said. ''Look, everybody involved in this movie, with the possible exception of me, thinks it's the greatest work of art since the Sistine Chapel. Maybe it is, but the fact is, we're desperately over schedule and over budget, and no one—not me, not the studio, not anybody but Mark and the editor—has seen a frame of it!''

''So?''

''So, this could go on forever. With him doing fifty takes of every scene, and in the case of the crowd extravaganzas and the war scenes—God . . . I mean, Terry, why isn't someone *curious* about where all this money is going?''

''Hmmm.'' I was absently running my hand up and down her leg, too spellbound by her ferocity to remind her that she'd asked for all this.

''And, personally, I'm just sick of the whole thing. I can't work with him because he keeps changing his mind. I do a scene one way, then he says its no good because he's decided he wants it done another way. Jesus! And, of course, he pays absolutely no attention to me off the set. Except to get mad. Or, rarely, to make up and get laid.'' The anger was drifting toward tears. ''I had a perfectly good career before all this started, and it's going to hell because he's got to have me around all the time for no good reason.''

''So?''

''So.'' She lowered her leg to the floor, kicked the cabinet hard, then turned her attention to me. Taking my hand, she urged me off the counter until we were standing very close. ''So,'' she half whispered, ''I'm sick of this movie. I'm sick of this life, and I'm sick of dreaming about being somewhere else doing something different. You know what I always wanted to do? Be a runway model for Philippe. And he wants me to do a videotape of his fall collection, which Jackson is going to direct in Paris in a couple of months. It's a great idea for selling the collection everywhere. They don't have to stage a show; they can just run the tape, and it'll be big and splashy. And I'm just dying to do it. And you know what else?'' She took my hand, and together we started back toward the living room. ''I'm turning over a new leaf.'' She chuckled at the cliché. ''I'm not going to act up anymore. I'm not going to cause any more trouble. I am going to be a veritable geisha to Mark, on the set and in the bedroom. And,'' she said, tossing her hair back passionately, ''and if we don't wrap by the end of May, love or no love, I am quietly and in a most refined fashion, going to walk off the picture.''

She turned toward me, looking firmly at me, bravery and anger forming an almost visible aura around her. And it occurred to me then that Mark might be wrong about Gaby, that she must be an actress of enormous skill, because I very nearly bought all that courageous talk of rebellion and resistance; God, she bought it all herself. But the trouble was that I knew too much about her, maybe more than she knew about herself. And what I now believe I should have told her then and there, what I couldn't bring myself to say because I still hoped against hope that I was wrong, was that it would take more than an act of courage to get Gaby to walk away from Mark; it would take a goddamned miracle.

chapter thirty

CHICAGO, *March 1981*

SHE had only had time to check into the hotel, start to unpack, and order and receive a Perrier from room service before the phone rang. For a moment, she decided against answering it, then bowed to the force she knew commanded her on the other end of the line.

"Hey, babe, how's it going?" Mark sounded like his old enchanting self, which probably meant he was high but maybe meant something else as well.

"Hi," she said noncommittally.

"Hi," he echoed her, then stopped.

"How's it going?"

"Couldn't be better. Wait a minute, yes, it could be better. If you were here, it would be perfect." Not a hint of condemnation in his voice despite the fact that she had bolted from the shooting as soon as she was finished, desperate to get away. He hadn't been pleased, but she'd left Washington before there was time for a major battle.

"Gaby, I miss you."

"But it won't be long, Mark," she soothed him, "You'll be here tomorrow, won't you?"

"Well . . ." he paused. "That's why I'm calling. We're still shooting the monument stuff. I just can't see any way we'll be able to get to Chicago before Monday."

"Monday! Mark. You mean I've got to kill a whole weekend in Chicago? For Christ's sake, Mark!" She didn't know, might never know, whether he was really running long or delaying just to punish her for leaving him. The temptation to throw a tantrum rose up in her, unbelievably strong, but she pushed it back, firm in her resolve to handle this like an adult. Only a hint of the disappointment, of the confirmation that they'd arrived at a point where nothing went right, showed in her voice. "Well, okay. When do you think you'll be here?"

"Scheduled to land in Chicago Monday at noon." He sounded relieved. "And I can't wait to see you, babe."

"Likewise," she managed, then fell silent.

"Gaby, baby, don't sound so sad. This is a job, not a vacation, right? And I'll bring you a great present."

"From Washington?"

"Just wait and see. Listen darling"—he was clearly anxious to cut the conversation short—"I've got to go. We're shooting in five minutes. Love you and see you on Monday. Okay?"

"Okay."

"Love me?"

Grudgingly. "Love you."

And he was gone. She put the receiver back on its cradle, hurled herself onto the gigantic, soft down bed, took a sip of the Perrier, then shocked herself by hurling the glass against the wall, where it had the audacity not to break at all, just plunk softly from the heavily papered wall to the thick carpet.

"Damnit," she mumbled aloud. "I can't even break a fucking glass when I want to," then burst into tears of fury, hurt, and frustration and buried her face deep in the plump and comforting pillows. "Enough." She forced herself up, decided to shower, did, then, feeling marvelously self-destructive, ordered a pack of cigarettes and, when they came, tipped the bellman five dollars.

As she strode up and down the room, puffing furiously on cigarette after cigarette, she felt assaulted by the anger and the desperation that came at her like body blows. In the brief pause between punches, she chastized herself, and bitterly, for being such a brat, such a crybaby. You're so damned lucky, she lectured herself sternly. You've got everything in the world everybody else wants, and here you are, acting like the poor little match girl, just because you're alone for a couple of days. She was almost at the point of convincing herself when, out of nowhere, a fresh burst of despair forced her right back to square one. She felt so vulnerable, it was scary, so sensitive that a door slamming down the corridor or the sound of distant laughter made her wince.

Her watch read seven thirty. Seven thirty on a Friday night in Chicago, and already she was frantic. What the hell was she going to do with a totally empty weekend in a city where she knew absolutely no one? She had heard the restaurant in the hotel was splendid, but she had never been one for dining out alone. There was also a health club with a pool, sauna, masseur, all the services of relaxation, but she didn't want to have to come back and shampoo her hair. Now she moved to the floor-to-ceiling mirrored closet doors, moving and posing, assuring herself of her physical excellence. She turned on the TV, then switched to the radio, then sat down again on the bed and decided to order a drink, but already the room was inducing claustrophobia. She was furious at Mark, enraged that somehow their relationship had turned into guerrilla warfare—snipes and sneak attacks, booby traps and terribly low blows. And yet her growing hatred of his selfishness, his ruthlessness, didn't even touch the part of her that had always adored and needed him. Even as the enemy, he was the object of her devotion.

Like they said, she couldn't live with him but she couldn't live without him. She and Mark had gotten too close to each other, had shared much too long and intricate a history, to just let go. She realized now that their years apart had merely been a delaying tactic, that he had been with her in some terrible form throughout the separation and now, even now, living in his shadow, in his keeping, made her feel whole. Except that, for the first time, it was beginning to occur to her that so driven, so driving an intimacy might be harmful. As a girl she had believed that all love was good. Now she was wondering if maybe she had been wrong; maybe there were some loves that hurt and destroyed. Or maybe she just couldn't handle the fact that he had once again disappointed her.

She didn't know what to do, but by now she was convinced she couldn't stay in the suite, with its hideous, mocking silence. A drink. That was something to do. Have a drink at the bar. Take off the terrycloth robe, put on something nice, like the little black suit Philippe had done for her, fix her makeup, walk into the bar, and just see what happened. That would be really audacious, proof that the peculiar shyness that jibed so badly with her appearance and her reputation was passing at last.

And so it was that forty-five minutes later, she crossed the small lobby and entered the dark, distinguished bar.

"Okay, Gaby, you're a girl on your own," she told herself as she walked to the bar and ordered a Kir Royale. There was a crowd at the bar, mainly well-dressed couples from out of town, enjoying a cocktail before their dinner guests arrived. Not prime stalking territory. Still, you never knew. Seating herself on a stool, she enjoyed the satisfaction of the bartender's recognition that he'd seen her somewhere before. She sat alone, brooding and nervous, sipping the champagne and cassis, and feeling it instantly go to her head. Well into her second drink, she sensed someone approach her, felt the chase begin, and slowly, languidly, she turned around to face a quizzical but smiling Terry Barron.

"Hey lady, buy you a drink?" he beamed.

"Terry Barron! It can't be!" She captured him in an embrace to make sure. "What are you doing here?"

"I might ask you the same question," he told her. "In fact I think I will. Over a drink." He slid onto a stool and ordered a Johnny Walker Black. "I'll go first," he began. "To be honest, Denise stood me up. We were supposed to spend the weekend together before you guys start shooting, but she called to say they're going to be delayed until Monday."

"Play it again, Sam," she said. "I just got the call from Mark. Terry, I just cannot believe you're here!"

He laughed and, seeing her glass was nearly empty, motioned to the bartender to bring her another.

"I'm such a baby," she admitted. "I was so worried about what I was going to do all weekend in Chicago."

"Yeah. Now we can worry about what *we're* going to do all weekend in Chicago."

"Oh, hell, we'll find something. We always do,"

and for a second, a lovely acknowledgment passed between them. "So what should it be?" she smiled greedily.

"How about dinner? Before you get even more tipsy and fall off the stool?"

"How dare you!" She exclaimed in mock outrage, then girlishly, "Am I tipsy?"

"Well, there must be a reason why you can't stop smiling."

"I'm just so glad to see you! I feel as though I conjured you up!"

"Maybe we conjured each other up. It's what they call a karmic friendship." He motioned to the bartender for the check and signed it, then helping her off the stool proclaimed, "Let's do Chicago."

"As it's never been done," she announced, her head held high.

"As it's never been done," he concurred, and arm in arm, they strolled through the doors of the bar.

"Where to?" They were standing on the sidewalk with all Chicago before them.

"Beats me." Gaby surveyed the territory, which encompassed the huge slab of brand new condominium across the street and the sleek vista of Delaware Place stretching grandly in the distance. "Let's just start walking . . . ummm . . . this way . . . okay?"

"Great." He took her arm and off they strode.

"It's like spring out," she said. "I thought Chicago was supposed to be the Siberia of the Midwest."

"They warmed it up for us," he said, smiling at her.

"But of course."

"The least they could do. Hungry?"

"I'm not sure." She laughed at what she'd said. "Can you believe that? I am in such a state of culture shock that I don't even know whether I'm hungry. Hey, you know what I want?"

"Piña colada?" he asked, and a surge of nostalgic affection hit her with delicious force.

"Oh, God, remember that night at the museum?" She said. "It seems like a thousand years ago."

"It was great." He offered his arm, and she accepted it.

"It was. It was great," she felt glad, suddenly, to be where she was, in a place she didn't know, with someone she did know, very, very well. She felt, for the moment, safe.

"So," he continued, "a piña colada for the lady?"

"Not anymore. We've outgrown them." She dropped his arm and turned to face him. "We're rich and famous. A piña colada wouldn't even touch where I'm thirsty. I want . . . champagne. And immediately."

"No sooner said." He hailed a cab. "The Ritz-Carlton, driver."

And so it began. At the Ritz-Carlton bar they enjoyed twin splits of Mumm. At the Hyatt-Regency, Terry sweet-talked the sommelier of the restaurant into transporting a whole bottle of the excellent California Schramsberg into the cocktail lounge. At the Ambassador, in the legendary Pump Room, they moved on to Möet et Chandon, but didn't quite finish the bottle. It had gone from dusk to evening to night, and by the time they found themselves at the Drake, sipping a lavish Roederer Cristal, they had gone from tipsy to high to some level of intoxication so gay, so giggly that Gaby wished she could feel that way for the rest of her life. Until the room began to tilt ever so slightly.

"Hey, I think some air is needed here," Terry announced, reading her perfectly.

"But we haven't finished the champagne."

"We'll take it with us," he suggested, summoning the waiter.

"And I'll go to the ladies' room while you make a total idiot of yourself."

"Coward." He hurled the accusation affectionately in her direction.

"You bet. Actually, I'm doing you a favor. I want to see if I can still walk."

And, somehow, she could. She could even patch up her makeup and arrange her hair, although, looking back, she would never know how. By the time she floated back to the lobby, she saw Terry waiting for her, napkin-clad champagne bottle nestled firmly under one arm. "We're going to have to brown-bag it. They wouldn't spring for the glasses!"

"You are unbelievable! You are really a great date!" she marveled, then danced through the door and, instinctively, headed to the right. "So are you," he called, catching up to her.

"Where to?" she grabbed the bottle and took a swig.

"Lakeshore Drive. Only the best for madame," and when she half tripped, he flung his arm over her shoulder, steadying her.

"Hey, this is *fun*! I love this!" she exclaimed, and was prepared to walk on when, all of a sudden, the sight before her stopped her before she began. "Jesus! It's like a city version of the South of France."

"That's why they call it the Gold Coast, darlin'."

"Oh, right. They do?"

"They certainly do." Even at night, the shining ebony lake in the distance curved in the famous horseshoe of all great beachfronts from the Côte-d'Azur to Malibu. But, most miraculous of all, fronting the lake, rising above it like sea gods, were gigantic towers of residences—some brand new, some old and dignified, but all so huge, so open, so grand, they seemed to suggest another galaxy.

"Oh, is this ever something!" She took another pass at the bottle, then passed it to him. Without removing his arm, without stopping, he continued walking her down the thoroughfare, as the strangely mild night breezes of the windy city drifted by them.

"Everything's so big, I get dizzy when I look up!" she told him, to which he replied, "Just like a provincial New Yorker to gawk at a tall building."

She broke from his grasp and danced ahead, around a corner to a broad tree-lined back street of what, in her New York neighborhood, would have been townhouses, but in this giant-scaled place were towering, vast apartment buildings.

"More champagne, you rude fellow," she commanded, and instantly her will was done. "I think I killed the bottle." She stopped, weaving slightly, facing him.

"We'll hide it here, behind this hedge." He took the bottle and deposited it. "They'll never know where it came from, and I'd hate to mess up the streets with refuse like this."

"Good thinking." She grabbed his hand and headed back toward the lakefront with him in tow.

Standing in front of the tallest, grandest slab of skyscraper, watching the moonlight twinkle on the lake, loving the sound of the cars rushing by them down the drive, Gaby, weightless and careless and totally happy, looked toward the lake. His hand still cradled in hers, she threw back her head, inhaled the night breeze, and half wept with rapture. "This is it! This is what I want." She turned to him.

"Are you sure?" The sparkle in his eyes had turned to something else, something infinitely softer.

She looked at him for a second, which seemed like a long, studied time, her smile mellowing to sweetness, "Yes. Yes, I'm sure." And slowly, lovingly, with great determination, she placed her hands lightly on his neck and drew his lips, ever so gently, down to hers.

chapter thirty-one

CANNES,
May 1982

THAT night in Chicago, we strolled back to the hotel, holding hands like teen-agers, easy in the knowledge that fate had taken over our lives. The realization that choice and will and ethics were finally only illusions freed us from all ties to anything or anyone else but each other.

Suffused in a mutual warmth, we didn't talk much, didn't even look at each other, for the magical transformation of our clasped hands into the center of the universe made each passing second into a consummate act of love. Once, sheltered by the great, sympathetic monoliths soaring around us, we paused at the same moment and embraced, her lips nuzzling my neck in a gesture of absolute sweetness, as we clasped each other with an innocence that made the breeze sigh.

There was no need to rush, no reason to paw, for we had all the time in the world to bring into being fantasies I, for one, had played out over and over in my mind for all the years we'd shared some strange, sequestered yearning. That our decision might have been the product of her anger at her lover, or mine at mine, was an idea that disappeared before it could occur to either of us. It just wasn't an issue; it was a concern generated from a level of existence we had already transcended.

Even time had donated its services to us, and we knew for sure that the night would last as long as we needed it. Strange, after all the years of nervousness and evasions, after all the missed signals, that the tension between us had utterly vanished, leaving us with the good part, the sunny and glorious intimacy that had kept us weaving in and out of each other's lives.

And as the Whitehall materialized before us, I thought of a line from Shakespeare: "Journeys end in lovers meeting," and I knew, with a relief that swept through me like the state of grace, that, for a little while at least, we had stopped traveling.

chapter thirty-two

CHICAGO,
March 1981

"YOUR suite or mine?" he asked her, straightening his tie in a good Cary Grant imitation. They were crossing the tiny lobby and heading for the elevators.

"What floor are you on?" she asked him as the elevator doors opened to admit them.

"Seventeen."

"I'm on fifteen. Let's get as high as we can," she tossed back at him as her finger firmly hit the button for seventeen.

Suddenly solemn, suddenly bashful, they watched the doors close and the floor indicator climb like a thermometer. When, at last, it released them onto seventeen, he took her arm to steer her to the left, then to the right, then down the length of a corridor.

The key turned easily in the lock, and they walked together toward the bedroom as naturally as if it were a habit.

She sat down, surprisingly primly, on the edge of the

huge bed, hands folded in her lap, looking up at him, asking nicely. Dropping down beside her, he didn't catch her up in an embrace, didn't kiss her ardently, just stared at her, smiling, as his hand caressed her hair. The kiss, when it came, was light and soft, and his lips moved quickly from hers, skimming her cheek, then coming to rest on her neck. "Champagne?" he murmured.

"Absolutely," she said a little breathlessly, before a thought came to her that brought her briefly back to earth. "Room service. Should I be here?"

What could have spoiled it all, wouldn't, not tonight. "Well," he mused, getting up and walking around the bed to the phone, "there's always the bathroom to hide out in if we're really being wicked."

"Yes!" She jumped up, giggling. "We *are* being wicked, and I'm going to take a shower."

Leaving him to order the champagne, she headed for the bathroom and enjoyed a long, languid shower, deciding, in a moment of wild abandon, to sacrifice the mane to the ecstasy of total immersion. The jets of hot water titillated her, urged her excitement on, in a kind of baptism. By the time she'd had enough, stepped from the shower, dried first her hair, then herself with the great, enveloping towel, which she then wrapped around herself, and opened the door to ask if the coast was clear, he was waiting to pour the champagne.

"To Chicago," she announced, lightly tapping his glass with her own.

"To Chicago," he responded, and they both drank, standing in the middle of the room, very close, but not touching.

"Give me your glass," he commanded her, and she felt, for the first time, a small tremor of fear, but she did as he told her, watching him set the glasses on the dresser behind them, then turn back to her.

"Gaby . . ." he said, and it was an invitation to which she utterly consented. Then his hands reached out and deftly, lovingly grasped her bare shoulders, tracing the smooth lines of her upper arms, then pausing, his grip tightening slightly, as he drew her to him.

This time the kiss was long and passionate and so easy, so graceful, she was astonished. Their tongues fit, their mouths fit, their bodies fit, as if they had always been here doing what they were doing.

Somehow they walked to the bed, somehow the towel dropped to the floor, and he sat on the bed as she stood before him, inviting his touch. As he studied her with his hands, she was flooded with a sweet weakness, a kind of desire she hadn't felt since she was very young, an ardor that impelled her down beside him and against him, having to hold him, having to touch him.

Somehow they both undressed him, making the act into a long caress, and then she lay back on the bed, admiring the fine lines of his body. "I've never seen you undressed before," she murmured in wonderment, as he moved against her, and the feel of his skin against hers, the weight of his body on hers, made her gasp.

Somehow, as they turned and felt and joyously tumbled, the fear fled, and the past, all the good parts, came rushing to blur the boundaries between herself and him. He entered her almost by accident, so ready for him was she; he glided into her, and his presence inside her—so perfectly fit, so natural—made her relaxed and ready to receive on a level she'd never even imagined. When he moved, it was as if he were stroking her, and the sublime blending of passion and gentleness made her mouth reach for his and find it, wonderfully.

In perfect rhythm, they were floating together, going

somewhere, bodies molded together because they had to be, because she'd forgotten where she stopped and he began. And then a foreign feeling started deep inside her, and she was puzzled and amazed and overwhelmed as it began to grow and spread, until she felt it all over herself, and instinctively, she arched her body against his, hearing, infinitely near and galaxies away, his crying out, and then she felt, really could feel, a hot, wet stream flowing into her.

They stayed like that, even afterwards, loath to let go until they had to, and her body, still pressed against his, glowed with a new kind of peace.

When she awoke the next morning, aware, before fully coming awake, of the warmth of another body beside hers, she turned and was first surprised, then pleased, that it was Terry. He slept like a child, on his stomach, burrowed deep into the mattress, his arms embracing the pillow, and the sight so delighted her that she moved toward him, kissing the soft vulnerability of his neck as if he *were* a child. Most surprising of all, that slight touch stirred him, and without raising his head from the pillow, he opened his eyes and, seeing her, smiled. He murmured some words in his half-sleep, and as she laughed and asked, "What?" he rolled onto his back, stretched his arms languidly and said, "Wasn't dreaming." Then reached for her and trapped her in a hug, his body, still hot from sleep, warming hers against the luxury of the cool, cool cotton of the sheets.

There had been a moment, very, very late the night before, as they had finally surrendered to sleep in each other's arms, when she worried about the next morning, about how they would greet each other, but now she knew with delight that the worry had been foolish and that their time together would be charmed. They were destined, for the moment, to make each other happy, to give each other pleasure, and that was that. And so their morning lovemaking was smiling and easy and, for the first time in her life, fun, like playing. And afterwards, they lolled about, nuzzling, saying silly things, until he drew apart from her, bounded from the bed, and called to her, ''Now *I'm* going to take a shower, and you're going to order breakfast!''

''Wait a minute!'' she called. ''What do you want?''

''Surprise me!'' he shouted through the rush of the shower.

''My God,'' she announced, having checked his watch lying next to the phone to find that it was after three in the afternoon. They must, it struck her, have fallen asleep moments before dawn, although it had seemed like night. Reaching for the room service menu, she realized that neither of them had eaten dinner and that she was starving, so she picked up the phone, dialed room service, and proceeded to order a feast. When the knock on the door announced the food's arrival, she was ready, having located and wrapped herself in his robe, which was much too big for her but which felt great. By the time he appeared, towel-clad and glowing, she was struck again by just how pleasing his body was, still a young man's body, lean and hard and graceful.

''What's all this?'' he asked, moving to the table as he dried his hair with another towel and, without stopping, kissed the top of her head.

''Just about everything I could think of,'' she told him, and it was nearly true.

There was champagne and orange juice, melon and strawberries, croissants and three kinds of toast, kippers and scrambled eggs with ham and bacon, lox and bagels, sweet rolls, and french toast with syrup. Pots of coffee and all kinds of jams and jellies, and in a more classical vein, three kinds of cold cereal.

"How many people did you invite?" he asked, seating himself opposite her at the table.

"Oh, just us. You refused to tell me what you wanted, so I ordered everything."

"Decadent creature." He grabbed her hand, kissed her palm and nibbled her fingers. "You'll corrupt me!"

"Fat chance, you rake!" She retracted her hand in mock outrage. "Come on, dig in. I'm starving."

They were both shocked by the amount of food they managed to consume amid the small talk and little jokes, less so by their subsequent dive for the bed. "It's the lox, it always does this to me," he murmured lecherously into the thigh he was studiously exploring.

"Oh, really, I thought it was the Wheaties," she countered, shivering with pleasure as his tongue lapped at her.

They made love as if they were memorizing each other, trying to learn as much as possible with every caress, and, as they learned, they discovered over and over new delights, new preferences. Like dancers or athletes, they found themselves moving into graceful and intricate new patterns, assured that they were natural partners, capable of mutual beauty, making love an art, a discipline.

Sleeping and loving and lazing, they were startled when, about five, the phone rang, but they instantly decided not to answer it.

"Nobody's in their room at five o'clock," he told her, and she agreed.

"But, you know"—she sat up massaging her shoulders, then running her hands down the length of her arms until she was stretching to feel the relaxation in her fingertips—"I've got to go back to my room. What're we doing for dinner?"

Reaching for a cigarette, he sat back against the pillows, dragged deeply, and thought. "Hmmmm. It's Saturday, and it's late. Let me try the place in the hotel."

She had gotten out of bed, collected various articles of clothing, and begun dressing. "Okay. Should I dress up?"

"Why not? We're royalty today."

She stepped into her shoes, walked over to the bed, and sat down, drawing him to her one last time, not wanting to go, loving the feel of his hand on her uncoiffed hair. He kissed her with grand sincerity, then slapped her playfully on the ass and commanded her to get going. "I'll come by in an hour. What's your room number?"

"1510. I'll be waiting." She teased him playfully, but he good-naturedly moved her hand away.

"Hey, kid, gimme a break. See you in an hour, you sex-crazed creature."

"And I owe it all to you." She pecked him on the cheek, then walked to the door, blew him a kiss, and left.

When she got to her room and saw the red button flashing on the phone, she called the desk and found out that Mark had called sometime during the day. Overwhelmed, for a second, by either fear or guilt, she reached for her address book and called the Watergate in Washington, but of course, he wasn't there. Once she had left a message, she put down the phone and forced herself to feel good again, reliving, as she bathed and dressed, moments of the lovemaking so delicious they made her hungry to see Terry again. On the stroke of an hour, he was there, perfectly elegant in a blue suit, white shirt, and knit tie. As she opened the door, she posed, for an instant, secure in the perfection of her smoky blue slip of a dinner dress. "Wow!" was all he said, but it made her incredibly happy to be so lovingly admired. He took her hand, then kissed her, his free hand gliding across her breast and around to her back.

"Get the reservation?" she asked as they both stepped back.

"Yeah, let's go."

"Already?" She gazed demurely at him.

"Yep!" he said. "We've got all the time in the world, remember?" And in a way they did. But, remembering Mark's phone call, she knew for a tiny, sad second, that in another way, they had no time at all.

chapter thirty-three

CANNES,
May 1982

I COULDN'T have written it, that weekened. And, if I had, the critics would have called me a maudlin fool for enjoying such grossly romantic fantasies. But it happened with such magic, such wonderful sensuality, that every movement—passing a bit of pâté across the table, rising as she went to powder her nose, sharing a brandy—became an act of love. Standing in line at a midnight show was as romantic as gliding down a flower-filled stream, she resting, I rowing—and once in the movie, *Stir Crazy*, we hooted and laughed with a naturalness belying the fact that we even knew what a soundstage was.

And then it was two, and we walked out arm in arm like all the other couples, hit the street and took a cab to Lakeshore Drive, where we strolled, holding hands, speaking seldom, dreaming of the night ahead.

"Are you in love with Denise?" Her question knocked me off balance.

"What?" I turned to her, surprised that, by bringing up the recent past, she was bringing up the future—a future I'd fantasized for years, but never dared to contemplate.

"Don't say I shouldn't bring it up," she told me rather gravely. "I should. I've never understood, and I always wanted to know. You can't hurt my feelings—I'm as sure of you as I've ever been of anybody—so I want to know you totally."

"Fair," I admitted, lighting a cigarette and pondering the possibility that she was beginning to see an "us" beyond this weekened. "This is cheating, but let me answer a question with a question." But she spoke before I asked, enhancing my hope, exciting my expectations.

"Mark? You wonder whether I'm in love with Mark?"

"Well, yeah."

"You tell me first," she demurred, letting me know this discussion was going to be serious, and tough.

As I started to talk, I released her hand and slipped my arm around her shoulder. "Hmmm. I asked you about Mark because I think you still feel bound to him in the way I've always felt bound to Denise. You know, sometimes when you're young and new at the world, and unsure of how the world sees you or how you should be seen, you meet someone who receives you totally, who sets the pattern for you. When I met Denise I was a real brat of a boy, arrogant, greedy, a real smart ass. Things had always come pretty easily to me, and I was spoiled rotten, but I'd always gotten away with it. But the grownups in Manhattan didn't accept my natural genius as a given, and their remarkable failure to see me as I really was forced me to behave even more . . . callowly, I guess. But it was because I was scared. Still, I was running a real danger of becoming totally obnoxious. I met Denise at a dinner party—I think I told you that once—when I had had too much to drink too early in the evening, and my drunken baby macho impelled me toward her. I was going to make her mine, and easily, too, so I didn't waste any time coming on to her. Good old Denise, never one to mince her words, took about five minutes of my crap, then looked up at me, all Sullivan wide-eyedness, and murmured girlishly, 'Get lost, little boy.' She then turned to a world-famous financier, who'd been waiting around and who was clearly of much more interest than I could ever be."

"Oh, Jesus," Gaby gasped, "you poor baby. I feel terrible for you," and I could hear how deeply she meant that.

"Yeah, I felt pretty bad for myself," I continued, "but, see, Denise had done it all so quietly, so casually, that nobody'd heard. So I was able to get through to dinner where, horrors of horrors, I found myself seated next to her. I was mortified, especially when she saw my expression and started to laugh. She said something like, 'Ah, Mr. Barron! We meet again!' I managed to say something, but I suddenly felt worried about all the cutlery and the glasses, and I was sure I'd compound my earlier error by revealing the table manners of an animal. But somehow Denise, without doing anything other than giving my poor trembling hand a light pat, managed to inform me that she'd help me through it. As long as I let her lead, I'd be fine and forgiven.

"What a dinner. She talked more to me than to anybody else, but when she wants to be, she's one of the world's great dinner guests, so she also drew me into the general conversation, even making my remarks seem charming and astute, indicating to the bigwigs around us that I was a young writer well worth considering for their various magazines and newspapers.

"After dinner, when I'd managed to make some contacts that still pay the rent, I walked over to her. It was pretty late, and I guessed it was time to go, and I wanted to thank her for the most profound act of generosity I'd ever experienced. Also, I guess, I wanted to bathe for one more second in that aura of incredible glamor. She was talking, I remember, to Stephen Sondheim, but when she saw me approach, she excused herself and walked over to me.

" 'Miss Sullivan,' I sort of stammered, 'I just wanted to say——'

"She said, 'I'm leaving. Walk me to the elevator.'

"When we hit the elevator, I was puzzled to hear her say, 'I go up,' and when she saw my surprise, she said—I'll never forget it—'I live in the building, and, you lucky boy, you're going home with me.' "

"And you've been going home with her——"

"Ever since." We finished the sentence in unison.

"Even to this day, when I'm with her, I feel like a kid. I guess that's part of the appeal. But, you know, in a way I'm *hers*. She styled me, she finished me off properly. I guess in a way she had a vision of me, and she fought with me and loved me and brutalized me into being what she wanted. Which was the best thing for me."

"Are you saying you owe her?" Gaby asked.

"Yes, in a way." I pondered the question. "But in a very loving way. Listen, she made me become the person who perfectly suited her, too. We have long enjoyed," I quipped in an intentionally stilted fashion, "each other's company."

"But she leaves you all the time."

"Yeah, but you know, I wonder. Looking back, I

think there was a time when Denise would have married me, maybe even wanted to, but I took care of that by making myself oblivious to the fact. I don't think I ever wanted to marry anybody at all.'' I omitted, of course, the misbegotten afternoon when I'd intended to propose to Gaby. ''And Denise was a good cover. She kept me loose and gave me a reason to be . . .'' I searched for the word.

''A playboy?'' She grinned.

''God!'' I was shocked to hear her choice of words. ''Yeah, I guess so.''

''Okay. And what do you do for Denise?''

''The obvious. Make her feel young. Make her feel wanted. Give her somebody to take care of her when the marriages break up. I think long ago we both acknowledged that we're loners and that our relationship is an alliance of solitudes.''

''I think you're very good to her.'' Gaby kissed me on the cheek, a reward for the goodness, and I was pleased that whatever we had together had at some point taken us past jealousy.

''Well, yeah, I'm good to her.''

''I think you're a nice man.''

''And I think you're sexy.'' I kissed her emphatically.

''Don't change the subject.''

''Hey, wait,'' I challenged her, ''it's your turn. Tell me about Mark.''

She sighed, then began. ''You know. Every once in a while, you walk into a room and see someone—not necessarily the best-looking or the most famous person, just someone—and the moment is imprinted on your memory for ever after?'' She looked at me for acknowledgment, and I nodded. ''Well, that's how the thing with Mark started. I was a very shy, relatively inexperienced sort of girl—you know, too tall, too quiet, too studious, actually. No big deal. I nourished a secret dream that I could be beautiful, but it was the kind of adolescent fantasy that just hangs on too long. I was very unaggressive, even in the sixties. And very bad at snagging guys. But for once in my life, with Mark, I did everything right without even thinking about it. All the other girls threw themselves at him. I didn't even acknowledge his existence. And that got his attention. Etcetera, etcetera. But that first time, it was absolutely *carramba*, so I fooled myself into playing it cool. And it worked. Like a charm. I couldn't believe it, but Mark was actually laying siege to me. Nobody had ever wanted me so badly, gone to such great lengths to learn every nook and cranny of my personality so that I would be so totally enchanted, so that I'd never be able to escape.'' She laughed a little at the memory.

''You were in love?''

''Like gang busters. He was so passionate, so demanding of my presence, I felt absolutely needed—a princess—and so beautiful.''

''How long did that last?''

''I don't know, Terry.'' I was suddenly aware she hadn't used my name for a day, and it was startling to hear it. ''The good feelings began to turn into desperate needs. If I wasn't with him, I wasn't beautiful, wasn't desirable. I was the old me. And, you know, that's still true. I almost can't stand him anymore, but I need him, I crave him, to make me feel like me.''

''Mark Groseman: the heroin of love.''

''Unfair.'' She tried to pull away from my arm, but I held her fast.

''Sorry''—I kissed her hair—''but what you're describing sounds like addiction.''

''Yes,'' she mused, relaxing, ''I guess you're right. I guess that's what I was thinking right before I ran into you last night. But the problem is, you have to want to get over an addiction, and I'm still not all the way there. We were apart for a couple of years, and I thought I was cured, but . . . well . . . I wasn't. But you know what I hope?'' She looked up at me, and I realized this was the closest we'd ever get to alluding to some mutual future. ''I hope I really *am* beginning to want to.''

''Okay, enough already.'' I turned us around a corner and back to the hotel.

''What are we going to do tomorrow?'' she asked, making me feel like a honeymooner.

''Are you suggesting we leave the room?'' I pretended to leer.

''Oh, well. We should have something to tell. . . . You know, local sights.''

''Actually''—I had grasped her hand automatically, without thinking about it—''we should hit the Art Institute. The Impressionist collection is really unbelievable, too big to be done in a day but definitely to be seen. Too many great paintings to be real, with a price tag that puts it in about the same league as all the major banks in Geneva.''

''And?''

''And there's a fabulous shopping center called Water Tower Place. You've probably seen it, it's only a block away—that big grey slab of a building down Michigan. It's on seven or eight floors. Marshall Field covers a lot of it, but the rest is every expensive shop you can imagine. If you're lucky, I'll buy you something wonderful.''

''How can I refuse? And I'll buy you something wonderful back.'' Suddenly, indiscreetly, she brought his hand to her lips and kissed it lightly. ''Remember, I'm liberated. I can buy you presents, too.''

He smiled. "Never turned down a present from a lady yet."

"And then?"

"Maybe tea at the Ritz."

"And then?"

"Definitely pizza."

"And then . . ." She looked at him wickedly.

"Anything your little heart desires."

"I can't wait till tomorrow!"

"Hey, lady, I can't wait till tonight!"

She stopped right there and threw her arms around me. "You jerk!" she exclaimed. "You are too damned much! I'm so glad I know you!"

And, for some reason, that remark almost made me burst into tears because if the truth be told, I was struck by the unfairness of it all. By the awfulness of Mark Groseman and how bad he was for her. By the irony of how good we were for each other and how, at this point in her life, goodness and love and comfort just weren't enough. And I also realized that if she ever decided to grow up and love me, I'd be there on a moment's notice. And all I had to be content with, until then, was the knowledge that my true love had my heart and I had hers, if only for the next twenty-four hours.

chapter thirty-four

CHICAGO,
March 1981

THEY awoke the next day to sunshine streaming through the windows, making Gaby feel for an instant as if she were awakening in Venice. It was only eleven, and they hadn't fallen asleep until well after four, but somehow, in the course of little more than a day, they had grown so accustomed to each other, had so quickly developed a kind of mutual behavior that was almost conjugal, that she had slept easily in his arms, a deep and thorough sleep, and awakened utterly refreshed. She kissed him gently awake, and they'd frolicked a little before he went back to his room to change. Besweatered and blue-jeaned and tweed jacketed, they met at noon, preening themselves on their shared style, brunched at the hotel on the best corned beef hash in memory, and hit the Sunday streets.

At the Water Tower, they pushed their way through well-dressed crowds, enjoying the bustle and the packed elevators that comprised the center of the building, all glass enclosed and very glamorous. They stopped for french fries and cokes at a MacDonalds with hostesses who seated you, admired the style and radiance of the affluent Chicago adolescents who congregated in the restaurants and breezed through the shops, then cruised from floor to floor in a building that was a museum of expensive buyables. In the stuffed animal shop, she fell in love with a preposterously funny-looking creature of prehistoric origin called a woolly mammoth, half-buffalo, half-elephant, but with a sweet face, fat feet and ridiculously lovable soft white horns. Of course, Terry insisted on buying it for her. It was absurdly overpriced, but he pointed out that on this particular day money was no object. She, on the other hand, presented him with a silly, orange plastic fish whose maw was a cigarette lighter. ''It's too big,'' he'd protested, ''what'll people think of me with a fish sticking out of my pocket?'' But she pointed out he would give it class.

At Marshall Field, she bought a pair of huge, tortoise sunglasses with tinted lenses so no one might recognize her, and found to her delight that, instead, everybody noticed them, they looked so great together. Exhausted from resisting the temptation to buy each other everything in sight, they fled to the Art Institute, admiring the costume-party quality of the passersby, garbed in a high bohemian style neither of them had ever seen in New York. She was stunned by the magnificence of the Impressionist collection, which stretched gallery after gallery like a great prairie of masterpieces, each one a treasure, the whole too vast and heady to be studied in one viewing, but they ran through the rooms, picking up the glow of the priceless wonders around them. By then, it was after four, and they took a cab to the contemporary Florentine grandeur of the Ritz and enjoyed an absolutely jolly tea, then practically ran the short distance to the Whitehall.

There were messages from Denise and Mark, but when one perfunctory call to each found them not at their hotel, they promptly forgot and fell on each other, making love to the sultry strains of rhythm and blues radio. When they woke from a warm, entwined kind of nap, it was after nine, so they both showered and dressed and took a cab to the pizza place Terry had heard about.

The pizza was fantastic, and, a little high on beer, Terry suggested they go for dessert to an Italian restaurant on Goethe Street.

"Goethe Street? They have a street called Goethe?" she marveled.

"Not only that, but even the kids pronounce it right."

"Amazing," she mused, as the cab dropped them off before a new and stunning condominium. The restaurant, which occupied the street floor of the building, was cheery, crowded with parents and kids, and feeling like kids themselves, they ate rich cream-filled pastries with chocolate tops and skyscrapers of ice cream, then switched to cappucino and amaretto, and laughed and told embarrassing stories on themselves, remembering the ridiculous scene at Charles de Gaulle when she'd had coffee all over her dress. At last, they could delight in confessing to the silly tension they'd felt for so long and all the times he'd made her mad when neither of them had admitted it. The night grew later and later, but, as if to keep it from passing—because it was their last together—they lingered, until the sweetness of the amaretto began to cloy, and with unacknowledged regret coupled with enormous yearning, they made their way back to the Whitehall.

"How 'bout a nightcap?" They were walking into

the hotel, clearly glowing and a little high, more recognizable as lovers than as a famous cover girl and a best-selling author.

''Why not?'' It was the last stage in prolonging the pleasure, the final pretense that this was just another night in a long series of nights stretching way into the future. And then it was time to go.

''Your room?'' Terry asked her, as they waited for the elevator.

''Yes, my room, I think,'' she said, and pressed the button as the doors shut. They took advantage of the empty elevator to kiss and touch, jumping apart when the car stopped at eleven, then drawing together again when nobody entered and the doors closed again.

''This way, remember?'' she indicated a turn to the right when they stepped off the elevator, and arm in arm, nuzzling, they strolled toward their destination.

''Got your key?''

''Here.'' She pulled it from her purse and handed it to him. They shared one more kiss as the key turned in the lock, and he whispered, ''You are such a joy.'' And then, banishing the thought that this night was the last, they parted as he pushed open the door.

It was then that her heart stopped in horrified disbelief, for sitting in the room were both Mark and Denise, looking definitely annoyed. As they entered, Mark jumped to his feet, exclaiming, ''Where the hell have you guys been? We were about to call the cops,'' and, as the rapture flowed from her heart, she knew that their time had run out.

All at once, they were lying, covering tracks. All of a sudden, the joy was over. Assuring herself that it would have happened anyway and that the shock only made it harder, Gaby concentrated on the hope that their togetherness was so intense, so genuine, that they could see it through without causing so much as a ripple in the mainstream of their lives.

"Are you guys a mirage?" she asked coolly, walking to Mark and receiving his grudging embrace. "Or is this Monday?" In the periphery of her vision, she saw Terry greet Denise with a kiss, and, only for a second, she felt furious at this invasion of their privacy.

"We wrapped early. On purpose. We actually *ran* through the rest of the Monument stuff so we could squeeze out an extra day with you guys. Where the hell were you? We've been trying to reach both of you for two days." Her attention was calming him a little, but he wasn't letting go just yet. "Where were you?"

"Oh, Mark, calm down," she said softly, hoping that her words would be covered by Terry's own explanations to Denise. "There are people here."

"All I want is an explanation."

"We've been walking around and eating and drinking and trying to kill time. What do you think we've been doing on a weekend in Chicago, for Christ's sake?"

She knew, of course, what would soothe him. It was all so simple that she was surprised at how difficult it was to force the words out. "But I'm so thrilled that you're here. I'm so thrilled that you did it for me," and she squeezed his hand and looked down at him, smiling. Immediately, she turned to Terry and Denise, who seemed the slightest bit uneasy with each other. "Doesn't this call for champagne?"

"Absolutely," Terry insisted, following her lead by reaching for the phone. "On me!"

And so it went. Two bottles of champagne later, good feelings seemed at least superficially restored, and

Terry and she had publicly collaborated on a scenario that would stand up under individual interrogation.

When Terry and Denise got up to leave, Gaby felt a kind of despair, a real surge of anger and disappointment that they should have been cheated so cruelly, but she was surprised at how casually, how convincingly, they had managed to hide all traces of their intimacy. Things were momentarily back to normal, and she wanted to run away and hide from that normalcy because she feared what would follow it. But she couldn't hide because she had to pretend how thrilled she was to see Mark.

If she was an actress, she would prove it now. Prove it in bed, when Mark's greedy and selfish brand of lovemaking seemed obscene and heartless compared to Terry's sweet caresses, prove it by pretending she was satisfied, as she had always pretended before she understood the extent of her pretense, prove it by overlooking the fact that his passion was a function of the Quaaludes he'd dropped and that he cared more about his own pleasure than her own. And it was then, as he came too hard and too fast, forcing her to murmur words she didn't mean or feel, that she began to wonder who she was and where she was and whether there are places from which there really is no turning back.

By Tuesday, the weekend, hard as she tried to cling to it as the prime reality, was inevitably moving into memory. But by Tuesday, she was glad. Glad that preproduction meetings and local interviews took up all of everybody's time and that there was always a minimum of five people in the suite, sipping, snorting, or smoking. Glad that she was always seated next to Mark, not Terry, and that by some unarticulated agreement, they never allowed their gazes to meet and linger across a room or a table. This mutual restraint warmed her because it seemed so clearly proof of trust. Glad that what she had to do, she had to do alone, without Terry's presence or knowledge but with his deep devotion to give her the courage to act.

And by Tuesday, it was time. Mark and she had come back from a late dinner with Terry and Denise and Chuck Garson and the actress he was dating. The meal seemed to stretch on for hours, hours in which she ate little and spoke seldom. Now that she had decided to leave Mark, she wanted it over with, just wanted to make it through the thick, smothering terror that caused her heart to pound and her head to throb.

Once they were back in the suite, Mark had immediately done up four generous lines of coke, and for once she was glad. Boosted by the drug, Mark was strong enough to accept any news, no matter how bad or how shocking, and as she changed out of her jeans and sweater and into a nightshirt, she could sense his euphoria building steadily. For some reason, she felt impelled to escape into the bathroom to wash her face and cream it, to brush her teeth, comb her hair, and take out her contact lenses. She wanted to feel clean for this, clean and pure. And then, gazing at herself in the mirror, seeing the fear in her eyes coupled with a strange glint of exhilaration, she felt she was ready.

"Mark—" She found him sitting on the bed by the phone, busily thumbing through his address book.

"What time is it in LA?" he asked her idly, not looking up from the book.

"Not late. Nine-thirty. Why?"

"I gotta call some people. Business. Top-level stuff . . ."

"Mark—" She went to where he sat and stood before

him, blocking his view of the phone. "Mark, please. I've got to talk to you. It's important."

"Right now?" He was clearly up for an endless coke rap with some other mad genius in California. Or maybe his dealer. Whoever it was, he definitely didn't want to be sidetracked.

"Yes, Mark," she insisted. "Right now."

"Oh, okay, Gaby, what is it?" He put down the book with an exaggeratedly annoyed shrug and looked up at her.

"Well—" Now that she had to do it, she realized she'd never rehearsed the scene, had no idea how to begin.

"Out with it kid. I've got work waiting." He motioned her to sit beside him.

"Mark, look," she began firmly. "This past weekend . . . this weekend, I . . . I came to a decision . . ."

"And . . ."

"And——"

Her brave start was abruptly cut off by his saying, "And you're going to leave me, right?"

Her shock was so profound, she couldn't speak.

"Right?" he persisted.

"Well . . ." She was astonished at his perception, even more astonished that it was going to be miraculously easier than she could ever have dreamed. "Well . . . yes."

"You know how well I know you, kid?" he babbled on cheerfully. "This is how well I know you. Tell me if this isn't just what you've been thinking. You, Gaby Blake, are going to just plain walk out on me—if we don't get married in the next week. Am I right?"

So telling wasn't going to be easy after all. It was going to be a nightmare. "No, Mark, I——"

"Oh, baby, baby." He slung an arm about her.

"Don't play hard to get. Not now. Because, Gaby, my girl, we have just taken the meeting and the deal is all yours, on your terms. A real sweetheart of a deal." He pulled her close, seemingly not sensing her reticence. "You won, Gaby, you won. Those days in Washington, I wanted you there, you know. Really wanted you. So, see," and he briefly nuzzled her neck, then held her at arm's length, beaming all the while, "in different places, we were coming to the same decision. Listen, before the plane landed, I had the scene all blocked out. We're getting married, Gaby. Here in Chicago. During the shooting. I told a couple of guys at the studio, and they're thrilled. Great for you and me, great for the picture, great for the studio. So it's gonna happen the first of next week, okay? Happy?"

"Mark," she demanded, "Mark, is this going to be in the papers? In the columns?"

"In the columns! The PR guys think they can get Rona Barrett to feature us on her TV slot! We've big news."

"When?" She was frantic. "When is it going to break? When is it going to be on Rona Barrett?" She had to know, had, somehow, to get to Terry to warn him.

"Let's see. Today's Tuesday. They agreed to wait until Wednesday to spring it. Thursday, yeah, I think Thursday. Baby, don't look so worried. You don't have to do a thing but look beautiful and pass the blood test. The studio's arranging everything."

"Mark"—she was crying, but she realized it only when he raised his hand to wipe away her tears—"Mark, I——"

"Gaby. You're just crying because you're happy. All brides cry."

Oh, God, she screamed to herself, oh my God. Why

hadn't he told her this yesterday or the day before? Before he told all of Hollywood? Before leaving him became a business decision? She simply didn't know what to do or what to say. She had to get to Terry, had to tell him what was happening so he could help her, so he could help them both. There was no way she could see him alone tonight, but she had to get to him fast, before it all fell apart.

Her chance came, blessedly, at a hurried breakfast next morning in the suite. It included the four of them plus, for a frenzied while, the art director and costume designer, nibbling on croissants as they angrily hurled conflicting cases at Mark who, Solomon-like, was expertly managing the dual roles of host and dictator. Only half listening to the argument, although it concerned what she would wear, Gaby played with her food and longed for Terry, although he sat only inches away from her.

She was in the process of spearing a strawberry when Denise shrieked, "This afternoon! What do you mean you're leaving this afternoon? My God, darling, I just got here!" And Gaby's heart plummeted.

"Denise," Terry said, his voice unusually brusque, "*you* just got here. I didn't. I told you I'm interviewing Dave Winfield today, and I'm not about to miss it."

"Dave Winfield," she repeated loftily, "whoever he is!"

"Denise, don't tell me about baseball, and I won't tell you about acting, all right?" It was the closest Gaby had ever seen him come to outright anger.

"What'd I hear?" Mark was bounding back to the table after escorting the designers to the door, one arm around each, Coach Groseman at his most persuasive. "You're splitting?" He looked at Terry.

"Yep." Terry pushed back his chair and lit a cigarette. "Gotta get back to work."

"When are you leaving?" Gaby risked it and was proud of her off-handedness.

He met her gaze. "One P.M. flight to La Guardia."

Denise was clearly not pleased. "I simply cannot believe this. We've barely seen each other. There was no reason for you to come out here at all."

"No reason at all. Well, as they say in the great world of sports, you lose some . . ." He smiled wryly. The conversation stopped for a moment but was interrupted by the phone, which Mark reached over to pick up. "Tell him I'll be right down."

"Come on, Denise, let's get going!" Mark jumped up, grabbing her hand. "That guy from the *Trib*'s waiting in the bar. See you guys in an hour or so."

"Don't you need me?" Gaby asked, pretending concern.

"Not for this one, doll. This guy's a *cinéaste*. He wants an actress who's worked with Truffaut and a director who's a post-auteurist. Hey"—he beamed with great largesse—"order anything you want," then he escorted Denise through the door and was gone, leaving Gaby stunned by the advent of the one situation of which she hadn't dared to dream.

Time seemed to stop for her in those first few seconds. Too stunned to move, she simply sat still, waiting for him. Waiting for him to smile at her, to rise and come to her to take her in his arms, and all those images crowded into her mind, dizzying her. For the briefest time, she closed her eyes, to clear away the layers, but when she opened them, she saw him rising from his chair, but standing by it, not moving to her, not smiling.

"Well," he said expressionlessly, "I guess I'd better

go pack." She was so dazed that it must have shown in her face, but he refused to acknowledge that transformation.

"What did you say?" she asked, sudden tears pricking her eyes, demanding release.

"I . . . I've got to get packing. As they say." His grin was hideously wry, absolutely impersonal.

"Oh. Okay." She heard herself say the words, not believing she was saying them.

"Yeah. Okay." He had turned around and was walking to the door, was reaching out for the doorknob, was going to leave her, was strolling out of her life. She was dreaming, she must be, because this made no sense, no sense at all. It was too cruel, the cruel action of a man with no cruelty in him.

"Terry!" She was on her feet and halfway to the door before she even realized she had moved, reaching for his arm with all her strength, trying to turn him around toward her. "Terry, what are you doing? You can't go. Please, don't go!"

And, when he did turn, she saw the horrible, the mystifying coldness in his eyes. Desperately, she threw her arms around him, trying to force him to become himself again. He didn't fight her, didn't push her away. It was worse than that. He simply didn't respond, absolutely refused to yield to her.

It was she who finally drew back, stabbed with an overwhelming grief as she realized Denise had won again, that Terry, out of cowardice or, worse, out of clear-cut preference, was walking away from her. And through her sorrow, she heard somewhere far away, the strange new voice of her lover say, "Not today. I've got a headache," and then she heard the sound of a door closing and then only the terrible silence.

chapter thirty-five

CANNES,
May 1982

I WANTED to hurt her, I wanted to wound her deeply, I wanted her, for once, to feel the agony of absolute rejection. I wanted to show her that no one could get away with savaging another human being, certainly not with such casual ease.

As it turned out, my future had come tumbling down Tuesday night, after dinner, when I'd found a message to call Liz Smith in New York no matter how late the hour. I couldn't imagine why Liz wanted to get hold of me so urgently, but I returned the call at once, not only out of curiosity but out of fondness for a lady who manages to be both a gossip columnist and a warm and terrific human being. And I guess it's true what they say about love improving the disposition; I was a man in love, all right, and my altruism was as boundless as my joy. So I picked up the phone while Denise was showering, dialed Liz, heard her pick up and sat there, smoking calmly, as my good nature shattered with my dreams. Liz had heard, through a contact on the Coast, about the coming wedding of Gaby and Mark, and she wanted some confirmation from a person close to the source. I truthfully told her I didn't know anything about it, but from the wealth of details she'd already accrued, I was sure the story was correct. So that was that. I had been screwed, played with by a super scam-artist, and the shock of her falseness raced through me with a heat so intense it made me sweat.

I must have turned white or red or some unusual color because when Denise walked into the bedroom, she asked me if I was sick. I picked up on her cue and told her I didn't feel great, so she put me to bed, convinced that I'd caught some kind of rare Midwestern virus, and I just lay there wondering if I should mention what I'd heard to her, knowing I couldn't without giving away the real cause of my affliction. It was so goddamned ironic: An hour ago, I had been praying for the opportunity to bring up Gaby, to talk about her in any context, just to bring her closer, had even been fantasizing that our weekend had given her the courage to break with Mark and started planning how I was going to give Denise the news as gently as possible. But suddenly, everything was changed. Now, and ever after, I would never mention Gaby unless it couldn't be avoided, would purge her from my thoughts and eliminate her from my daydreams. As Gaby was addicted to Mark, I was addicted to Gaby. She'd fooled me into thinking she was half-way cured, but she hadn't been, probably hadn't even wanted to be; but I was going to beat her at her own game. I, Terry Barron, was going to do the impossible. I was going to get over the woman I loved, if it took a lobotomy. But, for now, I sought refuge in my silent, black rage, soothing my hurt with the balm of vengeance.

I lay awake that night, constructing an elaborate game plan to shock her out of her brattishness, to force her to feel pain for the pain she'd caused me. Now, looking back, I wonder. Now my actions seem much simpler and far less noble. Now, I think I wanted to destroy her because I couldn't have her, wanted to punish her for making that fact so abundantly clear to me.

At the time, I seriously wondered whether she had used me to make Mark jealous enough to agree to marry her or whether the very sight of him made me simply cease to exist for her. Finally, it was the latter reason that drove me back to New York; I couldn't stand her obvious indifference anymore than I could deal with my own shame, for I, a consummate student of human nature, had been taken but good by a consummate actress, one who had proved herself the most accomplished of hypocrites as well as the most wanton of lovers.

That unspeakable thought led me further asea, into an examination of what she'd actually used me for. As a last-minute substitute playmate for a decadent couple of days? As a tool to use against Mark? As a sexual release? A trick? And if that last was the reason, it was monstrous, for she demanded from her playmates not merely love but endless adoration.

In more lucid moments, and they were few, it occurred to me that I was acting like a teen-ager, that we had gone to some lengths not to promise anything definite to each other, and that, if only in my heart, I had quickly broken my part of the bargain by hoping too much, thereby deserving what I got. But when I got to this argument, my thoughts always took the following direction: that somehow, to her, the consummation of our affair had totally canceled out the long years of our friendship; that, having used me, she was casting me aside. She was, after all, truly the ice princess of our first, turbulent meeting, incredibly manipulative for reasons I would never unpuzzle. And that last morning in Chicago, her automatic assumption that we'd have a final roll in the hay made me hate her with a violence I didn't know I was capable of. She had ruined me in some unfathomable way, robbed me of my innocence and my belief in love. I wished for her only the worst kind of future. And, to my subsequent dismay, I was to get my wish.

chapter thirty-six

LOS ANGELES,
May 1981

WHEN she awoke at twelve, Mark was gone, but in the place where his head had recently rested lay a stack of thousand dollar bills—quite a lot of them. At the bottom of the pile was a note:

> *Turning thirty should be fun. Take the day off and buy yourself something nice for the party. Your hubby.*

She would, of course, have preferred a more intimate surprise, but given the fact that his meetings with the studio were taking up more and more of his time, Gaby was impressed that he'd bothered at all.

Rising from the bed, grabbing for the bills and letting some of them flutter to the rug, she'd padded to the windows and looked out over the lugubrious expanse of a Los Angeles devoid of sunlight. Such a May morning would, in the East, have been sparkling and fragrant and filled with springtime revelers. But in LA, only in LA, it was overcast, threatening rain but never delivering, promising to burn off the smog but never getting around to it—the kind of disappointment that came to Southern California in week-long stretches, at the end of which four or five hours of half-hearted sun did little to improve the disposition or brighten the heart. Observing the gloom, she had felt a stab of something like terror at the bad birthday omen.

Now, at three, nestled in the cushy confines of a Rodeo Drive boutique dressing room, she still felt vaguely uneasy. She had half-heartedly rejected a green Grecian Galanos—too matronly; a pink taffeta de la Renta—too Academy Awards; a Lagerfeld, a Blass, a Givenchy, and a St. Laurent. In between gowns, vaguely uneasy, she had called the house to see if Mark had checked in. He hadn't. His office at the studio reported that he'd stopped in before his luncheon meeting but hadn't returned since then. His behavior had always been nothing if not erratic, but something about his mood lately had her worried. Since Chicago, since the wedding, he'd treated her with an almost psychotic possessiveness mixed with a barely disguised antisexual fury, which baffled her. The closest she could come to deciphering it was that he was taking out on her his increasingly dire anxieties over *Sirens' Song*, which was now so far over budget she could no longer even guess at the figure. The stockyards set that Mark had reconstructed on a studio backlot had cost well into the millions. Much more elaborate than it had to be, it was clearly a mad waste of money, but Mark had demanded, and the studio had gracefully gone along. It had continued to amaze her, this big business eagerness to throw good money after bad. Maybe that was what was wrong. Maybe Mark sensed her unarticulated but profound disapproval of what seemed to her the squandering of somebody else's money. Maybe he felt she was waiting for the ax to fall on his great and glorious thirty-million-dollar folly, anxious to say I told you so, and that shook his manhood along with his grandiose paranoia.

He considered himself an entrepreneur, but she wondered. He was, finally, too spoiled to compromise, too impatient to negotiate—a brilliant bullshit artist supremely well-equipped to snow front offices out of millions. But he had flourished in the seventies, that halcyon time of creative accounting when the bottom line was as open to interpretation as the *I Ching*. Now, two years later, the baby moguls were floundering—Coppola's Zoetrope Studios had gone broke, *Heaven's Gate* was a debacle for United Artists, and so on. But Mark Groseman, made defiant by flattery and cocaine, just kept filming, refusing even to consider the possibility that time was running out and that somebody soon—maybe even a clerk in the accounting department—would happen across the burgeoning budget of the celluloid sandbox on the backlot and call it to the attention of someone above him. Maybe somebody already had. Mark's manic joviality of the last few days, coupled with his frantic planning of the Bistro party—ostensibly for her birthday, but really for his "people"—made her think that something was up. That meeting today with the studio—he'd down-played it, but his behavior made her feel it was serious.

Staring disaffectedly at herself in an Armani satin dinner suit, she tried to concentrate on the fact that, although she neither needed nor wanted a new gown, she'd have to buy something to satisfy Mark and to reward the saleslady's hours of sugary solicitude. She could, of course, settle for one of Philippe's new dinner dresses, but to pay for a Valmont seemed an inexcusable extravagance. Still, such extravagance was absolutely in keeping with the town in which she found herself and the company she kept. Mark was the king of squandering, and she, as his consort, could hardly do less than follow his head. What she really wanted was to go home, so the Valmont was requested, brought out, and tried on, and, of course, it was "her" because it had been designed with her in mind.

She looked ravishing, and she knew it, but for some perverse reason, she resented being told that by a commission saleslady. Still, she announced she would take it, stepped out of it and handed it to the saleslady who, beaming triumphantly, left her alone at last.

Studying herself in the mirror, she found she was close to tears. It was tough, turning thirty. She had been taught, in the sixties, to fear it, but only abstractly, because "thirty" lay so far in the future that she had centuries before she would have to grapple with giving up being young.

Yet, mystifyingly enough, it had arrived, and at a time when she had everything everybody else wanted—fame, beauty, celebrity, wealth, even the marriage she'd dreamed of years ago—but had somehow lost, incomprehensibly lost, the one single thing she yearned for—to be loved not because she was valuable as a beauty, as a celebrity, as a wealthy woman, but just because she was herself, because she was delightful and smart and smart-ass and would be all these things, and therefore just as valuable, when she was eighty. She wanted somebody who would hold her, no matter what, who would always make her feel young, but all that had terminated abruptly in a hotel room in Chicago just when she was on the verge of freedom.

And now, left alone, facing a future of collapsing

expectations and imminent disasters, she thought she saw the sinister softening of her jaw line, the fledgling crow's feet when she smiled, a certain diminishing of the luster of her hair and eyes, and the vision hurled her into absolute despair.

Dressing hurriedly in jeans, sneakers, and sweat shirt, she paid for the dress in cash, Arab-style, threw the change into her bag, grabbed the box, and rushed back to the car. As soon as she got home she would fall immediately alseep, she thought, as she drove quickly through the morbid afternoon.

Turning into the driveway and getting out of the car, she was struck by an unnatural quiet. A third bad omen. The front door was open, but the Mexican maid was nowhere to be found.

Maybe she had gone shopping. Gaby couldn't remember giving her the afternoon off, but was actually relieved not to have to talk to anyone. Making her way along the tiled corridor to the bedroom, she was conscious of a silence so profound that the slight sucking sound her sneakers made against the tiles echoed jarringly. To her surprise, the bedroom door was shut, but she turned the knob and pushed open the door, preparing, as she passed into the room, to hurl the dress box onto the gigantic bed. The box, as it happened, was already in flight when she noticed she wasn't alone.

A vision of a tall, lean, nude woman rose to her view before the windows, not moving, not at first, until the sound of the door shutting caused her to turn with a breathy, "Mark? Mark, baby?" So she was no wraith. She was real, real as the joint in her hand, real as the shock in Gaby's eyes as she stared across the room at a mirror image of herself.

* * *

As if in defiance of Gaby's shocked immobility, the double slowly raised the joint to her lips and dragged deeply. Allowing herself a moment of long, slow pleasure, she then flashed a broad smile, gaily chirped, "Happy birthday!" and began to walk toward Gaby, hand extended in a burlesque parody of good breeding. "I'm Amy," she said effervescently, then, as Gaby's hand failed to grasp her proffered one, she allowed her effusiveness to simmer down to disappointment. It was then, at close range, that the extraordinary resemblance broke down into clever makeup, identical hairstyle, studied expressions and gestures—into a performance of Gaby in a drama whose script Gaby couldn't even imagine. Torn between confusion and rage, Gaby was too baffled to respond, and the two might have stood there, faced off in a weirdly restrained encounter, had not Mark's voice echoed from the front door and down the length of the hall to the bedroom. "Hey, Amy, darlin', I'm back! It's here, and it's fantastic!" And he strode through the door, clearly as high as a kite, brandishing a champagne bottle in one hand and a bag of cocaine in the other.

The sight of Gaby stopped him short, but only momentarily. "Gaby, baby!" He was so high that he was flushed and his pupils were huge, obscuring focus, aiming for the entire room. Hurling the sweating champagne bottle onto the bed, he grabbed her in a fevered embrace and almost panted, "Juanita didn't think you'd be home before five!" His attempt at contact made her suddenly pull away, surprising him. "Hey—" He looked for clarity to Amy. "What's the matter here? Aren't you two getting along?"

"Mark," Gaby managed to say, despite a growing panic, "Mark, what *is* this?"

"Baby, baby, baby," he crooned, trying, and failing, to link both women in a single embrace, for Gaby moved swiftly out of range and he was left with one arm around Amy's shoulder. "This here's your big birthday present!" His second grab for her failed.

"Mark." Gaby had moved to the door and stood her ground, unyielding as a statue. "What the hell is going on?"

"Honey—" He let his hand drop from Amy's shoulder to her hand, clasped it, and walked with her in Gaby's direction. "For my wife, the woman who has everything"—and he held Amy at arm's length as if he were presenting her—"the ultimate gift for my adorable little narcissist. A once-in-a-lifetime chance to get it on with the person she loves best in the world," and he placed his free hand on Amy's back, firmly but awkwardly thrusting her directly at Gaby.

"Really, Ms. Blake—I mean, Gaby," the girl, who was very young and very intimidated, blurted, "I really think you're *beautiful*!"

"So, go on girls, let's all be friends." Mark had deposited the bag of coke on a table and extracted from his bomber jacket pocket a small vial with a spoon attached to the cap. Filling the spoon with cocaine, he moved closer to where the two women stood, Amy breathless with anticipation, Gaby simply frozen to the spot.

Helping himself to a couple of spoonfuls of the coke, he then served Amy, who snorted eagerly, tossing back her head, then said, giggling, "Hey, this is really fun!" Refilling the spoon, Mark moved close, very close, to Gaby, who made no move to resist him. When he reached for her to pull her toward him and down to the spoon she was so compliant, he smiled, "All right. My little brat has decided to behave like a regular girl. And we're all going to have a great time. Now let's just get her high.'' He was raising the spoon to her nostril just as her hand flew up, interrupting his, knocking the spoon and the vial from his hand, but continuing on, weakly, to make contact with his face. But he wasn't discouraged. ''Oh, baby, baby,'' he crooned, this time grabbing her hair and somehow, by surprising her, forcing her down to the rug. ''Just look at this naughty, unappreciative little brat, Annie——''

''Amy,'' came the correction from the breathless girl standing above them.

''Yeah, Amy, just look at what my ungrateful girl did. She spilled our coke all over the rug. Now she'll have to lick it all up.'' He had Gaby's neck in a wrestler's lock, and he was forcing her head down toward the spot where most of the coke had spilled. ''Lick it!'' he commanded, ''Lick it up!'' She was so flush to the floor, she could barely turn her head to breathe when, at the last second, he changed his mind and grabbed her up, roughly cradling her in his arms. ''Oh, forget that. Hey, Amy baby, hand me the baggie!'' and the girl complied eagerly, exclaiming, ''You play like this all the time?''

''Not enough. Not until now, Amy dear, but now is a whole new ball game. Help me, sweetie.'' He directed her to retrieve the spoon and fill it with the cocaine, while he kept his grip on Gaby. ''Okay, hand it to me, darling. Let's make sure our naughty girl takes her medicine!'' And restraining Gaby's head, he shoved the spoon up her nostrol. ''Snort it, cunt!'' he screamed. ''Snort it all up, you whore!''

And she did because, suddenly, she was terrified. Mark was mad, for whatever reason, and he was strong, really strong, strong enough to kill her if it caught his fancy, and it might, because he might enjoy it, because he was berserk. So she snorted. Then, after he refilled the spoon, still holding her, he shoved it up her other nostril, and she snorted again.

"See, Amy, isn't she a doll when she obeys? A perfect little lady, but a snob, Amy, a real snob, I'm sorry to say. Thinks she's too good for me. Makes it plain that money can't buy her. She's got her own," he mumbled as he refilled the spoon and force-fed her more cocaine. "She's got all the money in the world, but you know what they say about the rich—she hoards it and cries poor. You know, I bet the rich bitch wouldn't even deign to help her husband out of a little jam. No, she'd never do it for Mark Groseman. Maybe for that fag of a writer she's always been wet for, but not for me. Not for a real man," and he released the spoon, letting it drop down to the floor next to the baggie, and pinioned her, applying his hands to her neck. "If she won't play, what do we need her for? I ask you, Amy? Why do I need her, when I've got you?" The girl had bent down to retrieve the spoon and the coke and now was merrily helping herself to more—a Mark Groseman fan, turned on by the drug and the game.

At last, the adrenaline of fear and the energy induced by the drug reached Gaby, making her strong, making her strong enough to gather all her power together and to shrug Mark's hands massively away from her neck. Her movement was effective, but not as effective as the reaction it produced in him, for he seemed to collapse. When she rose to her knees, he was curled up on the rug, a fetal madman, weeping. Surprised by her own clarity, she got to her feet and faced the still-excited replica of herself.

"All right, Amy, I think you'd better leave now. Does he owe you any money?"

Instantly, the girl bristled. "Of course not," she insisted proudly. "I'm no whore. I'm an actress."

''Well, then.''Gaby walked to the bed, took up the dress box, and handed it to the other woman. ''I assume we wear the same size. Take this.'' And as she handed Amy the unworn gown, she knew everything she must do, in the next few minutes, the next few days, the next few years.

''Now, do you have your car? No? Okay. Get dressed. There's a bathroom down the hall. Third door on the right. While you're dressing, I'll call a cab, and I want you waiting outside when it comes. Do you have money for a cab?'' The girl was hustling around the room, grabbing her clothes, without letting go of the dress box. ''Here,'' Gaby dug in her purse, pulled out a hundred dollar bill, and handed it to her. ''Now get out of here,'' she said, and the girl disappeared.

In about ten minutes, Gaby heard the front door slam. A car door opened and shut, the cab departed, and then there was only the sound of Mark's weeping.

''Mark''—she strode over to him determinedly—''Mark, stop this at once and get up. We've got to be at the Bistro in two hours, for your . . .'' she paused just a second, ''for your . . . party.''

At once the tears subsided, and red-eyed and broken, he looked up at her. ''Forget about the party. There isn't going to be any party. There isn't going to be any party ever again.''

She had given herself until the turn-off—about five minutes—to decide. She'd left the house with her mind made up, but once behind the wheel and out on the freeway, she'd weakened, allowing all the conflicting feelings of the last awful day to blur her clarity and diminish her resolve. In a now-or-never situation, she had let herself get stuck in a then-or-soon evasion, but time was running out, so she'd set a limit for herself—the turn-off, a perfect symbol of her predicament.

Mark's party had happened after all. She had managed to calm him down enough to admit that nothing had actually been cancelled, so she fed them both some tranquilizers and set to work. She quickly did her make-up, rummaged through her closet, settled on a single-shouldered Valmont midnight blue satin column, then pulled her unset hair back into a topknot, grabbed up large diamond pendant earrings, and dressed fast. Then she had virtually dressed him and gotten them both to the Bistro on time, absolutely astonished at her own strength. For it had come at last; the studio was shutting down *Sirens' Song*. Well, yes, Mark grudgingly admitted, as she drove them toward Beverly Hills, there had been warnings, but they hadn't seemed serious. There were nothing but philistines in the front offices now, business school graduates, for Christ's sake, unbelievable assholes. Would they let the print go? she had asked him. Jesus Christ, he had replied, digging in his pocket for the vial of coke, what if they would? He couldn't raise that kind of money. What about the ranch and the house? It was then he confessed that the earlier warnings had been very serious, indeed. In fact, a month ago, the studio had refused further financing, so he had put up the house and the ranch as collateral for a short-term bank loan at 17 percent to finish the picture by the outside deadline the studio had given him. But the picture wasn't finished, and the loan was due, and he was going to have to default. He could sell the plane and the car, but the money they would bring didn't amount to a drop in the bucket. He had obliterated his lines of credit, and he couldn't raise a fucking cent. There was just no way. His only hope, he lectured her wildly, was to snow another studio into picking up the picture. He'd have to start shopping it at once, before those assholes who'd betrayed him started bad-mouthing the film. He figured he had till the end of the weekend to cook up a deal. Three lousy days, when everybody was hard to reach. They had really fucked him over, really raped him.

It was good, though, that he hadn't canceled the party, he said, as if the decision had been at his whim, not at her insistence. That would have been the worst thing to do. He had to be there, had to assure his people that whatever rumors they might have heard were totally unfounded. Then, tomorrow, maybe even late tonight, he'd put in a call to Barry, get in touch with Sherry, maybe even take a meeting with George Lucas—he had all the money in the world. It broke his heart that they were so close to wrapping. Those dumb bastards!

The closer they got to the restaurant, the more he raved, which made his transformation, when he finally greeted his devotees, all the more remarkable. His ebullience was so overwhelming, his largesse so boundless, that Gaby felt, for a split second, as if she'd hallucinated the last six hours. What had happened in the bedroom, what had taken place between them, seemed as unreal as a nightmare, a recurring nightmare perhaps, but a nightmare nonetheless. For here, before her eyes, was the old, glorious Groseman. Groseman as Olivier as Henry V, jollying up the troops before the battle of Agincourt. Groseman full of piss and vinegar and bursting with ideas and appreciation. Groseman the champ, a man who threw himself on no one's mercy, least of all hers. So, as he began to glow, she was again relegated to the Siberia of everyone's attention, birthday or no, last-minute, vulgar but expensive presents aside.

Only Denise, as it happened, had gone to any real trouble, presenting her with a pair of jade and gold earrings that Gaby had admired in passing during one of their infrequent shopping forays, which happened only because Mark enjoyed the idea. Gaby wished Denise hadn't done it because Gaby didn't like her, hadn't liked her at their first meeting, didn't care for her tonight. It had taken her years to put a name to the feeling, and, when it turned out to be as base a sentiment as jealousy, she only resented Denise more for it. She resented her because of Terry, because the older woman had secured a lifetime lock on his affections, because—she'd seen it happen in Chicago—he couldn't, or wouldn't, give up Denise for any other woman. That she, Gaby, had been the other woman and had been harshly, rudely dumped, made her wish Denise the worst, if only to deprive Terry of the one thing he needed. Denise was the last person in the world she wanted to be remembered by. Thinking of Terry, missing him, especially tonight, still wanting him although he didn't want her, made her feel even more hopeless, even older, than she already was feeling. And lonelier, increasingly lonelier as, almost in defiance, the party whirled around her.

Mark had taken over the entire upstairs of the lavish restaurant, and Gaby for the first time wondered how he was going to pay for it. He couldn't charge it to the production. If he didn't find another studio fast, she'd end up paying for it. Excusing herself from a conversation in which she was not really being included, she made her way to the ladies' room. From beneath each of the two stalls, two sets of expensively clad feet were visible, and the silences punctuated with laughter meant that the ladies were preparing for the second half of the evening with a cocaine booster. When they exited, they flashed her polite, distant smiles, and she realized that they were young, very young, and that they regarded her as another generation, as an adult. It was unbearable. As unbearable as everything else that had happened on this, the worst day of her life. She was an emotional mess, exhausted from the afternoon's episode, edgy from the coke and fuzzy from the tranquilizers. Those decisions that had seemed so clearly right at four seemed almost too daring at eleven thirty. Well, she still had time to mull it all over. And at least she didn't *look* haggard; she'd get through tonight and then, as they say, tomorrow would be another day.

Leaving the ladies' room, distracted, she made a wrong turn and found herself in a short corridor of pantrylike rooms. She was about to turn and head back when she heard Mark's voice from inside the shelter of one of the rooms. "I can't. I can't tomorrow." God, he was already on the phone, wheeling and dealing. She was dying to know who he was talking to, to what sort of wild agreement he was consigning all their lives, so she hovered just long enough to be surprised when a woman's voice cooed, "But why, darling? Why can't you, Mark? You've never turned me down before." She lingered just long enough to recognize the voice as Denise Sullivan's.

She hadn't had the energy to be shocked, just mildly surprised at this latest piece of evidence in the case against Mark Groseman. It had often occurred to her, although she had always quickly dismissed the idea, that Mark probably slept with all his leading ladies—good art and intimacy and all that jazz. He probably also boffed every girl in the cast and on the technical staff. He probably always had, even when the two of them were more or less getting along, and he would have defended his actions, had she ever accused him, on the grounds that a film was a communal enterprise. That she was not allowed the same artistic license just meant that Mark was the boss, that criticizing her performance and shooting down all her ideas was merely a further acknowledgment of his macho double standard. Which meant that if she were to leave him, she would have to do it very carefully.

And so, she'd set out early the morning after the party, before he had slept off the pills of last night, which had first made him teary and then melodramatically apologetic for the afternoon scene. Slamming the door of the BMW, she'd taken a long look at the house, honestly not knowing whether she'd ever see it again. She'd sped around hairpin curves and down long, thin freeways, trying to force herself either to go or stay. What did she owe him? He'd deceived her, mistreated her professionally, even physically abused her, although, admittedly, she felt no fear toward him now. Then why did she still feel dread at the thought of severing him from her life? Maybe he represented her youth, and leaving him would bring the early onset of middle age. That was part of it. If she had Terry . . . but she didn't. Denise did, that was all too clear. Good old Denise, she thought, you'll follow me beyond the grave.

The prospect of a future without real shape and definition was also terrifying. Even the awful but familiar seemed preferable to the unknown, and the horror of being alone again. Maybe she was famous, but she was definitely alone, loved and cared for by many, as long as the loving and caring didn't interfere with a lover or a wife to whom their first loyalty was pledged. Maybe there was something in her that made her less than lovable. If so, she was soon going to find it out and have to face her own failure.

But, all that aside, there was the guilt. She could

always have justified walking out on Mark—except now. How could she when he was really down? There had to be a way to bail him out, to approach the studio with a reasonable plan for securing the print, and together they might figure it out. If he'd listen to her. She'd have to get him out of LA, away from the coke and the craziness. That, at least, would clear her karmic balance sheet and allow her to exit with a clear conscience—if she was willing to go through another couple of circles of hell to get back to purgatory. One last turn around the track and then home free? Right? And yet . . .

Decide, she scolded herself, *decide*! You have changed directions five times in the last half hour, and time is running out. Decide. Don't wait till it feels right. It won't. Probably ever. You've got to decide by the time you get to the turn-off. And as the exit sign loomed up ahead, presenting the stakes of her decision in great, black letters, she took the deepest breath of her life and made up her mind.

BOOK IV

chapter thirty-seven

CANNES,
May 1982

I WAS minutes out of Mougins. My heart was thundering against my rib cage, my mouth was dry, and I could feel the insistent staccato of the pulse in my neck. I was minutes away from getting what I had desperately wanted, and for the first time in my life, I doubted my own courage. I was scared the way kids get scared at ghost stories, and admitting that brought on a *frisson* to add to my other physical symptoms. I was scared because you never just get what you want, never get it on your terms. This was a quest, and I was coming to the end of it, but up ahead, the tiny medieval skyline of Mougins, not unlike the castle of the Grail, marked only the beginning of the fight. What waited there, what truths would be horribly revealed to me, what sadnesses would spring to life, what uglinesses would rise to the surface of my strangely innocent memories? And the pain. I didn't want to feel the pain again that I'd felt on that Saturday evening, just about a year ago. May sixteenth, it was. A little before eleven. I was in Brooklyn, I recall, feeling cranky.

There'd been something weird all along about the day. I was trying not to smoke, my teams had been losing, and then, during a long, tortured phone call from LA, I'd lost Denise—maybe for good, perhaps to fate, but possibly to a gentleman both unnamed and unclaimed. In the last year, we'd been growing apart, so I wasn't stunned; it was the method, not the fact, of her dismissal that got to me. Her method—generous to the last, the bitch—was to suggest that I should find a nice girl and get married. Clearly, a fatal first. The entire conversation was conducted on a level of brittle banter that, by the end of an hour, had left me drained, if relieved. Well, hell, I told myself, it's not as though you've lost everything. My publisher, after all, had praised my new novel as twice as good as *Sirens' Song*; I still hung out with the best, the most lucrative, and the most beautiful; Calvin Klein and I were on a first-name basis, and Brooke Shields blushed whenever she saw me.

Granted, losing Gaby was still so raw a hurt that I physically cringed when I saw her picture in the columns, but even so, I'd been able to keep on functioning, relatively unimpaired. No, Denise's rejection got me on a more vulnerable spot, right on my male ego. I had always been loved, and I was used to it, expected it, always found love when I needed it. And now, I hated the guy Denise had fallen for, just wanted to off him, because he commanded more love than I did. I resented him considerably more than I resented Denise, and getting in touch with that resentment opened up an old and agonizing wound. Gaby. Gaby and Mark. I felt the pain and the confusion as if it had happened yesterday.

My arrogance, born of years of indulgence and cultivation by women, had always blinded me to the superior nature of Mark Groseman's charms, to the reason for his Svengali-like powers over a girl who could have loved me if she'd let herself. He treated her like garbage, exploited her fame and elegance for his own crass purposes and, to top it off, cheated on her every chance he got. I, on the other hand, was faithful, fun, indulgent—and not short. So why was I always runner-up? I had waged this argument with myself for years, never arriving at a conclusion, never appreciating why I'd been bested. And here was the possibility of a second Svengali, depriving me of my security blanket when I needed it most.

After the phone call I'd gotten up, idly turned on the television, and mumbling, "Fuck 'em all," gone to the kitchen to grab a beer. I was back in the living room when a provocative line of copy in the news announcer's opening teaser caught my attention. I had sauntered over to the couch and managed to get comfortable, so I was lying down when the TV guy related the story behind the "Hollywood tragedy." Production had been shut down by the studio on the $32-million *Sirens' Song* and the distraught director, Mark Groseman, while flying to his ranch that evening, had crashed his Cessna into a mountainside, a probable suicide attempt, killing himself and his wife, the international cover girl . . . Gaby Blake.

I was too numb to reach for a cigarette, too blasted to remember I'd stopped smoking, too blown away even to hear the phone until what must have been the tenth ring. Denise, sobbing wildly, surprised by my apparent calm, assumed I hadn't heard, then, discovering that I had, cursed me for my icy indifference. "My God," she wept, "I thought you and Gaby used to be . . . so close. Have you no heart? And that talented man, that genius—gone. Oh, Terry, I'm so distraught.'' Through the thick haze that separated me from my feelings, the thought occurred to me that Groseman had been the latest man in Denise's life, but I quickly buried it, along with the stab of exhilaration mixed with despair that must always accompany the defeat—or demise—of an enemy.

I managed a ''Well,'' mainly to give her a chance to conquer the choked sobs that had, for the moment, deprived her of the opportunity to mourn on.

''Terry, I simply can't be alone. I just can't. I'm flying in on the Red Eye tonight. . . . Can you meet me at River House?''

''What time?''

''Oh, I don't know. Check the airlines. Whenever the Red Eye gets in. Oh, Terry, be there, please,'' and her grief again overwhelmed her. Denise, always a star performer, had pulled it off again. How could anyone, including a guy she'd kissed off fifteen minutes before, refuse to come to the aid of a woman in that kind of misery?

''Okay, Denise, try to pull yourself together.'' My words, in a crisis situation, careered toward cliché. ''I'll be there. Don't worry. Okay?''

''Okay, darling, and thank you,'' and she was gone.

I didn't call the airlines, whichever one it was, because I realized I couldn't take the yogi-calm answering-machine voice of the airline personel, because I was too distracted to be put on hold or to have to wait so much as a minute for information. I didn't call because, as I sat on the couch, not hearing the weather report, not caring if it rained or was sunny the next day, I became aware that I was slipping into a state where words, any words, hurt my ears, hurt my throat, hurt my nervous system. Eventually, figuring I'd just head toward River House, bound to arrive before Denise did, I arose, grabbed a heavy fisherman's sweater, foraged in the desk drawer for the keys to Denise's, finding, to my relief, an unopened pack of Camels at the back of the drawer, and fled the room where I'd first heard about Gaby.

The night, when I walked out into it, was mellowed with just a hint of a tang from the river, and that surprised me. I think I'd expected winter to have come with the news, and the lushness of the night seemed inappropriate, fashioned for joy not sadness.

My steps took me, without my ever having to decide, to the Esplanade, still busy, late on a beautiful spring night, with strolling couples and stray men looking for love. I stood by the river, leaning against the railing, lit a cigarette—my first in three weeks—and although it tasted awful, I forced myself to smoke it down to the tip, expecting the tobacco to steady me. That the nicotine clanged against my nerve endings, almost making me twitch, was less surprising than the lump that arose in my throat as I inhaled. By the time I arced the butt over the railing, I was on the verge of tears. For this was the spot where we'd ended up on another spring night, some four years in the past, when everything was just beginning, a moment when we'd both been high on our mutual invulnerability.

The grief still unspent, the mistakes yet unmourned, ran up my spine like a chill, and I suddenly felt hostile toward the easy, pleasant scene around me, resented the lovers, even resented the playful dogs and the glow of the skyline before me. Why were the lights still on, anyway? Abruptly, I turned away from the river and strode aimlessly on, my memories directing my steps, my loss craving the morbid satisfaction of cigarette after cigarette.

In the middle of the Brooklyn Bridge, where my memories brought me, I bawled like a baby, smoking all the while, utterly alone and grateful for the huge arena for my grief. As I walked north from Wall Street, throat aching from the years of tears still to be shed, I collected myself enough not to be singled out as a crazy by a passerby or a cop. Through Chinatown, through the dark and depressing streets first off the Bowery, then off the East Village, I walked in a daze, then, passing the scene of our first shooting, almost wept again. By the time I reached Twenty-first and Third, the tragedy of my folly struck me, for even though I'd forsaken Gaby, I'd done so with absolute assurance that some time in the future we'd make it right, that I'd write a book so fabulous she'd have to love me for it, even that turning thirty, which she had, ironically, the day before, would shake her to her senses and send her running to the timeless comfort of my arms. Now there was no future, no glory she could share with me, and what struck me next was that men, for all their advantages in this society, are allowed no socially permissable outlet for grief. I'd cried, but only in the cosmic privacy of the Brooklyn Bridge. I, like all other men, I guess, was shy of showing feelings, and that made it hurt the more. So, to kill the pain, I stepped into a bar in the high twenties and downed a double Jack. Likewise at a bar in the middle thirties, the forties, and the fifties, and by the time I turned east toward the river, I was drunk and my sorrow had turned to rage. On a deserted street, I kicked a garbage can with the force of an out-of-shape ex-soccer player, barely restrained myself from slamming my fist through glass windows and into wooden doors, crossed First Avenue rebelliously against the light, waiting until a few cars appeared and had to stop short. I had planned not to walk past her house, but somehow I ended up in front of it, dumbfounded, pretending nothing had happened since the afternoon I'd dropped her off after her shattering experience of meeting Philippe's lover. I should never have left her that afternoon. If I'd stayed, things might have—would have—been incredibly different, I accused myself. Walking up the steps, seeing her name on the bell, made me remember the first night, when I'd rung and rung, and she, not knowing it was me, had refused to answer back. A cute meeting—with an unspeakable ending. I turned and walked toward River House, overshooting it in favor of the steep and dangerous steps that led down to a park, then up across the transverse of the East River Drive, down which we'd raced on our way to Brooklyn, then to the narrow benches that bordered the river. Breaking into another pack of cigarettes, I restrained myself from shouting obscenities at the occasional mindless jogger rushing past me. Insulted that life was going on, unfazed, around me, I cried a little more, and then, when, to my dismay, a couple, clearly young and in love, chose the bench next to mine on which to make out, I left in a hurry, ran all the way back to Denise's, and made it to the apartment just in time to puke my guts out.

Denise arrived, like Niobe, all tears, and I took care of her. I guess that was good because it gave me something to do, but somehow, the rupture that had begun by phone the night that Gaby died, had been signed, sealed, and delivered by the tragedy. We pretended it was like the old, easy days, but it wasn't. And when she flew back west for the memorial service, we both knew we were freer than we'd been since the day, ten years ago, when we met. We would still be friends, maybe even occasional bedmates, but not lovers. We were no longer obligated to each other, for, in those first days, we'd had to face facts: We'd both lost someone.

It was all true, our respective suspicions—Mark, I was positive, has been the person in her life, and although we never discussed any of this, I was sure she knew, through my grief, that there had been someone I'd loved more passionately than I loved her. So we'd slipped to second place in each other's affections, but our refusal, maybe only my refusal, to see that had prevented us from having what could probably have been some shot at happiness. Now, in that lackluster period of aftershock, I had to deal with the suspicion that it was my fear of intimacy that had guided me in the wrong directions, had choreographed my bad timing and misconceptions, had led me away from Gaby just when we were closest, and that what had defeated us was my own cowardice. It was only six months later, when my Vietnam novel, *Hellfire*, had both skyrocketed to the top of the best-seller lists and been extravagantly praised by the critics, when Denise had found herself the Italian nobleman and we were celebrating our mutual good fortune with a bon voyage lunch at Le Cirque, that I found my suspicions were true.

It was autumn, a glorious autumn, and we had just finished a luncheon laced with witty conversation and clouded, happy memories. Denise, clad in the latest, multilayered horse-blanket outfit, glowing with renewed youth, maybe even a face-lift, and the promise of a whole new fortune to spend, suggested we stroll through Central Park. Out of the blue, as we walked she asked me, "You were in love with Gaby, weren't you?"

"Denise," I was honestly shocked, "what——"

"Come on, kid, I always thought so, but I wasn't sure. Then in Chicago, I was positive."

"You were?"

"Everybody was. It was obvious that you were wild about each other."

"Sure we should be talking about this?"

"I'm sure if you are, babe," she said, smiling bravely.

"Well, yeah, I guess . . ." I was having trouble going on, "yes. I guess I was . . . in love with her."

She guided me toward the reservoir, where late lunchers were idly reading their newspapers, where children's shouts could be heard across the expanse of the water, and sat me down.

"So what happened?" she asked.

"Huh?"

"I mean, when you two walked through that hotel room door, you were glowing, both of you. I could see it. Mark must have been able to see it. But then you left, and then there was that wedding announcement. I couldn't understand it—one minute you could barely keep your eyes off one another and the next minute you were gone and she was marrying Mark. It wasn't that you fooled me, but you confused me, buster, yeah, you did that. I've always wondered if you confused yourselves."

"Yeah," I meditated, "maybe so. You know, Denise, I thought she was using me to get Mark." I looked at her, with a gaze as callow and sincere as in the months after we first met, all those years ago.

"Is that what you thought?" she asked me, growing tougher with every syllable. "Is that what you really thought? After all your experience with women? After the way you made the Karen character exactly like her? You knew her so well, how could you understand so little?

"Barron, you are such a turkey! Didn't it ever occur

to you in Chicago that maybe Mark had sprung the whole wedding thing on her, that she was as horrified as you were when I came out of the bathroom and found you in a state of shock?'' I was dazzled by her insight, impressed by her years of restraint. ''My God, the wedding was a major media event before he ever proposed to her. Pretend you're her, back then. She must have been desperate, trying to figure out some way of pulling out without embarrassing Mark.''

And, of course, that hadn't ever occurred to me.

''It was so obvious that she loved you,'' Denise continued, mercilessly. ''Let me tell you, kid, I was at the wedding. She was the most melancholy bride I've ever seen. She was mourning you.''

''God, Denise,'' I snapped. ''Why didn't you say something then?''

She smiled ruefully. ''Because it wasn't my place to bring you together. Don't imagine that I wanted to give you up. Not then.''

Since we were now into confessions, I pressed on. ''What about you and Mark? I always thought there was something between you.''

''Right again, baby. There sure was.'' She was too larger-than-life to back off. ''Mark. Hmmm. Okay. Seeing you and Gaby was making me feel old. He made me feel young. And he made me feel like an artist. I made him feel established—and glamorous. And he is—he *was*—good, Terry. There's genius in that movie. It's a tragedy it'll never be seen.''

''Yeah,'' I mused, then asked her, relieved now that I *could* ask, ''Denise? Was Gaby any good in the picture? I mean, in the little I saw of the shooting she looked terrific, but Mark continually worked her over and criticized her. Why?''

''Well . . .'' She stopped to think. ''It's hard to tell

when you're right there in the middle of things, especially when you're jealous of a younger, more beautiful woman who's mixed up with your own man . . . but, yes, I think she was very good, but I also think she was fighting for your version of Karen, not Mark's, the same way she was always urging him to keep your version of the script, not his."

"I didn't know that."

"Yes, so their squabbles could be considered an artistic disagreement, but, really, I think he resented her—and resented you. She made a pretty good case, and he didn't want to hear it. I don't altogether blame him."

"Who was right?"

"I don't know, Terry. She had a point; the movie was getting so big, it was losing the love story. But Mark was the director, and the producer, not Gaby. Maybe she could have done it better, but that wasn't what she was hired for. And, you know, the more she pushed him one way, the more he went in the other direction. She kept trying to keep it small, he kept trying to make it bigger. So they were always at cross purposes, but I think he was a tremendously gifted director, and I bet she looks swell."

"You haven't seen any footage?"

"No, nobody in the cast did."

"Hey, Denise"—I had a brainstorm—"what's happened to the print?"

"I have no idea. I guess the studio still has it. I never thought to ask."

"Denise"—I realized I was hurrying her along, the force of my idea speeding my steps—"Denise, how would your future husband like to get into the movie business?"

"What do you—are you suggesting . . . ?" She was wide-eyed.

"Well, if nobody's seen the print, and you suspect it's great, and it's just languishing somewhere, why don't we try . . . ?"

"But, Terry, first of all, it's not finished——"

"There are ways, I bet there are ways."

"And, second, nobody wants a last film, you know, after the people are——"

"Maybe they don't, but what if it's a masterpiece?"

"Oh, well, maybe . . ."

"Listen, Denise," we had walked, without noticing it, all the way down to St. Patrick's. "Denise, listen, will you just talk to him? I'm sure they don't expect to recoup the enitre cost of the negative. If somebody promised them part of the potential profits, they might be willing to make a deal. It's not doing them any good the way it is. Will you try?"

"Well, all right," she promised, then looked at her watch. "Oh, Lord, it's four o'clock. Guido's due in any second. I've got to get back to the apartment. Good-bye, darling," she kissed me gently. "Walking east?"

"Not just now," I told her. "I've got a couple of errands."

"All right, then, I'll be in touch," and as she strolled away, I walked into St. Patrick's—the first time I'd been in a church since high school—and to my great surprise, in honor of a future that lay entirely in the past, I put my money in the box, lit a candle, and prayed.

So I had a mission, a grand passion, properly consecrated and prayed over. Denise, as good as her word, prevailed on her fabulously wealthy husband to pursue the possibility of purchasing the negative from the studio. The more I thought of finishing the movie, the more obsessed I became with what would be a memorial to Gaby—to our screwed-up, star-crossed love story, right up there on the silver screen. It had to happen, and as I awaited word from Denise, my grief, my numbness, actually began to lift a little. On every interview for *Hellfire*, I managed to mention *Sirens' Song* as well. When the movie offers started to come, I talked to every director who called, hoping I could kill two birds with one stone, and I actually was on the verge of mentioning the project to one or two big name guys, pending only Denise's call. So, with the rebirth of *Sirens' Song* to keep me going, the holidays weren't going to be quite so dismal as I'd expected, and the New Year held a promise of something better than mere loss because we were going to finish the picture, goddamnit.

And then, one day in December, the call came from Denise. "Hey, baby, got some word?" I veritably crowed.

"Yeah." She sounded less than thrilled.

"What's up?" My impatience was too uncontainable for me even to ask how she was.

"What's up, darling, is not going to make you happy."

Through plunging spirits, I managed to ask, "What's the problem? Too expensive?"

"No, Ter, it's not about money. It's about the print. It's gone."

"Gone? You mean somebody stole it?"

"No, dear, nobody stole it. Somebody bought it."

"Somebody bought it? Who? When?"

"Last fall, sometime in October. A European outfit named Phoenix Productions. Swiss-based. Nobody's heard of them, but they were solvent enough to put down a lot of dough."

"Why?"

"Nobody knows. Came as a big surprise to the studio."

"How can we get in touch with them?"

"We can't. Guido tried to contact them in Geneva, but there's no listed number. If the studio knows more, they're sure as hell not telling."

"It doesn't make any sense, Denise, none at all."

"Right, it sure doesn't. But at least somebody's bought it. Maybe we'll see the movie yet."

"I just can't let it go at that."

"Darling, sweetheart, you've got to let it go. You've got to. Promise me. It's out of our hands, Terry. It's over."

"All right, Denise, it's over," I told her grudgingly.

"All right, love, talk to you soon," and she rang off, knowing, as she must, that I didn't mean a word of that promise, that at that very moment I'd taken the vow and set off on the quest.

Months went by, and I talked to anybody who knew anybody who was connected to the studio, the film industry, foreign film companies, all to no avail. I did manage to find out the terms of the deal. Phoenix, whoever they were, had made a deal with the studio to the effect that the foreign company would take over the bank loan of about $21.5 million and the interest would be waived until completion of the film, which had an outside date of three months. That meant that, in effect, Phoenix and the studio were now partners. But that's all I could find out. I, a reporter with damned good credentials, couldn't make so much as a little tear in the veil of secrecy.

Until one day in the spring of '82 when I played back my answering machine to find a message that an administrative assistant to a Monsieur Corday of Phoenix Productions had called from Cannes. I hadn't found *Sirens' Song*, but *Sirens' Song* had found me. This Monsieur Corday, having heard of my interest in the picture, wanted to inform me that a finished print was now ready to be screened but that I would have to come to Cannes to see it. The assistant said no more, offered no information as to Phoenix's motivations, but she did mention Gaby and alluded to the fact that Monsieur Corday was aware of our friendship. And so it was that I drove into the walled city of Mougins, with the waves lapping languidly below me and the end of the quest directly above, in a little café inside the walls.

The hubbub from the film festival down the coast hadn't extended into the medieval solitude of Mougins, for the lovely little village was securely nestled in its own sense of the past. I found the café, parked on the street, and entered, hoping that the shaking in my knees and the croak in my voice weren't apparent to the proprietress.

"Ah, yes, monseiur, you're expected." She smiled and led me out onto a terrace where I saw a waiting figure, seated alone, facing the water. "Monsieur Corday." I approached the table as the figure turned toward me. Even in the starlight of the terrace, I could see he was handsome and elegant, dressed in a polo shirt and jeans. As I drew closer, I sensed we'd met before, and by the time I reached the table I realized that "Monsieur Corday" was Philippe de Valmont. Of course. Philippe. Of course. He, too, had loved Gaby.

"Monsieur Barron . . . Terry." He rose and shook my hand, "please excuse the masquerade. For business purposes, it was better that my name be kept out of the dealings with the studio. . . . Oh, don't bother to sit.

We're going on.'' Taking my arm in a gesture of easy camaraderie, he led me from the café.

''We're going to my house, up there in the hills. I thought it better if we met here so I could guide you. The house is, intentionally, difficult to find without aid.'' He proceeded to his Porsche and I to the De Lorean, and true to his word, he led me up and around, through forests and along tiny twisting roads, until we pulled up at an exquisite, almost medieval farmhouse.

We parked in the driveway, and he escorted me into the most beautiful and serene place I'd ever seen—flower-filled, with whitewashed walls against which centuries-old polished oak furniture gleamed exquisitely.

''Now, Terry, please come this way,'' and I followed him down winding steps into what I assumed would be a cellar.

I was still anxious as a cat, but the enchanted beauty of the house and the calming grace of Valmont's presence made me feel as though I'd wandered into a wizard's world where I was protected from harm, from pain, even from longing. For the first time in a year, I let myself feel pleasure, and when he admitted me to an exquisite little room, lit by electric torches in sconces, filled with couches covered in subdued but exquisite tapestry fabric, it took me a few moments to notice the far wall and realize I was in a screening room.

''Make yourself comfortable,'' Valmont told me. ''Can I get you something to drink? Champagne, perhaps? Because this is, after all, a kind of celebration.'' When I merely nodded yes, he disappeared and almost immediately returned with the champagne in a chilled, paper-thin crystal glass.

''The ashtray is here in front of you.'' He indicated a table. ''And a servant will refill your glass in so quiet a fashion, I promise you that you will not even notice.''

As I looked up at him, expecting him to sit, he shook his head. "No, I won't be joining you. As you can imagine, I've seen the film quite often enough. But I'll expect you afterwards in the living room. As the producer, I am most anxious for your opinion. All right, then, shall we begin?"

I nodded wordlessly, and as if by a magic command, the sconces dimmed and *Sirens' Song* began.

Two hours later, when the lights came back up, I just sat there with waves of something like ecstasy coursing through me. For the movie was a masterpiece. Even better, it was *our* masterpiece, Gaby's and mine—and Mark's—our shared vision come to life. Whoever Philippe had found to finish the picture was an artist, for the mysterious director had eliminated some of the cumbersome big scenes and the ones that were left gave the story just the right amount of scope, just enough sense of time and place to border the love story like the outer panels of a great triptych. It wasn't even that new scenes had been added, it was rather that every moment, given this exquisite economy, shone like a jewel—brilliant, unforgettable, tremendously affecting.

And Gaby. Gaby, in this treasure trove, was the greatest, the most priceless jewel—Karen, my Karen, more than my Karen, *our* Karen—a siren of such spirit and innocence that, had I not already loved her, I would have fallen in love with her that night. Only after five minutes, when the spell had worn off just a little, did I realize the miracle that was the last scene. Out of what bits and snatches—other scenes cut from the film—had they managed to fashion the ending, managed to put together an image of Gaby that had not existed and had, in fact, been done after she was gone? Finally, I rose and went up the stairs, searching for Philippe, searching for anyone in this enchanted castle. I was standing in the magnificent living room when I saw, on the terrace leading off from the living room, a misty figure leaning against the parapet, and I went toward it. A fog had fallen, and as I moved toward the terrace the figure—now I could see it was a woman—seemed to drift like an apparition in the other direction, away from me. But I continued toward it, the breeze and the fog strangely comforting, completely magical. And then the figure stopped moving, allowing me to come toward it, no longer fleeing. It turned to face me, and I saw, as if I'd lost my mind or stumbled into a spell from which I had not yet been released, that it was Gaby. Gaby, hair loose and caught up by the breeze. Gaby, tall and lean and graceful, all in lilac. Gaby, first solemn, then smiling, then radiant. Gaby.

chapter thirty-eight

CANNES,
May 1982

SHE had seen him walking from the car to the house, and even from that distance, she was warmed by the comfort of his physical presence. Even without seeing him smile, without receiving his touch, she could feel her heart literally leap. She had been waiting so long to see him that she was surprised by her calm—no adolescent nervousness, no fears of rejection, just deep anticipation and a contentment that built gracefully to joy as she heard his voice in the hall below.

Joy, because tonight was an ending to the misunderstandings that had conspired to keep them apart. Joy, because tonight was a beginning, and although it had taken a year of numbness and pain, then, slowly, of growth and maturity, she knew it had been worth it. Now, maybe only now, she was able to give him what he merited. Perhaps it had taken that time apart for them to be ready to meet again.

A year ago, the morning after her birthday, she had

decided against escape, had driven back to the house, prepared to bail Mark out one last time, only to find him gone. The single indication that he had been there at all was a number and a name scribbled on a matchbook by the phone. *Amy*, it read. Amy! The ersatz star who made Gaby, the genuine article, dispensable. Amy, the double, who made it irrelevant whether Gaby stayed or went so long as she appeared to have stayed. With Gaby gone, Mark could never interest another studio in the unfinished print, but if she seemed to be around, he was safe. So at the end, maybe all along, his need for her had been exploitation, not love. It was her services Mark had wanted, not her devotion or respect. And with that ugly revelation came absolution. Now, at last, she was free to go.

Within hours, her famous features hidden behind dark glasses and her mane of hair pulled into a small knot, she was on the Concorde, dazed, hurt, but exhilarated by the prospect of a new life in Europe. She found herself able to think of Mark without desperation, could look forward to a future with no strings attached. After all those years, she again belonged to herself.

Philippe was waiting at the Paris airport, the same place where she'd run into Terry so long ago. They hugged warmly and he'd whisked her to his townhouse, where they sat around, taking pleasure in being together, in being old and loving friends. Until the phone rang and an associate told him the terrible, crazy news about Mark and her. Gaby had managed to explain to Philippe what must have happened before the shock hit her.

Then she had gone to pieces, literally sickened by guilt and anger and a complicated and ambivalent grief. Later, Philippe explained to her that she'd cracked up, but at the time, all she felt was a profound listlessness, a lack of energy so profound that even walking across the room exhausted her. It had been Philippe's decision to take her to the house in Mougins, but it had been at her insistence that they'd not disclosed her presence there to anyone. Better to wait, she'd urged him, until she was strong enough to cope with the media madness that would ensue once it was known she hadn't died with Mark. And although he'd protested initially, he finally agreed.

The couple who lived on the grounds of Philippe's house saw to her daily needs, and he came down to be with her almost every weekend. Slowly, after months of constant care, she had begun to believe she did indeed have a future. To her astonishment, the irrational guilt and long-delayed anger were finally playing themselves out, and as she improved, she realized she owed Philippe more than she could ever repay him. His delight in her recovery touched her deeply and made her determined to grow even stronger to please him. The first time she snapped at him, he actually grabbed her and kissed her, and after their first argument, he'd ordered a bottle of champagne to celebrate. "Ah, Gaby," he'd told her that night, "how sad I am that soon I'm going to lose you to the world. I rather enjoyed having you all to myself."

"Philippe," she'd said, taking his hand, "you'll never lose me. Just you try!" And she'd meant it.

When she'd gotten to the point of contemplating just what her future should be, she revived her idea of finishing *Sirens' Song*. Shyly, she'd broached the notion with Philippe, and to her great surprise, he'd offered not only his encouragement but his money and international connections as well. During the languid Riviera evenings they'd sat on the terrace, planning. He was impressed with her thoroughness and ingenuity. "Gaby, does this mean I'm losing a model but gaining a business partner?'' he'd asked and she replied, ''No reason why I can't do both.''

''Of course,'' he'd agreed.

''Now,'' she continued, all business, ''I've made a list of the people we'll absolutely need. We've got to have Jackson. . . . How are we ever going to break the news about me?'' It was then that Philippe confessed he'd betrayed her. Jackson knew where she was, but he'd kept the secret and would make his artistic and directorial talents available whenever she wanted him. Gerald, her lawyer and the executor of her estate, had to be notified, so Philippe had flown to New York to tell him in person.

''He thought I was mad,'' Philippe laughed as he recounted the meeting at the Harvard Club. ''I could tell because he switched immediately from Perrier to martinis and began mopping his brow. Finally, assuming that creative people are all insane anyway, he agreed to sell the Beekman Place house and dissolve your assets to raise some of the capital.''

''There's one thing, Philippe,'' she'd insisted. ''Terry Barron must not be approached. If we need to rewrite the last scene, I'll do it myself.''

''But, Gaby—''

''Philippe, I refuse to discuss it. No Terry Barron.''

He had taken her hand in his and looked hard at her. ''Gaby, you're sure?''

''Absolutely,'' and that had been that.

And then they arrived at the real stumbling block. They had the capital, and the studio and the bank were ready to do the deal, but there was no way to shoot the last scene without Denise. ''Jackson,'' she'd complained in the course of a transatlantic call, ''I don't see any way in the world that we can approach that bitch!''

''Cool off, darlin' '' he'd told her. ''I'll get you

Denise on terms agreeable to all parties. She's not an absolute villainess, you know, any more than you're totally innocent. You two were jealous of each other from the first time you met. I should know, it was in my house. Seems to me you're both at fault, but I bet I can smooth everything over.'' True to his word, he'd handled it, and fast.

Two days later, Denise had rung up from her home in Cap-d'Antibes, ostensibly calling for Philippe but giving Gaby the most unconvincing performance of her career. In minutes, she came clean and contrite, wept on the phone, and offered, since she lived not far away, to drive over early the next morning with anything Gaby might need. From that first morning, Denise had been a lifesaver, raising morale, gofer-ing, contacting and hiring the best editor and composer in Europe, and contributing hefty amounts of her new husband's apparently limitless fortune.

It had been with Denise, formerly her enemy, now her confidante, that she'd first talked about Terry. The night was starry, after Van Gogh, and they sat on the terrace, satisfied with the editing work the crew had done that day in the miniature movie lab in the basement.

Made reckless by the anisette and the sense of professional accomplishment, she tried to sound casual. ''Do you ever hear from Terry Barron, Denise?''

Abruptly, Denise gave out with her smokiest laugh. ''Jesus, Gaby, I thought you'd never ask!''

''What in the world do you mean by that laugh, Denise?''

''Oh, nothing,'' and she'd gone back to sipping her anisette in silence.

''Well?'' Gaby couldn't resist.

''Well what?''

''Terry. Have you heard from him?''

"Yep. I saw him when I was in New York."

"So how is he?"

"Fine. The author of a distinguished and best-selling novel is usually fine. You really ought to read the book, by the way."

"I did read it, Denise."

"They say it's going to win the Pulitzer Prize. Brilliant, isn't it?"

"Yes, it is," Gaby said softly. "What did you two talk about?"

Denise looked up with a coy glance. "Oh, about some wild scheme he had for trying to get my husband to buy the print of *Sirens' Song*. I finally told him somebody else had beaten us to it. He was extremely rattled."

"He was? Why?"

"I'm not sure. I think he wanted something to remember you by."

"Remember me? He hates my guts."

"Gaby, you sound like you really mean that!"

"I do."

"Then you're not as bright as you seem. But, then again, I think I said the same thing to him."

Gaby's heart gave a totally unexpected lurch. "What do you mean?"

"I keep feeling I've had this conversation already. Oh well, at my age, any self-respecting temptress has to turn into a fairy godmother. Okay, here goes: You two are the only people in the world who don't know how you feel about each other."

"What?" Gaby poured herself another anisette and gulped it down.

"That first night in East Hampton at Jackson's, I could see it, plain as the nose on your face. You two kids were wild about each other. Pissed me off, let me tell you. Needless to say, I took a certain amount of comfort from the fact that you never got together, but I was always worried that one day, you'd wake up and I'd lose him. That time in Chicago, I was sure you'd both waked up with a vengeance. I'm sure Mark felt it, too. We were both so uptight—do they still say that? No? Well, we were both so furious that we had one of those little retaliation affairs because of it."

"Really?" Gaby actually felt a weight lift from her heart.

"Yeah, really. You two were so afraid of love. I could never understand it. What's to be afraid of? Hate is to be afraid of, not love."

"Why didn't you say something?"

"Screw you, young woman. That's against every rule in the book. You're supposed to figure it out by yourself, not find it out from a rival."

"God, Denise." Gaby couldn't stop smiling. "What should I do? Should I call him? I can't do that."

"Well, I wouldn't do it right this minute. The movie's almost ready. You've waited this long, wait a little longer. When the picture's finished, when you have something wonderful to share, get in touch with him. He'll come, I promise you."

"How is he, Denise? What's he like? Is he different?"

The older woman smiled wryly, sipping her anisette as she contemplated her answer. "He's more settled in himself, and not quite so easygoing. More serious. You read *Hellfire*. I don't think anyone can create something that powerful without having it change them some. But you'll like him grown-up, and he'll like you. Better even. You'll see. When you're ready, he'll be here for you."

Tonight Denise's prediction had come true. Even from the back of the screening room Gaby had sensed first Terry's approval, then his pleasure, without having to see his face.

She had left minutes before the film ended, walked upstairs and out onto the terrace, protected by the darkness and the mist, waiting for him, breathless to watch him approach. And he had, and he was older, a man secure in his excellence, at ease with himself, as Denise had promised, and dazzling, just dazzling.

She had seen him see her through the mist, had moved a little way away so she could watch him walk toward her, had caught the first astonished glimpse of recognition in his eyes, and then, as he spoke her name, she felt some new, high level of existence open up to her, like a curtain drawing back, and she knew that they were home.